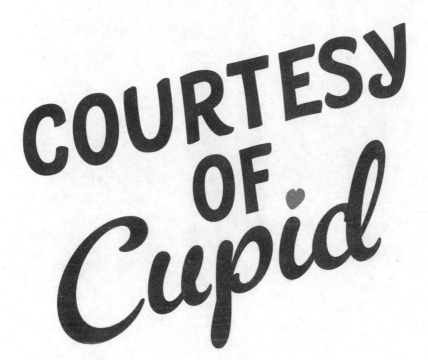

COURTESY
OF
Cupid

COURTESY OF Cupid

NASHAE JONES

ALADDIN
NEW YORK LONDON TORONTO SYDNEY NEW DELHI

This book is a work of fiction. Any references to historical events, real people, or real places are used fictitiously. Other names, characters, places, and events are products of the author's imagination, and any resemblance to actual events or places or persons, living or dead, is entirely coincidental.

ALADDIN

An imprint of Simon & Schuster Children's Publishing Division
1230 Avenue of the Americas, New York, New York 10020
First Aladdin edition January 2024
Text copyright © 2024 by Nashae Jones
Jacket illustration copyright © 2024 by Stephanie Singleton

ALADDIN and related logo are registered trademarks of Simon & Schuster, Inc.
Simon & Schuster: Celebrating 100 Years of Publishing in 2024
For information about special discounts for bulk purchases, please contact
Simon & Schuster Special Sales at 1-866-506-1949 or business@simonandschuster.com.
The Simon & Schuster Speakers Bureau can bring authors to your live event. For more information or to book an event contact the Simon & Schuster Speakers Bureau
at 1-866-248-3049 or visit our website at www.simonspeakers.com.
Designed by Heather Palisi
The text of this book was set in Adobe Caslon Pro.
Manufactured in the United States of America 1123 BVG
2 4 6 8 10 9 7 5 3 1
Library of Congress Cataloging-in-Publication Data
Names: Jones, Nashae, author.
Title: Courtesy of Cupid / by Nashae Jones.
Description: First Aladdin hardcover edition. | New York : Aladdin, 2024. |
Summary: When thirteen-year-old Erin discovers she is the daughter of the love god Cupid, she uses her newfound ability to sabotage her rival Trevor by making him fall in love with her, but she soon realizes love has a funny way of complicating things.
Identifiers: LCCN 2023017808 (print) | LCCN 2023017809 (ebook) |
ISBN 9781665939881 (hardcover) | ISBN 9781665939904 (ebook)
Subjects: CYAC: Love—Fiction. | Ability—Fiction. | Middle schools—Fiction. |
Schools—Fiction. | Elections—Fiction. | LCGFT: Romance fiction. | Novels.
Classification: LCC PZ7.1.J72365 Co 2024 (print) | LCC PZ7.1.J72365 (ebook) |
DDC [Fic]—dc23
LC record available at https://lccn.loc.gov/2023017808
LC ebook record available at https://lccn.loc.gov/2023017809

To Jean James for fostering my imagination,
and to Dave Noechel for encouraging me to
keep imagining things even as an adult

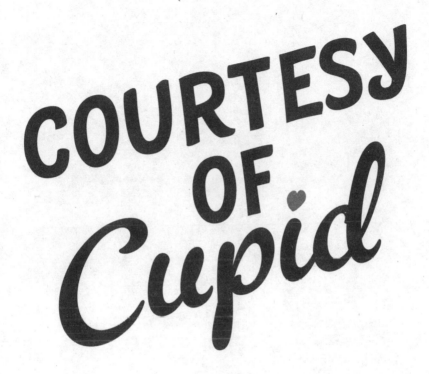

AN INTRODUCTION (SORT OF)

THERE ARE TWO THINGS wrong with this world.

Well, maybe not just two. There are obviously a ton of things wrong with the world, but just for the purposes of time, I'll talk about the major two I've observed in my life.

The first one is lack of ambition. I know, I know, it's weird for me, an almost-thirteen-year-old, to talk about ambition, but it *is* kind of how the world goes around. Think about it. What if early Americans had never held that Tea Party? What if Marie Curie had decided she didn't want to study science? What if Beyoncé was too shy to sing? Well, that would be a problem. A huge problem. And we're lacking ambition in the world today—not just in the world, but specifically at Paxton Middle School. *My* school. Most people here are perfectly content to be ordinary, and that is a tragedy. Or is it a travesty? Oh, who knows, it's one of those words. Or maybe both? Huh. I'll look that up later. But sadly, there is a lack of both ambition and talent in my school. Last year, my school got a project funded through a local car dealership that basically gave the students a budget to create something that would be beneficial to the school. All the students had to submit ideas, and then we had to vote on the top five. My idea, creating a dedicated space to host a tutoring center, would have obviously been super helpful for the school. But the rest of the students overwhelmingly voted to repurpose an old storage closet into a glorified nap room. Come *on*. I completely understand the need for rest and relaxation. But there's a time and place for things like that. Like when you're at home. In your own room. On your own time! Imagine if Marie Curie had decided to focus on meditation rooms instead of discovering radiation treatment.

The second thing that is wrong with the world is the concept of love. And I don't mean love, like between family members or even the love you have for your friends. I'm talking about romantic love, the type of love that you see in the movies. Hearts, flowers, grand gestures, the whole shebang. That type of love is a parasite, especially for middle schoolers. And oddly enough, all my classmates have been infected with the love parasite. It seems like every time I turn around, someone else is inevitably and completely consumed with what they believe is love. How many people do you know who actually fall in love in middle school?!

Love is nothing but a distraction. A distraction from the important things in life.

My best friend, Bruno, thinks it is highly ironic that I hate the idea of love, since my mom writes romance novels. But I don't think so, because logically, tons of people have moms who are writers.

Love hasn't done anyone any favors in life, and it definitely hasn't done me any. Love doesn't take away the pain of being roughly one of fifteen Black kids in your school or of losing a grandma to colon cancer or of never having a dad while growing up. Love doesn't help me forget—but ambition definitely does.

Which brings me to my next point. I have big dreams and even bigger ambitions. When I get older, I'm going to be a biologist. I have everything all mapped out. Howard University for college. Johns Hopkins for graduate school. Cure colon cancer in my twenties. Win the Nobel Prize (à la Marie Curie) when I'm an old woman like my mom (so, about thirty-five). It's a solid plan. A plan I will definitely achieve as long as I can overcome one obstacle. Well, not so much an obstacle as much as a person.

Trevor Jin.

Actually, I would like to revise my earlier statement. There are *three* things wrong with the world: lack of ambition, love, and Trevor Jin.

Trevor Jin and I were born to despise each other. I don't know if people are born with archenemies, but I definitely feel that

I was. I can't do anything—I mean, anything—without Trevor upstaging me.

For example, when we were in the third grade, we had this science fair that I was super excited about (obviously). I worked hard for three weeks creating a solar panel that powered a small paper windmill. It was a perfect complement to the clean energy unit we had just learned about. But Trevor Jin brought an actual robot that he had built from scratch. The robot could say "I love you" in forty different languages. Yuck. But of course, Trevor won first prize, and my perfectly perfect solar panel only won second.

That wasn't the beginning of things, though. Our feud truly started as most feuds do. With a stolen story.

Okay, I'm not actually certain that's how most feuds start. I'm not even 100 percent certain that I know anyone who is in a feud, but I'm certain this is how the feud started with Trevor. Trevor and I started kindergarten the same year, and we both had Ms. Colton, a bright young teacher who had only been a teacher for a little over a year. Trevor came to school in a bow tie and suspenders, and even then he acted like he was the king of the world. I was naive (because hello, I was five), and I attempted to make friends with Trevor.

For the first few minutes of class, Trevor and I sat on the round alphabet carpet. We went through normal kid stuff, favorite foods (mine: chicken nuggets, his: ice cream) and our favorite thing to play on at the playground (mine: the swings, his: the bouncing horse). After five minutes, we were the best of friends, or at least that was what I believed.

During our conversation, I told Trevor about my summer adventures, how my nana had saved up so she could take us on a trip to a lake house, where she taught me to swim and forage for berries. Trevor listened patiently, nodding his head during each part of my story. In return, Trevor told me about how he went to Disney World with his parents. When Ms. Colton clapped her hands a couple of seconds later, calling us to order, I was convinced that I had found a best friend that I would have for the rest of my life.

Ms. Colton decided that we should all do introductions since it was our first official day of school. She kept it simple. She just wanted our names and what we did over summer vacation. When she asked the class who would like to go first, Trevor immediately raised his hand, and Ms. Colton picked him. I was happy for Trevor. (Again, I would like to cite naivete.) I mean, why wouldn't I be? Trevor was my new best friend. He went up to the front of the room, a perfectly put-together child, not a hair out of place, his white shirt crisp and pressed.

He told the class his name and date of birth (not something Ms. Colton asked for, but whatever). When he first started talking, I was beaming with pride. After all, I thought Trevor was my friend. But then he started his summer story, and certain parts started to sound eerily like what I'd just told him. He talked about going to the lake and having to find his own food. And I sat there getting more flustered with each word. The icing on the cake was when he told the class that his grandma had saved up to take him on this special vacation, just the two of them. That was when I knew that he'd stolen my story, the whole thing. I was so mortified that by the time it was my turn to go up and present, I froze on the carpet, unable to move. From that day on, I only talked to Trevor whenever I was forced to.

And there are tons of stories like that. When it comes to Trevor Jin, I always seem to come up as second best. He makes sure of it.

But I'm working on that, and this year's the year that things change. Also, because I'm working on my scientific writing, you will see tons of things called footnotes. (These are used by real scientists when they give extra information that they don't have time to put in the main article.) So I will be using these handy devices to convey my most personal, most intimate thoughts. None of which will have to do with love or Trevor Jin.

CHAPTER ONE

Cupid Commandment Number 13: For a Cupid, there is nothing more noble than the pursuit of a quality education (except for maybe the pursuit of love).

PREPARING FOR THE FIRST day of school is similar to preparing for battle. At least, I think it would be similar to preparing for battle. I haven't actually prepared for battle before, but I imagine that preparing for battle would include plenty of planning, and if I'm known for anything, it's my ability to get things organized.

I'm the queen of organization. I already have my bookbag packed according to my class schedule (something we just got last weekend). I have:

1) Five binders (color coded for each of my
different classes and filled with paper)
2) A pencil pouch filled with ten
already-sharpened pencils, three highlighters,
and five pens
3) Two glue sticks
4) Safety scissors[1]
5) A pack of fresh note cards

Most students at PMS (Paxton Middle School)[2] will not have already gotten their supplies, because technically we won't get our supply lists until the first day, but it's the same supply list every year. It never changes.

I imagine that Marie Curie[3] would have always, always been organized. And that is motivation enough to buy my supplies early, even if my best friend, Bruno, says that I will end up being the only one who brings their supplies on the first day. I'm completely fine with that. Except I know that he's wrong. I won't be the *only* person who will come prepared. I know one other person who will be in class today in freshly pressed khakis and a button-down shirt (Honestly, who dresses like that in middle school? Who dresses like that if you're not a thirty-year-old man?), with

---

1. My mother still doesn't trust me with scissors even though this is my last year of middle school. It's not like I'm the one who stabbed myself with a toothpick last year.
2. Yes, our school initials are PMS. Yes, it is very embarrassing. Sometimes I wonder if there are actual adults in charge at that school.
3. Marie Curie is my absolute hero (heroine??). She was the first woman to win a Nobel Prize, and she won it twice. Honestly, if I could go back and be reincarnated as Marie Curie, I totally would.

all his supplies spread out on the desk in front of him.

Trevor Jin will be prepared, more than prepared, but this is going to be my year. This is going to be the year I best Trevor Jin.

A soft knock sounds, and my mom opens the door. I don't know why she even knocks. She never actually waits to be told she can come in.

Privacy is not something we have in the Johnson household.

She leans on the doorframe, smiling at me like a crazed raccoon. She looks absolutely ridiculous in a yellow poodle skirt, her hair pulled up into two poufs on either side of her head. I pull at my blue sweater self-consciously, giving her a withering look.

"You're not taking me to school like that."

My mom chuckles, coming over and giving me a playful hip bump. "Why not? It's a lot of fun. I'm getting into character. My newest heroine[4] is a love-shy girl carhop[5] who loves a boy from the wrong side of the tracks. You know getting into character helps me to write."

I roll my eyes.

"That's *Grease*. You're literally just writing the plot to *Grease*."

My mom scrunches up her nose, sticking her tongue out at me.

Honestly, sometimes I forget who the adult is in this house.

"The client is always right, Erin."

---

4. My mom is a romance writer (I know, I know). Well, technically she's what you would call a ghostwriter. Someone who writes a story for someone else, gets paid, and then gives all the credit to the person who paid them. It is, honestly, one of the stupidest things I have ever heard of. It would be like me writing a report for Trevor Jin because he paid me, and then Trevor getting all the recognition and credit. No, thank you!

5. A carhop is a fifties-style waiter/waitress who serves people at their cars. Sometimes they do this on roller skates.

"Whatever," I mumble, slinging on my backpack and glancing down at my watch. "We're going to be late if we don't hurry."

I look at her outfit again, groaning. "Mom, you can't get out of the car looking like that. Please don't get out of the car looking like that."

Mom laughs. Actually laughs. Like this wasn't some type of emergency that would tarnish my reputation as a serious student.

"Don't worry, peanut," Mom says, dropping a kiss on my forehead. "I won't embarrass you." She pulls playfully on my sweater. "Even though I would be the perfect complement to this grumpy librarian getup."

She wiggles her eyebrows at me as I swat her arm.

"Better grumpy librarian than over-the-hill sock-hop girl."

She snorts and we both laugh. My mom is definitely not over-the-hill. She had me when she was twenty, and she still looks like the living embodiment of some type of goddess. She is all smooth, even dark chestnut skin and perfect ringlet curls, where I'm short (honestly, when will I get a growth spurt?), pale brown (apparently, this is all thanks to my dad), freckled (again, thanks, Dad, whoever you are[6]), and I have impossible lionlike (reddish-brown) hair that refuses to lie down no matter how much gel I put on it. It really isn't fair that I have such a mismatched appearance, while my mom (who constantly goes out of her way to look like she's an alien from another planet) looks so effortlessly beautiful.

"Can you pick up Bruno?" I ask politely, even though I know

---

6. I have never met my dad. He left my mom right after I was born. My mom won't tell me anything about him, except that I look like him, which is not helpful at all.

she is going to pick up Bruno. Bruno's mom is her absolute closest friend in the world.

"Duh, of course I will," she responds, ushering me into the kitchen. She pushes a bagel into my hand, a dry bagel with absolutely no cream cheese. Who eats dry bagels?

"I'll get them both," my mom responds nonchalantly.

I put the bagel up to my mouth, preparing to swallow it down quickly, but I stop when I fully digest what my mother has said.

"Both," I say slowly, filling with dread.

My mom gives me an uncharacteristically sharp look. "Yes, both, Erin."

I groan. That means we're picking up not only Bruno, but also his obnoxious twin brother, Ben. Since our mothers have been best friends for most of their lives, Bruno, Ben, and I were raised together practically as siblings. Our mothers got pregnant with us around the same time, and our birthdays are officially five months apart. So Bruno has always been like a brother to me. We've always been attached at the hip. He is way closer to me than he is to his brother, who is meaner than a rattlesnake at a Fourth of July party. Ben is completely uninterested in me. To him, I'm nothing more than a pesky bothersome fly on the wall. But Ben absolutely loathes Bruno.

It wasn't always like this, though. There was a time when Bruno, Ben, and I were all close. But then when Ben and Bruno were eight, their parents got a divorce,[7] and it was like Ben turned into a

---

7. Ben and Bruno's dad now lives in California. So, they only see him during the first half of the summer, and every other Christmas break.

different person, surly and uncommunicative. It wasn't long before Bruno and I stopped hanging out with Ben. Ben can't understand how he and Bruno are even siblings, much less twins. He picks on Bruno every chance he gets. But when you're a talented lacrosse player with tons of charisma (and very little ambition), you can get away with being mean, especially when you're mean to your twin brother who doesn't own clothes in any color other than black.

Even though I typically carpool with Bruno, for the last two years Ben has been getting rides with his best friend and fellow lacrosse buddy, Xavier. But Xavier recently moved out of state. So, I guess we're now going to be stuck with Ben on morning rides to school.

When we pull up to their house, my mom leans on the horn, something that embarrasses me but makes Bruno and Ben's mom come to the door crippled over with laughter. They do this routine every time they take us to school. It isn't funny. It is never funny. I honestly would take the bus, if our neighborhood stop wasn't three blocks away. Bruno and Ben come out of the house, both of them scooting around their mother.

"Take good care of my boys, Jo!"

"Siempre,"[8] my mom shouts back.

This is also a part of their routine. They burst into a fit of giggles again.

I scoot over for Bruno, who climbs into the backseat, while Ben sits up front, grinning over at my mother.

---

8. Bruno and Ben's mom, Isa, is a second-generation Salvadorean, and she taught my mom some basic Spanish terms. This one means *always*.

"Hi, Joanna. You look nice today."

Ben purposefully looks back at me. I give him a biting look and he ignores me. My mother has started telling all the people my age to refer to her by her first name, even though it annoys me to no end. I roll my eyes.

"Thank you, Ben," she says, ruffling his light brown hair. "Ready for your first day of eighth grade?" my mom asks jovially, completely unaware of the death glare I'm giving her from the backseat.

"Yep, of course," Ben replies, fixing his letterman's jacket. I roll my eyes again. It's not even cold enough for a jacket, but Ben is a peacock. He loves for everyone to know just how popular he really is. As Ben turns around to face us, his mouth lifts into a smirk.

"Looks like the wonder twins[9] are ready too." He laughs. "The vampire and the librarian."

I see Bruno's cheeks redden out of the corner of my eye.

"See," my mom says, laughing. "I told you, you look like a librarian."

I ball my hands into fists. "Well," I say sweetly, "I will agree that I look like a librarian if Ben will agree to spell it."

Bruno snorts beside me, putting his head down when his brother turns around again to glare at us, his cheeks heating to a pale pink. Okay, I'm normally not this mean, but Ben is ruthless when it comes to Bruno, and it really isn't right.

---

9. Ben thinks it's highly original and amusing to refer to us as twins. It's neither original nor amusing.

Bruno, honestly, never does anything to anybody.

"Erin Marie," my mom admonishes. Her disapproving eyes meet mine in the rearview mirror. I sink back against my seat as Ben gives me a triumphant look. I huff loudly. Ben is definitely not worth it.

CHAPTER TWO

*Cupid Commandment Number 3: Cupids know that
there is a very, very thin line between love and hate.*

MOST PEOPLE HATE THE first-day-of-school introductions, having
to stand up in front of the class and give your life story in approxi-
mately thirty seconds, but I live for it.[10] I always have a speech
prepared, one that lets everyone know that 1) I'm going to be first
in our class, 2) I'm going to be the first Black woman to receive
the Nobel Prize in Medicine, 3) I'm going to cure colon cancer,
and 4) I'm going to do all of this in spite of Trevor Jin.

Bruno is one of the people who hates introductions and

---

10. Even though our school is fairly small, we still get a new set of teachers every year.
Because of this, the first class on the first day is devoted to introductions.

icebreakers. In fact, he pretty much hates any type of public speaking. Normally, I help him whenever he has to give presentations.[11] But this year I have all honors courses, and Bruno has a lot of art electives. He is a *really, really* talented cartoonist, though he won't show anybody but me his artwork. So because of that, we now have zero classes together, which is not how I wanted to start the year. Another side effect of this new schedule is that Bruno will inevitably have more classes with Ben, which is never a good idea. Furthermore, Bruno is really supportive when it comes to the melodrama that is Trevor Jin. He once skipped class to sit with me in the clinic when I fainted because I lost the student senate president seat to Trevor. Granted, it was the fifth grade. And maybe I was taking it a *tad* bit more seriously than I should have. But it was really unfair. The only reason Trevor got the position was because his mother brought in ice cream for the whole class. Obviously, the election wasn't based on any sort of merit.

I find my homeroom quickly and stop outside the door. I shuffle my premade note cards. While I have what I want to say memorized, there is no harm in being prepared. Also, whenever I'm in doubt of what I should do, I ask myself, *What would Marie do?* or WWMD for short. And I'm almost 100 percent certain that Marie would be prepared for all the different scenarios that could occur. For example, scenario number one: What if I suddenly develop amnesia and I can no longer remember my own name, or worse,

---

11. We have a secret system, where I pull my nose up so I kind of look like a pig, and then that always makes him smile and forget his nerves. When we were younger, we used to pretend we were pigs, and we were in charge of this pig kingdom. Honestly, it was just an excuse for us to roll in the dirt. Six-year-old me wasn't as well put together.

my own ambitions? The note cards will be necessary to help me remember not only what I'm supposed to be doing but also my own identity. Scenario number two: Trevor Jin heckles me during my entire introduction, and I get so flustered, I forget what I'm supposed to be doing, and I effectively forget my speech and end up flunking out of the course and having to live with my mom for the rest of my life (ugh).[12] So, either way, it pays to be prepared.

I blow out a breath and prepare to open up the door to the classroom. For homeroom this year, I have Ms. Richmond, an English teacher who is rumored to be a bit wacky but a lot of fun. Students who had her last year said she liked to dress up in silly outfits and read in weird voices. The most important thing is that she is the new sponsor of the Multicultural Leadership Club, and this year they are having elections for the new president. And I *want* that spot. I deserve that spot. I walk into the room fifteen minutes before the start of class. I like to be the first one in class in order to show my dedication, and also to be able to pick a seat that is front and center.

The room is blissfully empty. Not even Ms. Richmond is in the room yet. Good. Good, I can pick a seat, right up front, in the center, away from distractions. But as I near the perfect seat, I stop, looking down at a ramrod-straight back. I take in the jet-black hair, styled and coiffed without a strand out of place, a perfectly pressed collared shirt and boring khaki pants. He has the

---

12. To be fair, this really isn't something Trevor would do. He is a certified teacher's pet, which means he wouldn't necessarily heckle me, but he would find some other way to make sure I screwed up.

most bland wardrobe. It just doesn't make sense. I didn't even see him when I first came in because he pretty much blended in with the desks and the rest of the classroom furniture.[13] Dread floods through me. Trevor Jin turns around and smiles at me, but not a nice smile. Nooooo, that would be too much for Trevor. Instead, he gives me a smile like a shark who has just spotted a tasty minnow.

"Trevor," I say coolly, plopping my bag down on the (clearly less desirable) seat next to his.

"Erin," Trevor replies, turning away from me. On his desk, he has two pencils laid out next to one black pen and one blue one, and in the middle of the desk he has a clean sheet of notebook paper.

"Running late today?" he says.

I ignore him, starting to set out my own pencils and pens on the desk.

Trevor leans back in his chair, looking at me with his black laser eyes. "Typical. Some of us like to make sure we're on time."

I look around the room. There is still a good fifteen minutes until class starts. The late bell hasn't even rung yet. Honestly, he is so infuriating. Why is he so worried about me anyway?

"Well," I reply, "*some* of us have a life."

Trevor's eyes narrow for a microsecond, then flick to nonchalance.

"Well, why don't you tell me who that person is? I'm dying to meet them."

---

13. Though Trevor is my archenemy, it would be scientifically irresponsible not to mention that he is what most people would consider attractive. He has that tall, dark, and handsome thing going for him, I guess. But that is a strictly scientific observation on my end.

"Ugh. Idiot," I mumble, going through my bookbag.

Trevor smiles his shark smile again. "I'm a lot of things, EJ, but I'm not an idiot."

I flinch at the use of my nickname.

"Only my friends call me EJ. You can refer to me as Erin."

Trevor's mouth tenses. He turns around quickly. I ignore him, digging in my bag for the teacher gift I picked out for Ms. Richmond. I heard that she is a huge fan of Shakespeare, and I saved up my allowance to buy her a special edition of *A Midsummer Night's Dream.*[14] The book has beautiful illustrations and a foreword from some important Shakespeare scholar dude. Not really my thing, but whatever. It is important to start off on the right foot with Ms. Richmond, as she could possibly be the deciding factor in the upcoming election. I pull the book out of my bag and set it on the table. I see Trevor glance over, and I give him a triumphant smile. Ha, you won't be first when it comes to this, Trevor Jin.

We hear Ms. Richmond before we see her, a clattering of tinkling following each of her steps.

"My early birdies," she chirps happily. I look up at her in horror. Her entire sweater is covered with little bells. I look over at Trevor, who is also grimacing at her jingling ensemble. "I should have known the two of you would show up early."

She points at me. "Erin, right?" I nod. "And Trevor?" Trevor is obviously not amused that he has been called on second. He nods crisply. Vaguely, I start to wonder how she knows my name, but

---

14. Apparently, this is some lovey-dovey play about fairies and mismatched love. My mom helped me pick it out. She said any English teacher would love to have it. Yeah, okay.

then I remember that Trevor and I are pretty well known by the PMS teachers. So, really, it isn't too much of a surprise that Ms. Richmond knows who we are.

"Ms. Richmond," I say in my best student-of-the-year voice. "I'm so happy to have you for homeroom and for Honors English."

I know I was laying it on a bit thick, but honestly, WWMD? She would definitely lay it on thick to make sure she accomplished her goal. I bring the book up to Ms. Richmond, and I hand it to her.

"What's this—" She gasps, holding up the book like it is the holy grail of books. "*A Midsummer Night's Dream*, the illustrated edition," she squeals. "I've been dying to get a copy of this."

I beam at her. Success. Take that, Trevor Jin. Score one for me, zero for you. "It's just a little something I picked up this summer. I thought you would like it. It has some really diverse illustrations in there. Speaking of diversity—"

Trevor cuts in. "I wouldn't consider the addition of fairies diverse."

"It's a diversity of species," I hiss in annoyance.

Trevor pulls an envelope out of his bag. Wait, what is he doing? What is he pulling out of his bag? I try to slow down my skittering heart. It is just an envelope. It is just an envelope. It can't possibly be better than the book I saved up all summer to get. It just can't.

"What a coincidence, Ms. Richmond. I got you something too. It's just a little something, nothing like the book Erin got you."

He walks over to her and hands her the envelope. My stomach sinks. He is smiling like a shark again.

"Oh, Trevor," she replies, laughing. "I don't expect gifts. Not at—"

She stops for a moment as she rips open the envelope. I crane my neck to try to get a better look at what she is holding. A ticket? It looks like some type of ticket. Ms. Richmond screams, causing the other two students who have filtered in unnoticed to jump.

"A ticket to go see *Twelfth Night*[15] at Blackfriars Playhouse up in Staunton! I've always wanted to go. Trevor, you shouldn't have!"

Oh my god. She looks like she is on the verge of tears.

"I've wanted to go to this since I was in college, but I've never been able to afford to. Thank you so much, Trevor."

Now she is crying. Big, messy, snotty crying. Trevor hands her a tissue, the stupid smile still plastered on his face. "It's no problem, Ms. Richmond."

He looks so pleased. I just want to wipe the smugness off his face.

"My dad knows the artistic director there, and he was able to get a free ticket for the show."

Of course *his* dad,[16] the famous neurosurgeon, was able to get some fancy-pants play ticket.

---

15. This is another Shakespearean tale of mismatched love, which means Trevor and I kind of matched our gifts. Gross.

16. Dr. Jin and Dr. Jin are a true power couple. Trevor's dad is a renowned neurosurgeon, and his mom is a congenital heart surgeon. Apparently, they met during their residency and fell in love over a cadaver. His parents are so cool, and if I ever have to get married, it would definitely be to a person who is just as ambitious as I am.

"Cheater," I hiss under my breath. Because, honestly, it is cheating if you use your parents' money.

Trevor ignores me.

"I hope that's okay?"

"Oh yes," Ms. Richmond says, still blubbering. "It's my favorite play."

Of course it is. Leave it to Trevor Jin to get tickets for her favorite play. What a suck-up.

"I know class is about to start," Trevor says, "but I wanted to mention my intention to run for the presidential spot for the Multicultural Leadership Club. I know that you're sponsoring it this year, and I'm really excited to start sharing my ideas with you."

"Of course, of course," Ms. Richmond replies, wiping her eyes with the tissue. "I'll get you an application. They aren't technically due until October, but there's no harm—"

I jump up from my seat, my chair clattering to the ground. "I want one too," I yell.

Ms. Richmond looks at me and then the chair, eyes wide.

"Please," I say, a touch quieter. Ms. Richmond nods, grabbing a folder from behind her desk, producing two forms. Trevor and I each grab one.

"October first is the deadline, my early birdies," she tells us. She blows her nose into the tissue.

"Mine will be in before that," Trevor offers.

"Mine will be in by the end of September," I counter.

"Mine will be in within two weeks."

I glare at him. Two weeks isn't a lot of time to get together a quality application, especially considering that we have to gather teacher recommendations.

"Mine too," I answer coldly.

Trevor glares back at me, all dark laser eyes.

"Well, good," Ms. Richmond says, looking from Trevor to me like she is witnessing an unfriendly tennis match.

I huff and sit back down in my seat, looking at the first question on the application. An obvious one, but one that is necessary to answer. *Why do you want to be the president of the Multicultural Leadership Club?* I write in a flurry of scribbles as the bell rings, signaling the start of class.

To make Trevor Jin pay.

I look at my words, sloppily written in pencil, nothing like my normal neat handwriting. It feels good. Almost like a sense of freedom. I shake my head and sigh. When I erase it, I'm careful to get each and every stray mark.

CHAPTER THREE

*Cupid Commandment Number 10: A Cupid, much
like a person in love, must always be prepared for
the unexpected.*

AFTER THREE WEEKS OF school, I have pretty much settled into a routine. Five days a week of classes. Check. Peer-tutoring kids who are struggling with math and science on Tuesdays and Thursdays at the library. Check. Piano practice on Wednesdays. Check. Fridays hanging out with Bruno. Check. Spend every day planning my victory over Trevor Jin. Check. (Double check.) (*Triple* check.)

I have already turned in my application, exactly two weeks after school started, like I said I would. I have glowing recommendations, and I wrote stellar answers to all the essay questions. So now it is just a question of when Ms. Richmond will announce the candidates (which everyone knows will be Trevor Jin and me). I will win this campaign, no matter how glossy Trevor's campaign is.

"So, come home right after school today, no tutoring, okay?"

I forgot that my mom was trying to talk to me. She looks at me through the rearview mirror. Bruno looks up too.

I groan, but I tell her it's okay. Today is my birthday, and every year on my birthday my mom and I go out to eat at the local Chinese food buffet. My mom always ends up embarrassing me in some way, whether it is sobbing in the middle of her lo mein or getting the workers to sing me an awkward rendition of "Happy Birthday." Either way, it is absolutely the worst day of the year, and I do not look forward to it. Not at all. But I also don't want to disappoint my mom. She enjoys celebrating my birthday, and it gives us time to bond, so I guess it's not too awful. Bruno looks over at me. *Sorry,* he mouths.

"I can't believe you are finally thirteen," my mom muses.

I flinch. I hate my late birthday. I'm always the youngest in my class, turning the next age after everyone else has been that age already for months and months. Bruno and Ben have April birthdays, so they will be fourteen before me. And I won't turn fourteen until we're already in high school.

"Who's turning thirteen?" Ben pipes up from the front seat. He's staring down at his phone, his fingers flying over the screen.

"It's my birthday, Ben," I respond dryly.

"Oh really? I thought your birthday was in July."

25

"Nope," I reply as Ben snorts at something on his phone. "It's today. Like it's been for the last thirteen years I've known you."

Honestly, Ben does this every single year. Is it really that hard to remember your brother's best friend's birthday? Especially if said best friend is half a year younger than you. At this point, it's becoming a bit sad.

"You're, like, really young," Ben states.

Also something he's always known. I cross my arms, primed to come back with a witty retort, but Bruno speaks first.

"Her birthday has always been the same day each year, Ben. This shouldn't be a surprise."

He says it so softly that at first I think I imagined it. But then Ben lifts his eyes from his phone, and he slowly turns around to face Ben. He drops his voice, so only Bruno and I can hear him.

"What did you say, Dracula?"

Bruno's eyes immediately fall to his lap, shying away from Ben's stare.

"Nothing," Bruno mutters.

"That's what I thought, maggot," Ben hisses.

Bruno sinks farther down into his seat.

I bristle. "Hey. Don't talk to him like that."

Ben briefly turns around and rolls his eyes at me.

"Who even asked you? Why are you even talking?"

"Why you—"

My mom cuts me off.

"Children," she states with an exasperated drawl. "Can we get along for one day? One single, measly day?"

Ben yawns, shrugging his shoulders as he goes back to his phone. Bruno is still staring down at his lap, his fingers splayed open over his knees.

I hate that Ben makes him feel like this. I absolutely hate it. I wish I knew how to make Ben stop being so cruel to Bruno.

When we finally pull up to the school, my mom rushes me and Bruno out of the car.

"Have a lovely, lovely day, you two," she breathes. Her eyes snap over to Ben. "Hold on for just a moment, will you, Ben?"

I stop in my tracks. What is she up to? Better question: What can she be up to with *Ben*?

I don't have long to think about it because before I know it, Bruno is pulling my arm, steering me toward the building and our shared locker.

When we get to the locker, I dig into it to retrieve my literature textbook, sliding it into my bag.

"You really shouldn't let Ben run all over you," I admonish Bruno, but I soon realize that he isn't paying me any attention. His eyes are locked onto India Saunders, a pretty girl in our grade who has a sweet smile and stylish braids that hang halfway down her back. India is one of the fifteen other Black kids who go to PMS with me, and you would think that would give us some type of solidarity with each other, but I barely talk to the girl. Let's just say we don't hang out in the same social circles. And by different social circles, I mean that she is friends with Ben, which, in all honesty, doesn't say a lot about her taste in friends. Or her taste in general. But that doesn't matter to Bruno; he is head over heels in love with the girl and has been since she moved to town three years ago.

"Why don't you go talk to her?" I say, nudging his arm. He startles in embarrassment, his cheeks becoming a deep pink.

"No, no, of course not," he mumbles to me. "I mean, talk to who?"

I roll my eyes. Bruno likes to pretend that he doesn't have the world's most obvious crush on India, but I know it. He knows it. Heck, I'm pretty sure all of Paxton Middle School knows it. It isn't exactly a well-kept secret.

"Oh, I have something for you. For your birthday."

I grimace. Bruno knows I despise birthday gifts. And pretty much my birthday in general. Reasons why:

1) My mother goes out of her way to embarrass me each and every birthday.[17]

2) I don't need another reminder that another year has gone by and I'm still second best next to Trevor Jin.

3) Birthdays kind of suck, because every year I think about my dad, who he is, and what it would be like if he cared that I existed.

Bruno shuffles through our locker, finding his black sketchbook. He flips through several pages where I get a glimpse of the

---

17. I'm not exaggerating about this. Before the Chinese restaurant tradition, my mother used to throw me parties. Parties where no one but Bruno and Ben would show up. I know she doesn't mean to embarrass me, but my mother and I don't necessarily have the same definition of what is or isn't embarrassing.

newest comic he has been working on, *Diamond in the Rough*. He's already shown me a couple of panels, and it looks amazing. Apparently, it's a story about a reformed villain who wants redemption, and the villain goes around correcting the wrongs he did to all these people. It's a pretty awesome concept. Bruno pulls out a single sheet.

He smiles. "Close your eyes."

I promptly squeeze them shut. A thick piece of paper slides into my hands.

"Now open."

I open my eyes and gasp.

"It's me." Bruno has drawn me as a superhero. I'm clad in a lab coat that somehow floats behind me like a cape. In one hand I have a beaker, and in the other I have a microscope. I have never looked so amazing. Ever. The coolest part of the drawing is the heading in big graffiti letters: *What would Marie do?*

"Bruno, this is absolute perfection," I breathe.

"Do you really like it?" he asks shyly. "I know you don't normally do birthday gifts, but I have been working on this for a while."

"Do I like it? I love it! It's perfect! Someday when you're a famous graphic novelist, I'm going to show everyone this drawing. Can you sign it?"

Bruno smiles. He pulls a pen from his pocket and quickly scribbles his initials on the page. I bump his shoulder with mine and give him a smile back.

"I love it. I really do. This is the only acceptable gift I'll take for my birthday."

I glance behind us. Is India Saunders staring at us? Her face is scrunched up into this little pout that honestly really isn't doing much for her face. But yes, she *is* looking at us, and she looks almost sad. But just as I start to alert Bruno to her weird staring, she whips her head back around and continues talking to her friends. I shrug my shoulders, using a magnet to hang Bruno's picture up in our locker. I look down at my watch and make a small squeak.

"I'm going to be late to homeroom."

Bruno nods, his lips twitching. Okay, maybe I'm being dramatic. I'm not really going to be late, but I *do* like to get to class early. Really, being early is on time, and being on time is late. I wave goodbye to Bruno and make my way to Ms. Richmond's classroom. Of course, Trevor is already there, his pencils, pens, and paper laid out in a neat line. Honestly, one day I should just accidentally fall onto the desk or accidentally throw everything out the window or something.[18] Trevor looks up from his desk, giving me a cursory glance.

"A little late today, aren't you, EJ?"

I scowl at him, throwing my bookbag onto the floor beside my desk. "I told you that only my friends are allowed to call me EJ, and you're most definitely not one of my friends."

Trevor grins back at me, his teeth flashing.

"Whatever you say." He pauses dramatically. "EJ."

I slide into my seat, facing the front, and start to lay my own supplies out on the desk.

---

18. Okay, I wouldn't actually do that, but I'm very, very tempted.

"I don't have time for this today," I hiss.

"Oh yeah. I forgot. It's your birthday." He flings his hand up like it matters very little to him.

"Yes, that's right—" Wait a minute. Wait just a minute. How does Trevor Jin know that today is my birthday? In all the years I have known him, I haven't once known Trevor to mention my birthday at all.

"How did you know today was my birthday?" I ask.

A flush floods his skin. He looks away, chewing his bottom lip.

"Forget I said anything," he mumbles.

No, I'm most certainly not going to forget that he said something. Not when he's so obviously been snooping in my personal information.

"I don't know how you got that information, Trevor, but you better not tell anyone."

Trevor rolls his eyes. "Who am I going to tell?"

"My birthday isn't listed anywhere. I don't have social media. So I know you didn't get it from there. I *know* Bruno didn't tell you. So what are you doing, Trevor? Are you stalking me?"

Even as I say it, I know I've probably gone too far.

Trevor's eyes flash with a spark of hurt. His jaw tightens, and he turns away from me, ending our conversation.

Good. I don't need to look at your stupid, stupid face, anyway. Stalker.

I fume through the rest of homeroom and English. Trevor, for his part, avoids my gaze. Even though I know he can feel me staring daggers at him. By the time we get to biology (another class

I unfortunately share with Trevor), I've calmed down. Somebody probably told Trevor my birthday in passing. It probably just came up in conversation or something. Maybe I have a birthday twin, and they were just telling Trevor how much they are looking forward to their own birthday, and then they just casually mentioned that we share the same birthday. But as much as I like that theory, there are two things wrong with it.

> 1) Why would anyone besides Bruno know my birthday?
> 2) Trevor Jin doesn't have casual conversations, or friends, for that matter.

So that leaves me with this really odd, niggling feeling, like I'm missing something very important.

Determined not to think about it, I sit down at my assigned seat for biology. Biology is my absolute favorite class. I mean, that goes without saying for a future biologist. But it's not just something I'm forced to love because of my future career path; it's something I actually enjoy. When I was younger, I would save up my money from the tooth fairy[19] and purchase science kits online, where I could put together skeletons or do mini experiments to see how mold grew. So this is the best part of my day.

---

19. FYI, my mom was really bad at the whole tooth fairy thing. She'd forget to put the money under my pillow, and when I would ask in the morning, she would tell me that the tooth fairy was part of a union and she couldn't work after nine o'clock on weekends.

"All right, everybody. Settle down." Mrs. Evans looks around sixty years old, about four foot eight, and ninety pounds, but she is probably the most intimidating teacher at the school. And the most respected. Rumor has it that she has a wing named after her at the college she attended. Another rumor says that she turned down a job at NASA to come work for the school.[20] Either way, she is my absolute favorite teacher, and I have been dying to take this class since I got to this school.

"So, today we're starting our heredity unit. We're going to focus on DNA and the inheritance and variation of traits."

A couple of groans sound throughout the room. But not me. My heart picks up speed a little.

Mrs. Evans continues. "That will take us into biological evolution, but we won't get to that until well after Thanksgiving."

More groans. I peek over at Trevor, who looks just as interested as I feel. Ugh. I turn back around, focusing my attention on Mrs. Evans.

"So, everyone has completed the reading, correct?" Her eyebrows go up as she examines the room. Most people avoid her gaze. "Good, because you have partner projects that you will be working on, and I need to assign partners."

The groans are more audible this time, and though I don't groan, my excitement is ebbing away. I hate partner projects. Partner projects usually mean that I end up doing all the work and my partner shares the credit, or worse, my partner does the work

---

20. Not completely certain if this is true. I mean, what person with any sense would turn down a job at NASA? And Mrs. Evans is a very sensible person.

and it isn't up to my standards, and I have to redo the whole thing again anyway.

Mrs. Evans claps her hands to bring the class's attention back to her.

"Please pay attention. I won't be giving you your partner's name more than once."

I listen, waiting for my name to get called.

"Okay, and next, Erin Johnson."

Finally. It feels like I have been waiting forever. Who do I have? Honestly, does it matter? I'll end up doing all the work anyway. And that is just fine. That's exactly how I prefer it.

"And Trevor Jin."

I freeze, and out of the corner of my eye I catch Trevor doing the same.

No, nooo. This can't be right. Mrs. Evans must have made a mistake, a really awful mistake. I cannot be paired with Trevor Jin. Isn't there some type of memo or something in the teachers' lounge that prevents us from working together?[21] My hand shoots up, just as Mrs. Evans starts reading the next name.

"Mrs. Evans," I interrupt.

She purses her lips at me, not thrilled to be interrupted. "Ms. Johnson."

---

21. Actually, I'm pretty sure there is a memo. Every time Trevor and I end up sharing a class together, we're intensively competitive. And I'm not too proud to realize that maybe we do get a bit out of hand sometimes. There was one time during history class last year that I ended up smuggling in my cousin Tasha's pet rat for my presentation on the bubonic plague. Let's just say it ended with Trevor and me having to stay after school to search the first floor of the building for the less-cute version of Mickey Mouse.

"I think you might have made a tiny mistake[22] when you called my name."

Mrs. Evans glares at me, glancing down at her list.

"What mistake do you believe I made, Ms. Johnson?" She emphasizes each one of her words.

I flush.

"Um, it's just that you paired me with Travis—I mean, Trevor—and . . . ," I stammer.

As if I could forget Trevor. Ugh. Why did I even think that?

"Yes, I did, Ms. Johnson." Her glasses slip down her nose, and she is looking at me with a piercing, disapproving look.

"I just thought maybe we'd be best with other partners," I finish meekly.

"Oh, is that right, Ms. Johnson? You thought you knew best?"

The room is quiet now. I can feel everyone staring at me.

I slump down in my seat.

"No, Mrs. Evans. I think I was mistaken."

Mrs. Evans nods. "That sounds more accurate."

Great, now I will have to work with Trevor Jin. Happy birthday to me.

The rest of the day goes fairly smoothly, though for some reason I feel like people are staring at me. It is the weirdest thing. Every time my back is turned or people think I'm not paying attention,

---

22. To be honest, this was really quite brave of me to say. Mrs. Evans does not make mistakes, nor does she like it when students imply that she has made one.

I catch them staring or whispering behind their hands. One girl even waved to me. Honestly, it has just been the world's weirdest day. When I told Bruno about everything that happened in biology and the weird stares, he just shrugged. He said people were probably staring because they heard how I stood up to Mrs. Evans, but that didn't seem right because 1) I didn't really stand up to Mrs. Evans, and 2) most kids don't care what happens in an Honors Biology class. But maybe Bruno was right? I really don't have any other explanations as to why the majority of the school seems to find me fascinating all of a sudden.

Bruno and Ben's mom is waiting by the car in the parking lot to get us right after the last bell.

"I thought my mom was coming to get us." I frown, examining Bruno's mom, who is wearing a bright pink tunic scrunched together with a wide red belt. Her thick black hair is tied up in a red bow. She looks ridiculous, but she normally does. Just like my mom. That's probably why they are best friends.

"Hey, cool cats!" Isa says. Bruno and I look at each other and roll our eyes. Both of our moms are constantly trying to use slang, but unfortunately their slang is very, very outdated. Like, majorly outdated.

"Hi, Ms. Isa." She pulls me in for a hug. "I thought my mom was coming."

I look around her, thinking maybe my mom is playing a prank on us and hiding in the backseat. She used to do that to us all the time around Halloween. One time, I jumped so hard that I fell back against the car and knocked myself out. I had to be taken to the emergency room and treated for a mild concussion. After that, my mom decided it was for the best if she stopped with the pranks. Though maybe she's changed her mind in honor of my birthday. Maybe, just maybe, she wants to make my birthday extra cringey.

"Your mom had an emergency client call, and she asked me if I'd come and get you guys."

"Oh." I look over at Bruno, and his eyes mirror mine, laced with suspicion. My mom uses the same excuse whenever she is up to something, something that will inevitably end in disaster. The last time she used the excuse of an emergency client call, I was ten and she made me stay at Bruno's house for six hours. When I came home, she had painted my room a color she called bubblegum pink. I didn't have the heart to tell her that it looked like Pepto-Bismol.

"Come on, chickadees," Isa says, sliding into the driver's seat.

Bruno and I climb into the backseat.

"Seat belts," Isa chirps.

"Where's Ben?" Bruno asks as we start to pull out of the school parking lot.

"Oh, you know Ben," Isa replies. "He got a ride home with one of his friends or something."

Sometimes our moms aren't the most responsible parents in the world.

It doesn't take us long before we reach the front of my house, but something is wrong. Something is very wrong. Our driveway is full of cars, and there is a tiny pink heart balloon tied around the mailbox.

"What's going on?" My heart starts to race.

"Nothing," Isa replies in a singsong voice.

Crap. Something is definitely, definitely up.

Isa parks near the curb on the side of our house.

Bruno is also sensing that something is off. "We're getting out?" he asks in disbelief.

Isa is already out of the car, her colorful tunic ballooning around her.

"Oh, you know," she replies, looking away from us. "I just want to check on Jo. You know how clients can be."

"Mom, you don't have clients," Bruno says in exasperation. "Your last job was cashiering at the Global Mart." Bruno looks over at a red Toyota parked in our driveway. "Hey, is that Lou's car?"

Lou, as in Lucinda, as in Bruno and Ben's stepmom. Something is up. Something is *up*. I'm starting to sweat, and my breathing is coming out in choppy huffs.

Bruno looks over at me in sympathy. He grabs my shoulder and squeezes. Isa leads us up to the door.

"Mom, what's going on?" Bruno tries again. But his mother ignores him, throwing open my front door with a flourish.

The room explodes with noise. "Surprise!"

No. No. No. No.

I look around in horror at all the familiar faces. There are so many people here. Almost all the people I know. Kids from my grade, my great-aunt Agatha, cousins I haven't spoken to in years, even my next-door neighbors, who only talk to me to tell me to get off their lawn. All these people are in my house. On my birthday. And my mother is in the center of the room, holding up a piñata shaped like a heart, surrounded by what look like Valentine's Day decorations. Valentine's Day in September! I look around at the faces, all of them in various states of bemusement, until I stop on one face, the one face I didn't want to see in my house, didn't want to see ever again. Trevor Jin. Trevor Jin is in my house on my birthday, squeezing the life out of a plastic noisemaker. I will never live this down. Thank you, Mom, for ruining my life.

CHAPTER FOUR

Cupid Commandment Number 8: Cupids are ambassadors of love. They must be champions of all things related to love. Every day is Valentine's Day for a Cupid.

"SURPRISE!" MY MOM HOLDS the piñata up above her head and shakes it. "Are you surprised?"

I glare at my mom. "Surprise is definitely one of my emotions," I mumble.

My mom squeals, dropping the piñata heart, and pulls me in for a hug. "I knew you would *love* it. Get it? Love it, because of all the heart decorations?"

I grimace. Yeah, I get it. I hate it, but I get it.

My mom grabs my arm, pulling me toward the other side of

the room, where, to my horror, there is a huge heart-shaped cake sitting on the dining room table.

"The cake is filled with candy corn. I wanted to fill it with those little conversation hearts, but apparently they only sell those in February. Silly, if you ask me."

It isn't silly. It isn't silly at all. Normal people buy conversation hearts and other heart candy around, I don't know, Valentine's Day!

"Mom," I say, feeling sick. "You shouldn't have. You *really* shouldn't have."

"Oh nonsense," my mom says, looking pleased. "This is a big birthday for you. I wanted to make it extra special for my little love muffin."

Two of my classmates swivel around to look at us, tittering.

"Mom," I hiss. "Don't call me that in public. We talked about this."

"Yes, yes," my mom continues, ignoring me. "Can you believe I pulled this off? At first I was just going to take you to the buffet, you know, like we always do for your birthday, but I figured you'd want to do something you'd always remember." Well, she's right. I will always remember this.

She pauses for a moment so she can squeeze my cheek.

Before I can respond, my great-aunt Agatha comes up to me, planting a huge, wet kiss on my cheek, while enveloping me in a hug.[23] I sink into Aunt Agatha's arms, temporarily

---

23. Great-Aunt Agatha is Nana's older sister. And even though Agatha was less than two years older than Nana, she would always treat her like she was the much younger, less responsible sibling. And of course, Nana hated it. So they would bicker every time they saw each other. But even with their rivalry, when Nana died, Aunt Agatha was so stricken with grief that she didn't leave her house for a month.

comforted by how much she looks and smells like Nana.[24]

"Aunt Aggie," my mom squeals. "You made it."

"Of course," Aunt Agatha replies, moving away from me. "We wouldn't have missed EJ's birthday for the world."

She waves a hand vaguely in the direction of the enormous number of aunts, uncles, and cousins who are huddled together in the middle of the room.[25] I groan, because I know that most of my family would have had to come from out of town for this spectacle.

"And, look, Birdie made it too."

Aunt Agatha pulls over my cousin, the only one who is around my age.[26]

"Despite her mom wanting her to stay home." Aunt Agatha's eyes travel over to her youngest daughter, who is watching Birdie like a hawk.[27]

"EJ," Birdie squeaks. She envelops me in a hug.

Aunt Agatha smiles, pulling my mom away to give us some privacy. Birdie releases me from the hug, a ridiculous smile stretched across her face.

"OMG, EJ. This party is amazing."

I gape at her. She is the only, and I mean the only, person in this room under the age of thirty who thinks that.

Here's the thing. I love my cousin. Of course I do, but we're as different as two people can be. I'm practical and logical. Perfect

---

24. Both Nana and Aunt Agatha wore the same peppermint perfume.
25. Aunt Agatha has four daughters, and between her four daughters there are nine grandkids, and two great-grandkids. My mom was Nana's only child. And she was what Nana called a late-in-life blessing. Because of that, most of my cousins are older than me.
26. Birdie is a year younger; she also goes to PMS.
27. Birdie's mom is super overprotective, almost the complete opposite of my mom.

traits for a future scientist. Whereas Birdie is, well, Birdie.[28] I give her a noncommittal grunt.

"The decorations, the food, everything is so cool," she squeals.

Yeah. It's as cool as having all your teeth removed.

"And the boys. There are so many boys."

Birdie's big brown doe eyes dart around the room like she's hunting for prey. She absently fluffs her curly Afro.

"I haven't noticed," I mumble, trying to figure out a way to extract myself from her.

"Ooh." Birdie grips my upper arm. "What about that one?"

Birdie is normally about as subtle as a freight train, but I still didn't anticipate her blatantly pointing to a boy like she was picking out a puppy at the local shelter.

"He's cute. I mean, *hellooo*, gorgeous."

I'm suddenly very afraid to turn around, because somehow I know who Birdie is going to be talking about. I just know. I turn around slowly and look over in the direction Birdie is pointing. I find myself peering at Trevor.

Unaware of my silence, Birdie continues. "He's been staring at you. I mean, like, the whole time I've been talking to you."

Birdie's bubbly voice carries throughout the room, and I swear that Trevor has heard her. He turns to look over at me, and for the briefest moment we lock eyes. Horrified, I turn away. Trevor does the same.

---

28. Exhibit A: Birdie is currently wearing a sky-blue dress that is covered with abnormally large cartoon hearts. No one else decided to dress up to thematically match the party. Just Birdie. Sometimes I entertain the thought that maybe Birdie and I were accidentally switched as babies.

"Trevor wasn't staring at me."

Birdie opens her mouth to protest, but I stop her before she can rebut.

"Besides," I whisper, "Trevor may be cute, but so are polar bears."

Birdie looks at me in confusion.

"Polar bears are one of the most dangerous animals in the world."

Birdie lets out a low whistle. "Deep," she says.

I was tired of this. Not just of Birdie, but of this whole ridiculous party.

"Excuse me," I reply politely to Birdie. "I have to go find my mom."

I find my mom near the corner of our living room, fiddling with a string of heart-shaped fairy lights.

"Mom, why did you throw this party?" I ask in exasperation. "Why didn't we just go to the buffet?"

Because as much as I hated the buffet, that would have been a million times better than this. Mom turns around, surprised that I'm behind her.

"Well," she starts excitedly. "So, I had the idea for this party. This morning, I got Ben to send out the invites to your classmates. It was genius of me, actually, to ask him."

I grit my teeth, looking away from my mom.

Ben. Ben sent out invites to what looks like at least half our grade. This is entirely his fault.

"Right," I hiss through my teeth. "I should go thank Ben."

I spot Ben on the other side of the room, surrounded by his friends and in a deep conversation with what looks like Bruno. Is that Bruno? As I get closer to them, I notice that it is less of a conversation and more of an argument. Bruno's cheeks are bright red, and he is whispering fervently to Ben, who is crossing and uncrossing his arms in annoyance.

"Yeah, well. It's not my fault your little girlfriend didn't like the surprise her mom put together."

"She's not my girlfriend and you know it." Bruno's entire face is now a burning red. He casts a quick glance at India, who is on Ben's left side.

I march over to Ben and step between him and Bruno.

"Why, Ben? What have I ever done to you to deserve this?"

"Because he's evil, EJ," Bruno mumbles.

Ben barely acknowledges me before he turns to face Bruno again. For a second I see an unfamiliar emotion flicker across Ben's face. An emotion I caught once before, during a Halloween when we were all in the third grade. Until that Halloween, Ben and Bruno had dressed in matching costumes. Sometimes my mom would let me join in on the "fun" (for example, the gummy bear costumes from when we were three), but mostly it was Bruno and Ben who wore the cute matching getups. But the year we were in the third grade was different. Bruno and I were obsessed with *The Addams Family*,[29] and we had our hearts set on being Wednesday and Pugsley. Ben, on the other hand, had

---

29. Bruno and I still love *The Addams Family*. It taught us that being weird can be cool.

his own obsession. He loved superheroes, and he was dying for Bruno and him to be Batman and Robin that Halloween[30] (with him as Batman, of course). When he got home and figured out that we had come up with our own plan, one that didn't include him, he'd looked so devastated that I thought he would cry (and Ben never cries, not even after the one time he broke his leg falling from a tree). Bruno and I tried to make it better. We told Ben that he could be Cousin Itt or Uncle Fester, but he refused, deciding instead to match costumes with one of his good friends from class. This, along with the recent divorce, caused Ben to completely shun me and actively pick on Bruno.

Ben turns his back to me as if he's bored with the whole conversation. He yawns, dramatically covering his mouth.

"Why?" I ask again. "Why did you pass out the invitations? You knew I would hate this. You knew."

I felt a pang in my chest. We'd been friends once. Good friends. And now things were so different. It was like there were two Bens—the before-the-divorce Ben and the after-the-divorce Ben. And the after-the-divorce Ben barely resembles the Ben I knew from before.

Bruno scowls at his brother, and Ben scowls right back.

"Whatever," Ben says, throwing up his hands. "I was doing your mom a favor. I'm sooo sorry for trying to do a nice thing."

And suddenly I need space, away from the noise and clutter of bodies. I need an area where I can just breathe.

---

30. This was Ben and Bruno's first Halloween without their dad. He had recently moved to San Diego, which was over two thousand miles away.

I hide in the kitchen. Kitchens are safe. They are usually off-limits to partygoers, and people won't look for me in the kitchen. Right? I glance down at my watch. It has only been twenty minutes since I first came in the door. How long do parties usually last? One hour? Two? Three? How long can I safely hide in the kitchen before people notice I'm missing? I look around the kitchen, which mercifully remained undecorated.[31]

I slump into a corner by the pantry, sinking my face into my hands.

"Why is this happening?" I grumble into my hands. "This, this is why I hate birthdays."

"Oh, come on. This isn't that bad."

That voice. It's so very familiar. So very, very familiar.

I lift my face from my hands and look straight into the eyes of Trevor Jin. He is smiling, steadying a platter of heart-shaped sandwiches in his hands.

"What are you doing in here?" I quickly hop up, brushing off my jeans.

Trevor's smile slips, and he shrugs. "Your mom asked me to bring these sandwiches into the party. Apparently, she forgot to bring them out earlier." He sets the tray on the counter.

"Oh," I say in embarrassment. Of course my mom would ask my sworn enemy to come to the one place I was hiding from everyone.

Trevor doesn't respond; he just frowns at me like he wants to say something but doesn't know if he should.

---

31. When I say undecorated, I mean not decorated for the party. Unfortunately, my mother decided that yellow and lime green were appropriate colors for a kitchen.

I sigh. "It's completely appropriate that you're here right now witnessing my downfall. It seems almost like karma wanted to give me that final kick in the butt."

Trevor's face crinkles. He starts to say something, then stops. Then starts again.

"Is it really that bad? Having a mom who planned all this?"

There's an adorable wrinkle in his brow that accents his very serious frown. I could see possibly, maybe, how some people might find him cute.

"Did you see the decorations? The streamers above the stairs have dancing puppies and hearts on them. I don't see how it could get any worse."

Trevor's mouth quirks up at the corners, then slides down again into a scowl.

"You could have a mom who didn't have the time to even remember your birthday," he replies quietly.

I stand still, stunned by what Trevor has just told me. It feels strange, hearing him confess this, because it sounds almost like something you would confess to a friend. And we aren't friends. We're mortal enemies. But that doesn't stop the flood of sympathy that washes through me. Trevor is right. As much as my mom may have failed at certain aspects of motherhood, she's never failed in trying to make my birthdays special.

I move out of the corner, coming to stand right in front of him. Almost like an instinct, I feel an odd urge to comfort him.

"I—"

"Erin, there you are." My mom comes into the kitchen. I automatically move away from Trevor. "Why are you hiding in the kitchen?"

She sweeps past Trevor and grasps my hands.

"It's time to sing 'Happy Birthday.'"

My gaze flicks over to Trevor, who is now looking down at his shoes. I want to run. I want to tell my mom that there is no way on earth that I'm going into a room full of my classmates so that they can sing "Happy Birthday" to me while I blow out candles on a heart-shaped, candy-corn-filled cake. But something about how Trevor is looking down at his shoes, like he wishes this were *his* ridiculous birthday party, stops me.

"Okay," I mumble in resignation.

"Awesome!" my mother squeals.[32] "I have a special surprise for you."

I lurch behind her, trying to hide my grimace. "Really, Mom, you shouldn't have. Really."

I'm surprised to find Trevor not far behind us, following us out into the living room. He sets the sandwiches down on the living room table.

"I found her!" my mom trills. Everyone in the room turns to stare. It is painfully clear that no one has been looking for me. My mom ignores my protests and pulls me by the elbow up to the front of the room.

"Thank you for coming, everyone. I'm glad you could make it to Erin's thirteenth birthday bash."

---

32. I would like to note that for a grown woman, my mother sure does squeal a lot.

I stand still. Maybe if I stand still enough, I will kind of fade out of existence. Isn't there some type of scientific theory that proves that?

"Thirteen years ago, when Erin first made her appearance, I knew that my life would be changed forever."

Well, obviously. Everyone's life is changed when they have a kid. I breathe in deep, trying to steady my nerves.

"So, I wanted to commemorate this very special day as Erin makes her first step into womanhood."

"Mom," I hiss, my ears burning.

My mom pats my shoulder. "It's okay, honey. I went through it too. I know it is a confusing time."

This can't be happening. This can't be happening.

"So, I have a little surprise for Erin." Mom shuffles behind me, pulling out a stack of papers.

What is she doing? God, what could she be doing? Calm down, Erin. Calm down. She probably named a star after you or something else cool like that. It has to be something like that. It just has to be.

"So, I know that many of you probably know that I'm a writer."

None of them know you're a writer, Mom. None of them.

"Well, my newest client wants me to write a young adult novel, something sort of like *Twilight*. Vampires and werewolves. The whole shebang. And I'm sure all of you know that *Twilight* is one of Erin's favorite movies."

No, no, it's not. I hate everything to do with vampires, werewolves, and witches. I only watched the stupid movie because my mom begged me to.

"Well"—my mom turns around to face me—"I have already got my first draft written, and I'm excited to share the first passage with all of you."

Why? I must have done some pretty horrible things in my previous life, like catastrophically awful, to deserve this level of embarrassment.

"Annnd"—my mom turns back around to face everyone else in the room—"the main character is named Erin. Surprise!"

I want to disappear. Just disappear on the spot. I shrink down, trying to make myself as small as possible.

"Of course, I'm going to have to swear you all to secrecy. You aren't supposed to know I wrote this." She holds a finger up to her lips, giggling.

"Mom." I look up at her in desperation. "Please, maybe we should save this—"

"Nonsense," my mom states, pinching my cheeks. "I wrote this just for you."

She clears her throat.

"'Erin was an extraordinarily beautiful girl, who didn't know how beautiful she really was.'"

Oh god.

"'She was five foot two, one hundred pounds, scrawny, but with a smile that would light up a room.'"

Ben snorts from across the room.

My mother continues. "'She was painfully shy, and she found

it hard to make friends—that is, until the day she met Trevor Long.'"

I freeze, my mortification reaching a fever pitch. Did she say Trevor? I look over at Trevor, and he is staring at my mom, his mouth open.

"'Trevor wasn't from Erin's small town. He was a mysterious stranger who had just shown up one day and enrolled in school. He didn't talk to anyone. He was one of those boys who probably brooded for a living.'"

The room is quiet, almost deafeningly quiet.

"'Erin didn't know she was falling in love. Once she realized it, she had already fallen deeply and irrevocably in love.'"

I start to shake, my hands balling into fists at my sides. My mother has written a love story about me—not just about me, but a love story about me and Trevor Jin. I can't believe this is happening. I just can't believe it. Birdie lets out a squeal of excitement and claps. I shoot her a death glare.

"'If Erin was honest with herself, she knew she'd loved him from the first moment she'd set eyes on him. She knew it from the first kiss, how his mouth covered—'"

"Oh yeah, a nerd romance!" someone hoots.

I flee. I run from the room, not caring. Not caring if it hurts my mom's feelings or if it makes me seem rude or if it makes me look like a coward. I cannot take this humiliation any longer. I cannot. On my flight up the stairs, I think I briefly hear my name being called. But I don't care. I just want to escape. I run through the hallway until I get to my room. I open the door and slam it shut behind me. I no longer care if everyone hears the door slam or what they think about me. Honestly, what does it matter? My mother has ruined my life. Absolutely ruined my life. Sure, this party would have been perfect for someone like Birdie, someone who likes kooky, embarrassing Valentine's-themed parties and mothers who write ridiculous fan fiction. It's not the type of party appropriate for a future scientist. I fall onto my bed, too humiliated to change into my pajamas. Honestly, if this is what being thirteen is going to be like, I'd rather just go back to being twelve.

For the rest of my evening, I ignore everything. I ignore my mom when she softly knocks on my door an hour after I flee the party. I ignore the back-to-back phone calls from Bruno. I lie in my bed, arms crossed, planning a way to run far away, possibly to another planet.[33] I think about this plan until I fall asleep.

---

33. Mars is very close to being inhabitable. Maybe I can immigrate there and become an actual Martian.

CHAPTER FIVE

*Cupid Commandment Number 5: A Cupid's powers
normally manifest around the age of thirteen. A
new Cupid should be careful that they are not
unconsciously using their powers.*

WHEN I WAKE UP the next morning, I feel completely and utterly refreshed. I can't remember the last time that I slept this well. I get out of bed, somehow feeling stronger, more resilient. But then the memories from yesterday slam into me with such force that I pause in organizing my school outfit for the day. The party. My mother. The romance novel starring me and Trevor Jin. I push aside the gray sweater I just carefully laid out on my bed, and I fall back onto the mattress with a loud thump. I will not be going to school today. Heck, I might never go back to school. I might have to move schools or, even worse, get homeschooled.

I groan, pushing my face farther into my pillow. What are the chances of getting into a competitive high school program if I randomly switch schools in the middle of the year? Probably significantly low.

Honestly, what would Marie do? Would Marie quit because of a minor embarrassment? Well, maybe it isn't exactly minor, but still.

No, no, she wouldn't.

I climb out of bed and quickly get dressed. I will put on a brave face. I'm a future Nobel Prize–winning scientist. I can handle a little embarrassment. I mean, really, are these people even going to be important to my future? Probably not. So why should I care at all? That is the logical way to look at things. Breathing deeply, I prepare myself to leave my room. Unfortunately, I have forgotten one little thing about this whole scenario.

My mom.

I will have to talk to Mom. I groan again, opening the door, going down the stairs as if I'm marching to my death. One foot first, then the other. If I'm being honest, 1) I *do not* want to talk to Mom about last night,[34] and 2) I really, really don't want to go to school. No matter what I said earlier about my classmates at PMS, obviously they matter a teensy bit. I walk into the kitchen, swinging my bookbag onto the kitchen chair. My mother is at the stove, pushing around what seems to be some genuinely

---

34. I love my mom, but we couldn't be more different if we tried. My mom doesn't have very thick skin, and she doesn't take criticism well. I know she just wanted to surprise me and everything, but I hated almost every part of that party, and I don't know how to tell her that without hurting her feelings.

sad-looking scrambled eggs. She peers up at me when I come in, then quickly looks down at the now-smoking pan.

"Shoot," she says, pulling the pan from the stove top and putting it on the counter. She looks over at me dolefully, her eyes watering a bit. "I was trying to surprise you with eggs."

My mother is not a cook, and what this means is that some of the time I take up the task of making small meals, but the majority of the time we live on takeout. From the time I was born, my mom and I lived with Nana. When Nana was alive, it was different. Nana always cooked me hot meals. She believed that cooking was the perfect way to show a person that you loved them. And Nana showed me this every day through piping-hot biscuits made from scratch, whole hams soaked in honey, and collard greens that tasted both bitter and sweet. Nana would fill my plate with her version of what love was.

"It's fine, Mom," I answer slowly, as if speaking to a small child who is on the verge of throwing a tantrum. "I'll just eat cereal," I say, moving toward the pantry.

Before I can open the pantry door, my mom pulls my arm and spins me around to face her. She looks sheepish and almost slightly embarrassed. "I have a client meeting in twenty minutes. So I can't take you guys to school today. Lou is coming to get you."

I don't respond.

"Also, I talked to Bruno last night." My mom wrings her hands in front of her chest. "He told me about Trevor, and how you two are not on the best of terms."

That's putting it mildly.

"And that my story might have been a bit embarrassing for you. And I'm sorry."

A bit?? How about life-altering? How about future-changing? How about cataclysmic?

"Of course, I've heard you mention the name Trevor a time or two.[35] I just liked the name. It seemed like such a strong, romantic name, perfect for the male love interest."

"Mom!" I squawk. "Trevor is neither a strong nor romantic name. It's the perfect name for a suck-up. A suck-up who gets on everybody's nerves." I cross my arms.

"Well," my mom says, dumping the eggs into the trash, "obviously, I see that now."

"Uh-huh," I reply with obvious sarcasm. "So, you're changing the character, then?"

"Oh nooo, I've already sent pages off to the client. She loved it, by the way. So we won't be changing any character names."

I look at her in disbelief. "Then why are you apologizing?"

My mom looks at me as if I'm completely missing the point. Her watery eyes are now suspiciously dry. "Well, I'm obviously sorry about reading it out loud. I didn't know this Trevor person would be in the room."

"Mom, you had Ben invite almost everyone I know from school. Why would you think Trevor wouldn't be there?"

My mom wipes her hands on a dish towel. "Well, to be

---

35. I've literally been referencing Trevor as my mortal enemy since I was six years old.

honest, honey, I thought that you might have made him up. I've only known you to have one friend, and you've always had such a healthy imagination when—"

A horn sounds, and I have never been more grateful to leave for school.

I get into the backseat of the car, flashing Bruno a tiny smile. Thankfully, the front-side passenger seat is empty. Bruno's stepmother, Lucinda, sits at the wheel.

Where's Ben? I mouth to Bruno.

Not here, he mouths back.

"How are you doing today, Erin?" Lucinda asks, giving me a sympathetic look in the rearview mirror. She is looking at me like I'm one of those homeless puppies on television that look like they've never eaten a day in their lives. I purse my lips. I know Lucinda means well, and overall she is a lot less cringey than either of our moms, but it doesn't mean I want to go into a deep conversation about my hidden feelings or anything. And with Lucinda there is always a deep conversation about feelings. She is a trauma therapist, and while I appreciate having an all-access pass to my emotions (not), for today I just want to pretend like my life-changing, life-altering mess of a thirteenth birthday party never happened.

"We all thought it would be best if Ben rode to school with Isa today." Lucinda gives me another knowing look. "Bruno had a talk with us about the party and everything Ben did. And while I'm sure he didn't mean any harm"—I snort—"we think it's best if Ben rides to school today with his mom." Lucinda winks at me. I know she was the reason that I'm getting this very needed Ben-free ride. I give her a grateful smile. Lucinda is honestly the most sane out of the three parental figures.

When we arrive at school, I sit still for a moment while Bruno climbs out of the car.

"Good to go?" Lucinda asks, turning around to stare at me with a patient smile. I give her a tentative smile back. Even though yesterday was quite possibly the worst day of my existence, and even though there are probably videos and memes circulating around the school referencing a romance between me and Trevor Jin, I, for some reason, have never felt more alive. I'm vibrating with energy. My skin is a live wire, and I buzz with an overflow of what feels like electricity. I can't remember ever feeling this energetic, and it feels—well, frankly, it feels completely and utterly exhilarating. I feel that if I truly wanted to, I could lift Lucinda's car right off the ground.

I hop out of the car, this newfound energy both exciting and confusing. What was in this morning's cereal?

I give Lucinda a thumbs-up and jog to catch up to where Bruno is waiting for me on the sidewalk. I pull his arm into mine, and we start to walk toward the front door of the school.

"Hey, thanks for talking to everyone. My mom, your moms, just thanks."

Bruno nods solemnly. "I hate that Ben is such a troll. It's like he wants me to hate him or something."

I peer up at Bruno, who seems to be worlds away, lost in his own thoughts. I sigh.

"I don't think he wants you to hate him—I think—" I shake my head. "I don't know what I think."

Bruno is no longer paying attention. His eyes move over to where Ben is getting out of their mother's car. Ben hurries to open the car door for India as she climbs out of the backseat. He looks over at us, catching Bruno's stare. Ben gives Bruno a smug smile. India's eyes lift too. She focuses on our linked arms, then looks away at Ben in embarrassment. Bruno's mouth is a tight line, his shoulders as tense as a bowstring.

"Come on," I say, pulling on his arm. "Let's just go."

"Yeah," Bruno mumbles, making his way up the front steps.

"Just go talk to her." I pull his arm again. He stops, and I force him to turn around to face me. "Come on." He looks up, peeking over at India, who is now standing near the front of the school, talking to Ben. Bruno shakes his head.

"No," he replies quietly. "She's busy."

"She's just talking to Ben," I huff. "She's not really that busy. I mean, plus, I always catch her peeking over here at you. She does it when she thinks you're not looking."

Bruno's face softens for a moment, and he looks as if he'll do it, like he'll finally go and say something to India. Then he shakes his head as if he's coming out of a trance.

"No." He turns around, ignoring my grunts of obvious disapproval. "I said she's busy. Let's go."

I flinch at the tone of his voice and clutch his arm once again. Bruno is such a good guy. He deserves to be happy. He deserves it way more than his stupid twin brother. And India would make him happy. He's been pining after her forever. Longer than for-ever, it seems. I just wish he'd gather the courage to go and talk to India, to tell her how he feels. Honestly, I see the way India looks at him all the time. I just wish he would get over his fear.

Suddenly, I feel warmness flush through me, circling me like a hurricane. I clutch tighter to Bruno's arm as a warm tingling sen-sation crawls from the bottom of my toes to the top of my head. Suddenly, I see a swirl and pop of green surround Bruno. It mists his skin and gives him a sort of greenish glow. I hunch over Bruno, gripping his arm even higher.

"Hey, are you okay?" Bruno asks with concern, holding me up with both hands. I nod, straightening up.

"Yeah, I think so. I think I might have had a hot flash or something."

Bruno snorts with laughter. "A hot flash, like the things my abuela used to get."

"Shut up," I say, pushing his shoulder. "Look, it must have been something I ate. I've been feeling weird all morning. But I'm okay." I unhook my arm from his.

He gives me another once-over and nods. "Good, because I have something I have to do before the homeroom bell rings."

"Oh?" We have the same routine every morning. Walk into school together, go to our locker, and then I head off to class early, and he heads to the art room to get a couple of minutes alone to work on his comic.

He nods again, smiling. He looks different. Somehow, he looks brighter, as if the green mist refreshed him.

All right, I'm hallucinating. Obviously, I'm hallucinating. It must be the lack of sleep and the trauma from the get-together-that-mustn't-be-named.

Bruno hoists his bookbag on his back, spins on his heel, and heads straight for Ben and India. I stand there, my mouth gaping open. Is he—is he really going over there to talk to India? I watch in absolute fascination as Bruno saunters over to India with a confidence I never knew he possessed. When he finally makes it to the pair, both India and Ben share dual expressions of surprise. Ben says something, his mouth an ugly sneer. Oh no, he's going to push Bruno away. Bruno is going to come back over here and let Ben win. I hold my breath as Ben continues to gesticulate, moving his arms rapidly. But Bruno doesn't budge; he simply ignores Ben and holds out his hand to India. India stands there for a moment, stunned at whatever Bruno has just said. Then she puts her hand into Bruno's outstretched one. Bruno smiles at her, and they walk toward me. By the time they reach me, India is leaning into Bruno's arm. They walk past, Bruno opening the front door for India. He turns back to look at me and winks.

What is going on?

When I get to homeroom, it is a bit later than my usual time (fifteen minutes before the bell rings), but the classroom is still quite empty. There are only three students sitting at their desks, and of course Trevor Jin is one of them. Ignoring him, I sit down in my seat, turning my body so my back is facing his desk. I start to unpack when I hear a rough voice interrupt my process.

"Don't worry, I wasn't going to talk to you."

I flush in anger. "I didn't ask you if you were going to talk to me," I respond tartly.

"Well, you're turned around in your desk like you're afraid I'm going to attack you or something."

I whip around to look at him. "I'm not afraid of you, Trevor Jin."

Trevor keeps my gaze, a smirk stretched across his lips. "Well, stop acting like it, *EJ*."

If I could get away with slamming all his precious pencils, pens, and notebooks to the floor, I totally would. I would love, love, love to wipe that smug look off his face. But, hey, he probably has a reason to be smug. I'm the one who just had a pseudo birthday/Valentine's Day party where my writer mother read *Twilight* fan fiction that he has a starring role in. If I were him, I would be smug too.

The bell rings, and Ms. Richmond hustles up to the front of the classroom.

"Now, children. I have a special treat for you today. Many of you know that Mr. Fairview is the eighth-grade counselor here at PMS."

We all nod our heads listlessly in response.

"Well, today, Mr. Fairview is going to go over a presentation about life after eighth grade," she says.

Life after eighth grade. Ms. Richmond makes it seem like we're heading into war (which, to be fair—high school is sort of like war).

"Mr. Fairview will go into class options, paths you can take, diploma options, and clubs offered at the high school too."

I sit up, a bit more interested. Out of the corner of my eye, I can see that Trevor is now sitting up a little straighter too.

Ms. Richmond continues. "I shouldn't have to tell you how important your high school years are to your future. I'm sure you already know this, but I also want to emphasize the importance of having fun in high school. You're only young once." She laughs, like what she said was the funniest thing ever. Trevor and I sneak a peek at each other, each of us smiling.

Wait, hold up. I'm not sharing a laugh with Trevor Jin. I lurch back around, focusing on Ms. Richmond. I must be sick today or something.

"So, without further ado, or much ado about nothing"[36]—she stops and snorts with laughter again—"Mr. Fairview." She points over toward the door, where I hadn't noticed that Mr. Fairview was standing. Mr. Fairview is a quiet man, only about five foot five, and he has five different-colored sweater-vests that he wears for each day of the week.[37] Every time he talks, it sounds as if he is whispering, so we all have to lean in to make out exactly what he is saying. It's the strangest thing to have lessons from him, because we either have to 1) take up lipreading, or 2) ignore him, take a nap, and hope we don't miss anything important.

"Thank you for that introduction, Ms. Richmond." He looks

---

36. Apparently, *Much Ado About Nothing* is another Shakespeare play. I need this woman to go out and get a life.
37. Monday: blue, Tuesday: gray, Wednesday: dark green, Thursday: black, and Friday: checkered.

up at her, his eyes wide and adoring. His glasses slip slightly down his nose, and he pushes them up hurriedly, trying in the process to cover the blush that is creeping up his face.

Ms. Richmond winks at him, and he stumbles a bit, tripping over my bookbag.

"Sorry," I mumble, pulling my bookbag completely under my desk.

"Not your fault," Mr. Fairview says good-naturedly. "I trip over my own feet at least twice a day, and they are attached to my body."

He gives me a warm smile, and I give him one back.

"All right, class. I want to thank Ms. Richmond for allowing me the time to come to talk to you. It was very generous of her." He looks over at Ms. Richmond with such longing that I'm sure she will notice and blush from the embarrassment of it all, but she isn't even paying attention. She is looking down at her desk, flipping through the pages of our next reading assignment.

Mr. Fairview is totally in love with Ms. Richmond, like, head-over-heels obsessed.

The room has gotten quiet, waiting for Mr. Fairview to continue. Finally, Ms. Richmond puts down her book and glances up at Mr. Fairview. "Oh, I'm sorry. Did you need something else, Paul? Oops, I mean Mr. Fairview."

Mr. Fairview seems to glow red. "Oh no, I'm sorry. I mean, you can call me Paul, of course. I mean, I'll just start now."

The whole class can feel the weight of Mr. Fairview's

secondhand embarrassment. He gets through his presentation without any more incidents, though he does stop every couple of minutes to stare longingly at Ms. Richmond. I know most of the information that Mr. Fairview is going over, but one thing in particular definitely catches my interest. Warrior Academy High School has several different specialty programs for incoming students, programs that you have to apply for. We will learn more about most of those programs later on in the year. The program that I want to get into today, that I absolutely need to get into, is the dual enrollment program.[38] But they only take one student each year for the program. One. Which means that Trevor and I will be vying for the same spot.

"We will now start accepting applications for the dual enrollment program, but they won't officially be due until January thirty-first. Now, please raise your hand if you'd like an application."

About six hands pop into the air, but I'm not worried about most of them—well, nearly all of them. The only hand I'm truly worried about is Trevor Jin's. He is the only one who could conceivably take this spot away from me.

Mr. Fairview starts handing out the applications. When he gets to me, he puts his hand in his folder but comes up empty. "Oops, I need more."

With about as much grace as a giraffe doing ballet, he lumbers back up to the front of the room, where more applications are

---

38. The dual enrollment program allows you to take college-level classes while in high school. The classes give you a competitive edge when it is time to apply for college.

stacked neatly on Ms. Richmond's desk. When he crashes into her podium, I'm sure no one is surprised.

"I'm so sorry," Mr. Fairview says, picking up the spilled lesson plans from the floor.

"Oh no, I do that all the time," Ms. Richmond replies kindly.

Mr. Fairview becomes redder, which honestly doesn't seem entirely possible. He bends down farther, scraping up the remaining papers from the floor. It is at this moment that I catch a small smile flitting across Ms. Richmond's face. A smile! A smile directed at Mr. Fairview. They like each other, like, really like each other, but neither one can tell how the other person feels. A thought courses through me. I bet if they were dating, Ms. Richmond would keep him on his toes. She'd make sure he'd meet deadlines. I've heard horror stories from previous students about Mr. Fairview losing an important recommendation letter or forgetting to turn in their applications. I can't afford for that to happen to me.

Mr. Fairview maneuvers around Ms. Richmond, grabs an application, and slides it onto my desk. "Here you go, young lady."

I grip the paper, examining it to make sure it is the right one before I let go. I look behind Mr. Fairview, and I catch Ms. Richmond giving him a quick look of longing. I turn back to face Mr. Fairview, who is staring at me in confusion, his hand and my hand still gripped on the application. *God,* I think. *I wish you would just notice how much Ms. Richmond likes you. You should totally ask her on a date.* The warm feeling I felt earlier starts rapidly circulating throughout my body again. A light orange cloud outlines Mr. Fairview. I panic, snatching the paper from Mr. Fairview's hands. He gives me a small smile and moves on. What is going on with me? Do I have some sort of condition that brings on spontaneous hot flashes? Could I be sick? Like, deathly sick? Could I be dying??[39]

The heat crawls off my skin, leaving me feeling tingly and weak. I slump my head down on my desk. A ball of paper hits the top of my head, and I jump up to see that Trevor is staring at me curiously, like I'm some algorithm that he has yet to figure out.

Are you okay? he mouths.

Is Trevor really asking if I'm okay? I glare at him suspiciously, and the fleeting look of concern is quickly replaced with a scowl. He turns back around, facing the front. Amber, a girl in my grade who is a talented flutist but only a semi-talented academic, taps me on the shoulder. I turn my head so that I can peer at her, giving her a look that conveys that she is clearly wasting my precious class time with whatever gossip she is about to tell me.

Amber looks particularly smug. She gives me a huge, mocking smile.

"You have paper stuck in your hair."

I feel around in my hair and pluck the stray paper out. I knew it. I just knew Trevor Jin wasn't actually concerned about me. He was only feigning concern to have an excuse for throwing paper at me. I shoot a venomous look over at Trevor, who isn't even looking my way.

---

39. I can't die before discovering the cure for cancer. I just can't.

"Can everyone give Mr. Fairview a round of applause?" We dutifully clap. "Thank you so much, Mr. Fairview, for that amazing presentation." Ms. Richmond continues to clap, even after we all have stopped.

Mr. Fairview finishes handing out the papers. He walks smoothly up to the front of the room, not tripping, not even a little.

"Hey, class, I have one more tiny presentation, if that's okay with Ms. Richmond?"

Mr. Fairview looks toward Ms. Richmond for confirmation so that he can continue. She nods, slightly confused.

"Okay, class." Mr. Fairview claps his hands. He sounds louder, more confident. "I need help. I have a special date tonight, and I have to figure out where to take my date."

Ms. Richmond looks flabbergasted, her mouth forming a tiny O. But Mr. Fairview doesn't pay attention to her reaction; he just keeps on going.

"So, what's the best place to take a lady to impress her?"

Hands shoot up. My classmates start calling out restaurants, bistros, and cafés. My hand shoots up last.

"Yes, you. Erin, right?"

I nod. "How about a creamery? There's a dairy farm about thirty minutes away from here, but they are also a creamery. They show you how their ice cream is made, and then you get to eat the ice cream. It's pretty cool. I went with my mom last summer. Maybe you can take your date there."

Mr. Fairview doesn't respond. Instead he looks back over at

Ms. Richmond, who still looks confused but is now staring at Mr. Fairview with glazed-over, moony eyes.

He turns back around to face me. "Sounds like we have a plan, Erin. Thank you."

He turns again, grabbing a pen and blank sticky note off Ms. Richmond's desk. When he stands up straight to look at Ms. Richmond, she looks utterly confused. "Here," he says, pushing the sticky note into her hand. "Text me your address, and I'll pick you up at five."

Ms. Richmond's face flushes first with confusion, then with pleasure. She simply nods her head, and Mr. Fairview disappears from the room.

I stare at Ms. Richmond, startled.

I know this is something I'm saying quite a lot today, but what just happened?

CHAPTER SIX

Cupid Commandment Number 14: Love is patient.
Love is kind. So a Cupid must be those things too.

EVERYONE LEAVES ENGLISH CONFUSED. Chatter rings around me as my classmates try to figure out what happened earlier during homeroom.

Lucy, a girl with bright red hair and a penchant for talking louder than necessary, is chatting to her friend right in front of me.

"I think it was very, very romantic. Clearly, he had planned that for a long time."

I roll my eyes. No. No, he hadn't. I'm almost sure he hadn't. It wasn't until he handed me that paper, until I thought about him asking Ms. Richmond out on a date, that all of a sudden he became this different person. Braver. More confident. Kind of like what happened to Bruno earlier. I shake my head. It's impossible. There is no way that I had anything to do with either one of those situations. There are tons of explanations for what is happening. I mean, I once heard of a virus that burrows into people's brains and affects their personalities. Maybe it is something like that. It has to be. What other explanation could there be?

I come up to my locker just in time to see Bruno giving India a quick hug. She smiles from ear to ear, tweaking his nose while Bruno smiles wider than I've ever seen him smile before. Yep. The world has officially gone insane.

Giving them a tiny smile, I squeeze past them and spin the combination lock, pulling it open.

"Oh, hi, EJ." India holds up her hand in a friendly wave.

EJ? We've barely ever talked to each other before, and now she's using my nickname. Okay, good to know.

"Hello—" I pause. Should I give her a nickname too? IA, IS, Indie? I settle on her actual name. "India."

I slide my science textbook from the locker.

"So, you want to hear a funny story?" India asks, her eyes wide saucers of interest. Well, actually, no, I don't really want to hear a story, since 1) I'm not one for gossip (unless it's about Trevor), and 2) I do not want to be late for class. In fact, I want to be extra early today so that I can beat Trevor. My locker is significantly closer than his is to our next class, and it is honestly the only time I can beat him.

I open my mouth to tell India, *No, sorry, I have places to be,* but then I lock eyes with Bruno, who is looking at me, pleading. Okay. Okay.

"Sure," I consent, closing the locker with a thud.

"So, I totally thought you two were dating or something. I mean, Ben kept hinting at it, calling you guys an old married couple. Isn't that funny?"

India lets out a tinkling laugh. I press my lips into a straight line. No, not really. It isn't funny in the slightest.

"Uh-huh," I answer, cutting my eyes over to Bruno.

Is she serious? my face asks.

Bruno gives me a sour look as a response. *Be nice,* his eyes say.

"And, well, Bruno seemed to think that Ben and I were dating, like we're a couple or something."

"Yep," I respond noncommittally, staring down at my watch. "That's usually what dating means."

Ugh. Did I just say that out loud? I didn't mean to say that out loud. But honestly, I'm not going to make it in time to beat Trevor. He is probably leaving his locker right this moment.

"But I absolutely wouldn't date Ben," India continues. "We're just friends, like you and Bruno. So maybe we can all be friends?"

I burst out laughing.

India's beautiful, full-wattage smile falters a little as she blinks down at me. I slam a hand over my mouth.

"I'm sorry." I lock eyes with Bruno. "I'm sorry. It's just—it's just, have you run this plan by Ben yet?"

India blinks again.

This time I snort when I laugh.

Hang out all the time? With Ben??

"Well, good luck with that," I say, shouldering my bookbag.

Bruno frowns at me. I give both of them an apologetic smile.

"Look, I'm sorry," I say. "Today's been a really weird day. I'll catch you guys later."

I hurry away from them before they can respond, and I go into biology. I clunk down on my stool right next to Trevor. Of course, somehow, he managed to arrive before me. Why would anything at all go my way today? And why is he sitting in the seat next to me? His seat is on the other side of the room. Trevor doesn't look over at me. He sits still like some type of freaky statue. Like he's pretending that I don't exist.

"Why are you sitting here?" I pull out my supplies, careful that my pens don't touch his neatly laid-out notebook. "I didn't realize you had trouble remembering things, like where your seat is located."

He turns and looks at me, his eyes frosty with irritation.

"What I didn't realize is that you didn't know how to pay attention to directions." He nods his head toward the board where Mrs. Evans has written out an updated seating chart, placing us next to our new partners. I groan inwardly.

"Whatever," I mutter, snatching up a pen, my ears burning. "Just don't talk to me, okay?"

"You started talking to me first," Trevor points out.

"I just wanted to know why you were sitting here," I explode. My voice carries throughout the room.

Mrs. Evans looks up from her desk, her eyebrow raised in disapproval.

"Sorry," I whisper, shrinking back into my chair.

Trevor looks like he wants to respond, but just then the bell rings.

"Okay, class." Mrs. Evans holds up a stack of sheets. "You should be sitting in your new assigned seats. This is where you will sit for the remainder of the semester. Your first joint project is due Monday. So I'm hoping you will use your time wisely in and out of school to complete the work."

I steal a glance at Trevor. He is purposely avoiding my gaze. And I know he's pretty much the Lex Luthor to my Superman, but I have to admit that he's unfairly good-looking, with his perfect cheekbones and his long lashes. So maybe I understand a little bit of what Birdie was talking about at the party. Trevor whips around, his eyes connecting with mine. I flush, quickly avoiding his gaze.

Mrs. Evans starts handing out a stack of papers to every student in the class. When I get the assignment sheet, my stomach sinks a little. A DNA model. We have to create a DNA model. I was hoping that the project would be something that Trevor and I could complete separately and then come together for our finished product, because unlike most students, Trevor definitely will not let me do the project on my own. He has serious control issues, which—to be fair—so do I. Trevor seems to come to the same realization that I have, that there won't be any way to get out of working on this together.

He clears his throat, looking at the sheet. "So, it looks like we're going to have to work on this together."

I cross my arms, still unwilling to play nice. "Excellent deduction, Captain Obvious," I reply dryly. He ignores me, pulling out a yellow highlighter.

"It looks like it has to be a 3D model that includes the double helix[40] and all four base pairs. So that means because a double helix is—"

"I know what a double helix is," I snap. "Please don't tell me you were about to mansplain a double helix to me."

I cross my arms as he narrows his eyes on me. "I wasn't going to explain it. I was going to—you know what, never mind. We need to call a cease-fire if we're going to get anywhere on this project."

He is right. I know he is right, but today has been so weird, and maybe that is seeping into the way I'm handling Trevor. Or maybe it is the crippling embarrassment from last night's failed birthday party.

"Fine," I mumble, pulling my sheet closer to me, uncapping my own yellow highlighter. I examine the assignment sheet. "It looks like we can make it out of whatever we want to. Mrs. Evans put some examples down of materials we can use. We can use pipe cleaners, Play-Doh, or metal." I count the materials off on one hand. "What are you thinking?"

Trevor shrugs. "I think we should do something that really

_____

40. Double helix is just the description of how double-stranded DNA looks.

makes a statement. All those things are fine, but are they really going to stand out from everybody else's projects?"

I hate that he is right, but he is right. I don't want our project looking like everyone else's. "Okay," I respond reluctantly. "We can make a replication model[41] and get bonus points. Nobody else will think of that."

Trevor nods excitedly. "That actually sounds pretty smart." I wrinkle my nose at his use of the term "actually." "We could use my dad's 3D printer. He wouldn't mind if we borrowed it for school."

I raise an eyebrow. "Your dad has a 3D printer? What does he use it for, making 3D lungs or something?"

I laugh at my joke, but I stop when I look over and catch Trevor's serious yet sheepish expression.

"I mean, he doesn't really make 3D lungs, does he?"

Trevor shakes his head, a bit embarrassed. "Not just lungs, per se. He's working on a grant project where they are creating 3D-printed organs for people on the critical transplant list."

Well, then. God, sometimes I wish I had cool, successful parents who were changing the world. All I have is a mother who frequently puts her pants on inside out. Honestly, it's not that hard to figure out how to put your pants on the correct way.

"Well," I reply softly. "That's pretty awesome. You must be really proud of him."

"Yeah." Trevor looks away, his eyes narrowing. "Proud."

Is that bitterness I hear in his voice? Trevor's jaw is tight,

---

41. Just in case you need to know the definition of this term too, I'll put it here. DNA replication is the process of copying a double-stranded DNA molecule.

and he looks—well, he looks like he is uncomfortable.

"Well, that sounds like a good plan," I say, changing the subject. I think back to our discussion in my kitchen, the way he opened up about his mom. And I wonder if he feels the same way about his dad.

"I guess everyone has to have a good idea once in a while." I smile at him. "Even my mom."

I've got no idea why I just said that. Why would I bring up my mom? Or by default the awful story from the party?

I concentrate on my lap, not wanting to see Trevor's reaction.

Trevor clears his throat, and my eyes move up to meet his. His eyes are so warm. Have they always been that way?

"I think your mom is pretty cool."

"Yeah?" I ask.

"Yeah," he confirms. His eyes stay connected to mine. For a moment, it's kind of hard to breathe.

I look away, coughing into my fist.

"Besides," Trevor says, "I did enjoy your mother's story."

I know that my cheeks are hothouse-tomato red.

"Whatever," I mutter.

Trevor catches my eyes again, and there it is, me struggling to breathe.

Snap out of it.

"I'm serious." He goes back to scanning the assignment. "Besides, I think Erin sounds pretty interesting." He looks up with a blush. "The character, I mean."

I glance down at the assignment also.

"I think the Trevor character is kind of cool too," I say.

Trevor looks up at me and smiles, an actual smile, teeth and all. It makes his face look quite nice. Wait, what am I saying? Trevor's face absolutely does not look nice.

"So, Saturday, then?"

I shrug, but I can't stop the smile that pulls at the corners of my mouth. "Yeah, Saturday."

Trevor pulls out a sleek black phone, a phone that I have never seen before except on celebrity ads.

"Here. Put your number in. I'll text you my address."

I only hesitate for a moment before I key my number into his phone. I save my number under my full name: Erin Johnson. Trevor looks down at the phone. "You didn't have to put your last name in there. I know it's you."

The bell rings. We gather up our stuff, and I give Trevor a small returning smile. Honestly, this might be the first interaction where I have ever willingly smiled at Trevor Jin.

"Everyone knows that it's more professional to put your last name in people's phones."

Trevor laughs, following me out the door. "Well, you're nothing if not professional, EJ."

"What's that me—" I don't get to finish because while I'm talking to Trevor, I fail to notice the wall, a wall that has been there since the day the school was built. So, of course, because this day has been a weird anomaly of a day, it makes sense that I forget about the wall and walk straight into it.

* * *

All in all, today wasn't as bad as I thought it would be. Surprisingly enough, very few people mentioned the party or my mother's story, and the biggest surprise of the day turned out to be that Trevor Jin could actually be nice, and not just nice but helpful. When I had that immensely embarrassing incident where I ran into the wall (I still can't believe that happened), Trevor took the time to help me pick up all my pens and notebooks that had spilled out onto the floor. We even shared ideas that we had for the Multicultural Leadership Club. He asked me if I needed help getting to the nurse. I told him no, of course not. I would know if I had a concussion. He responded to this by saying that most people don't know that they have a concussion when they first get it. And I responded with "Okay, Dr. Jin." This made him get all red and upset. So he pushed my stuff into my arms and left. Though, honestly, that was progress for us. Most of the time we just grunt and give each other the evil eye.

But none of that matters, because we are back in Ms. Richmond's classroom, and she is about to let us know who the chosen nominees are for the role of president of the Multicultural Leadership Club. Honestly, it really isn't even a secret. Everyone knows that Trevor and I will be the nominees. And cinching the presidential role will go a long way toward me getting that coveted spot for next year's dual enrollment program. I look over at Trevor, who is waiting patiently, his hands steepled together. Feeling very diplomatic, I give Trevor a friendly *we're all professionals here* sort of wave. He stares at me, then gives me a stiff wave back.

See, we can be friendly with each other. We can get along.

Maybe Trevor and I are turning over a new leaf. Maybe, just maybe we can be something sort of like friends. After I win the presidency, of course.

Ms. Richmond shuffles into the room, looking quite flustered. She smooths back her thick black ringlets out of her eyes. What's up with her? Then I remember. Mr. Fairview. She and Mr. Fairview are going out on a date. *Because of you,* a tiny voice in the back of my head insists. *They are going on a date because of you.* I push those thoughts away, concentrating instead on my acceptance speech. I pull a set of plain white note cards out of my bag, my neat handwriting spanning the lined fronts of the cards.

"Okay, I think we're all here." Ms. Richmond looks around the room. We aren't the biggest club by far, but we have a fair number of students, thirty in total. "So we should go ahead and begin. I don't want to hold you up. I know that you children have lives and things to do after school."

"Don't you have a date tonight?" one boy calls from the corner of the room.

Ms. Richmond's ears grow red. "Yes, yes. Well, let's not talk about that."

Apparently, the whole school has heard about what they are calling the most romantic gesture of the year.

"So, I know many of you are aware that our previous president and vice president both graduated the eighth grade last year, and we have been left with two very important openings in our club. Applications have been made available to those who have asked, and after much consideration I have narrowed the candidates to two nominees. As is our normal process, we will hold elections, and the winner will become president and the person who comes in second place will be our vice president."

Everyone waits both quietly and patiently, even though we all know the names that Ms. Richmond is going to call out.

"So, without further ado, your nominees are Erin Johnson and Trevor Jin."

Light applause rings throughout the room. "Erin, did you want to come up here to say a little something to the club about your nomination and the direction you plan on taking your campaign?"

I jump up, my note cards in hand. Shuffling them a bit, I stand behind the podium Ms. Richmond uses to teach from.

"Hello, fellow clubmates. For those of you who don't know me, my name is Erin Johnson, and I have been a member of this club from the day I entered the sixth grade. This club is integral to PMS, as it provides a safe environment not only for minorities but also for their allies. Being from one of the only Black families in this town has taught me a lot about who I want to be as a person, and how I want to educate my community and help it grow. One of the first items that I will do if elected your president is to get rid of the chief mascot. Many Indigenous people in our community have come forward to object to the racist undertones of our mascot, and I aim to get rid of the mascot altogether. Thank you for your time."

Applause scatters across the room. I move back to my desk.

"Great idea, Erin. I love the initiative you are taking. Brava."

Ms. Richmond glances over at Trevor, who hasn't moved an inch. "Trevor, it's your turn, dear."

Trevor gets up slowly, unfolding his steepled fingers.

"Good luck," I whisper. Because we're turning over a new leaf. I need to at least try to be cordial. Maybe, just maybe, Trevor Jin isn't my sworn enemy.

Trevor steps up to the podium. "Thank you so much, Ms. Richmond, for this opportunity. Let's clap for Ms. Richmond." He swings a long arm over to Ms. Richmond, who is blushing again. Several of the girls in the classroom are giving Trevor these ridiculous puppy-dog eyes, like he's the prince of PMS or something. It really is unfair that Trevor is so traditionally good-looking. He never even went through the awkward stage that most people go through. Unfortunately, I'm currently still in my awkward stage.

"Also"—Trevor swings around to look at me—"I want to thank my opponent, Erin. It's always hard having to go after her. Great writing runs in the family."

I pause, glaring at him in shock. What did he just say? Several other students start chortling behind their hands.

"So, thank you, Erin, for your wonderful speech." The room erupts in rapturous applause, and a few whistles even sound from the back of the room.

I'm gripping my desk, almost to the point of pain. I do not move. I do not take my eyes off Trevor.

"While I find everything that Erin wants to do admirable, I also want to look at some more immediate things that the club needs, such as funding. When was the last time we took a field trip or hosted a multicultural festival? Well, according to a source, it has been five years since we have done any of these activities. So I want to bring the fun back to our club."

I stare at Trevor, my mouth hanging open. According to a source? That source was me! We were sharing ideas earlier when I was busy turning over a new leaf. I came up with those ideas he just used. Me! And now he's using them for his campaign. You know what? This is my fault, completely my fault. I let my guard down around Trevor, and he proved that he hadn't changed a single bit since kindergarten. He's still a thief.

"Who's with me?" Trevor Jin finishes his speech, pumping his fist into the air.

Everybody claps. Some people stomp their feet, and one girl gives him a standing ovation.

"And as a token of the things to come in my upcoming presidency, I brought everyone something to show my appreciation."

He goes over to his desk, where a large tote bag sits. What is he doing now? I have a really bad feeling about this.

He pulls out a black shirt with an electric-red logo that says A VOTE FOR TREVOR IS A VOTE FOR A GOOD TIME.

"Who wants a free shirt?"

I fume as he starts launching shirts around the room. Trevor Jin pretty much just declared war, and I'm ready to go to battle.

CHAPTER SEVEN

Cupid Commandment Number 2: A good Cupid knows that their Cupid Manual is worth its weight in gold. Cupids must know their manuals inside out.

I KNEW IT. I just knew it. It was too good to be true. All of it. Every bit of the Goody Two-shoes, nice routine that Trevor fed me. He was just buttering me up so that he could steal my ideas. I catch the activity bus, knowing that my mom has a "friend" date with Ms. Isa tonight. Every Friday night they go out to some local restaurant or art gallery or avant-garde play. They never go to the same event twice. Which usually means that 1) I'm on my own for dinner, and 2) I never know exactly when she will traipse into the house.[42] Usually Bruno and I hang out, but Bruno is

---

42. About a year ago, she ended up staying away for the whole night. We were all so concerned that we got Lucinda to call the police. It turns out my mom and Isa had fallen asleep at the local theater during an all-night Bollywood movie marathon.

hanging out with India tonight for the first time. But this is just fine with me because I don't want to talk to Mom or Bruno or anybody, for that matter.[43] I'm going to use this time alone to come up with a plan to exact revenge on Trevor. Oh, and I'm also going to come up with a plan for the election. A plan that will completely destroy Trevor.

I walk up to my house, pulling my key out of my pocket. It always feels good to come home at the end of the day, because even though it is cliché to say, home is really where the heart is. Even when you have a wacky mom who does things like throw you whack-a-doodle birthday parties without your consent. There's still our little two-story Colonial to come home to.

Some of my best memories happened inside this house. Spending early mornings with Nana. Waking up to the smell of bacon, grits, and grease. Helping her feed the chickens and then checking their coop for eggs. Before Nana died, we had a chicken coop in the backyard with six chickens. Every morning, Nana and I would get up with the sun to feed the chickens and collect the eggs. It was easily my favorite part of the day. When Nana died, I tried to keep up with the maintenance of the chickens. But my mom kept forgetting to buy them feed, and pretty soon the chickens started getting sick, so we had to give them away. A soft pang rings through my chest. If Nana were here, she would have dinner waiting for me. There wouldn't be weeds in the front garden, and she

---

43. Okay, maybe I'm not 100 percent fine with it. Bruno and I always hang out on Friday nights. Always. It's tradition, and you're only supposed to break tradition for emergency situations. I'm pretty sure that's written somewhere in the best friend manual for dummies. And FYI, first dates are definitely not emergencies.

wouldn't just listen to my problems; she would help me come up with solutions. I shake my head, clearing the tears that are starting to form at the corners of my eyes. But Nana isn't in the house. Of course Nana isn't in the house. Nana isn't in the house because she died two years ago, and now I have to be a grown-up and solve my own problems. I shake my head again, turning my key in the lock and pushing my way into the house and away from my thoughts about Nana.

I step into the entryway, making my way toward the kitchen. Friday is my favorite day of the week for many reasons. Not only do I get to eat what I want (banana-peanut-butter sandwiches times three), but Bruno and I get uninterrupted time to binge-watch our favorite shows (mine: *Dr. Fynn's ER*, and Bruno's: *Princess Hawke and the Nightrider*) and to talk about the week. But now Bruno is missing out on our ritual to take India mini-golfing. Mini-golfing is also known as the world's most boring sport. Honestly, I've never understood the need to do something in "miniature" when you can just go golfing for real. Well, it's his loss because I'll just eat his share of the banana-peanut-butter sandwiches.

When I get to the kitchen, I halt in my tracks, stunned into a few seconds of awkward silence. When I finally find my voice, it comes out in a whisper.

"Mom? What are you doing here?"

My mom is seated at our kitchen table, her hands clasped before her, a deep frown etched on her face. Her characteristically bright clothing seems oddly toned down, as she is in a pair of gray yoga pants and a faded shirt with the phrase PLANTS NOT PATRIARCHY. It is a positively tame outfit for my mother. In front of her, laid out on the table, are several items: a thick leather binder wrapped tightly with frayed ribbon, several yellowed envelopes, and a heavy-looking bronze heart-shaped locket.

My mom waves a hand toward the empty chair across from her. She clears her throat, wriggling like a rabbit caught in a trap. What is going on? I scan my mother, her nervous grin, her clasped hands, and I know that whatever it is, it can't be good. I slide into the open chair, glancing down at the weird hodge-podge of items on the table.

"I thought you were going out with Ms. Isa."

I fidget in my chair. Honestly, I really don't know what this could be about. I shuffle through the possibilities. Possibility number one: Mom is leaving with Isa so she can go to clown school, so she can prep for a life in the circus. No, that can't be right. I think my mom once told me that she thinks clowns are agents of the underworld (whatever that means). Possibility number two: my mom has discovered that I absolutely cannot stand rom-coms,[44] and she is planning to disown me and adopt a new daughter, one who wears pink and knows all the words to *Sleepless in Seattle*.[45] But that doesn't seem quite right either, because if that were the case, why would she have this weird array of stuff on the table?

---

44. "Rom-com" is just a fancy way to refer to romantic comedies, otherwise known as lovey-dovey movies where everyone gets a happily ever after. Scientifically impossible, by the way.
45. *Sleepless in Seattle* is one of those lovey-dovey rom-coms that my mom absolutely adores. For the life of me, I can't understand why.

"What's going on?" I try again. I clasp my fingers together, mimicking my mom. If she wants to be serious, I can be serious.

My mom lets out a slow breath, dropping her eyes down to the table. She fiddles with the bronze locket, which seems at first to be dull and unpolished, but the longer I look at it, the brighter it seems to get. In fact, now it almost seems to be glowing. My mom moves the locket over to me.

"This is yours," she says simply.

"Ooookay," I respond, taking the locket into my hands. The metal feels warm, as if it's somehow being heated from the inside. "Why is it so hot?" I ask. "Is it battery-operated or something?" I hold it up to my ear and jiggle it a bit. I put it back on the table.

"Open it," she states.

I cross my arms. "Why? What's going on?"

My mom lets out a tired sigh.

"I promise I'll tell you everything. Just open the locket, Erin."

I pick up the locket again, the heat pulsing against my palms. I jam the end of my nail into the clasp, pulling apart the two ends. The locket seems to grow even warmer, but it doesn't burn. In fact, the heat feels soothing, almost energizing. I slowly move my eyes across the picture on the left-hand side of the locket. The picture is of a freckled redheaded man, pale-skinned and smiling. There isn't anything that is necessarily special about him. He isn't overly handsome, nothing is particularly striking about him, save his red hair, but there is something about the picture that makes it impossible to look away.

"Who is—" I stop midsentence as my eyes land on the picture

opposite the redheaded man's. I study the picture; the man is present again, but this time he's sitting on a chair bouncing a giggling baby on his knee. A giggling redheaded baby with russet-brown skin.

"Is this—is this me?" I stammer.

It can't be. It just can't be. I've never seen this man before in my life, and here is a picture of me as a baby sitting on his knee, laughing like there is nothing funnier in the world.

"Yes," my mom says simply.

"Who is he?" I ask, even though I know what she is going to say. I just know.

My mom leans back in the chair, wringing her hands together fervently.

"Well." She pauses, taking a moment to clear her throat. "Well, that's your father."

The kitchen falls silent as I stare at my mom. My father? My eyes travel down again to the man in the picture. I take a moment to properly examine the photograph. At first it seems like it's impossible that we're even distantly related, much less father and daughter. But then I notice similarities, like the crooked tilt of his smile and the down-turned eyes that Mom used to tell me reminded her of crescent moons. The evidence is there. This man is my father.

For a moment we sit in silence, my mom watching me anxiously as I stare down at the open locket. I remember when I was small, how desperately I wanted to know about my missing father. I would beg my mom for any information that she could give me. What did he look like? What did he do? Why did he leave? And most importantly, was he coming back? My mother would always avoid my questions, telling me things such as *you're too young* and *I will tell you when you're ready*. I eventually lost interest in asking about my father. The mystery man felt like more of a myth than a real person, but now my mom is telling me this redheaded man who looks like me is my father.

"Say something," my mom whispers.

A thousand questions rush through me at once, but there is one question that I desperately want to know.

"What is his name?"

My mom hesitates, her eyes dropping to her lap. Okay, I didn't think that would be too hard of a question. It wasn't like I was asking about why he left. Why he left me . . .

My mom is still silent. I watch her as she wiggles in her chair. Finally, she sighs, relenting.

"Cupid."

I snort. Well, that's an unfortunate name. And of course, my mom would have a relationship with a man named Cupid. Of course she would.

"You fell in love with someone named Cupid?" I ask in disbelief, more than just a little bit amused. "Like a little cherub baby, heart arrows, God of Love Cupid?"

My mom wrings her hands.

She seems embarrassed or nervous or something. And for the life of me, I can't ever remember a time when my mom exhibited either of these emotions. For heaven's sake, my mom once spent two weeks dressed like a medieval tavern wench so that she could get an "authentic" experience for a side character in one of her novels. She refused to take off the costume even to go grocery shopping. But apparently the thing that makes her wriggle with embarrassment is the fact that my father's name is Cupid.

"That's not all," my mom continues.

There's more? How could there possibly be more? My mom has already been hiding this from me for thirteen years, this huge secret that is literally one half of my identity.

I give her an irritated nod. She huffs out a breath.

"So, going back to what you just said." She pauses. I stare at her blankly. What did I just say? What is she talking about?

"About the God of Love bit," she continues slowly. "You see, Cupid isn't necessarily who you think he is."

"Mom, I'm not completely hopeless. I do know who Cupid is. Besides, what does this have to do with my dad? His name is Cupid, but what does that matter? I've heard more ridiculous names before."

I don't know why I suddenly feel so defensive of a man I've never met before, but I do.

"It's not that."

"Well, what is it, Mom?" I bite out. "What's going on?"

"Your father isn't just named Cupid. He *is* Cupid," my mom blurts out. "He is the God of Love."

I look at my mom. What is she talking about? Is the headscarf she's wearing wrapped too tightly?

"Mom." I talk slowly, as if relaying something to a small child. "What are you talking about?"

"Your dad is Cupid. The God of Love," she repeats.

Suddenly, something clicks inside my head.

"Ooh, you mean he's like an actor or something. He plays Cupid on a TV show?"

I rack my brain, trying to figure out a show with a Cupid character. There has to be one. Could I possibly have a famous Hollywood father?

My mom shakes her head. "No, Erin, that's not what I mean. I mean your dad is actually a god, specifically Cupid, the God of Love."

I can't help it. I start laughing. I double over, pushing back from the table.

"Is this a joke?" I say. "Are there hidden cameras somewhere?"

My mom looks at me solemnly.

"Okay, Mom. Seriously. Is this research for a new book, or a joke? Because if it is, it isn't funny. Not at all."

My mom is never purposely cruel, so I don't think she would intentionally use my dad as a prop for her writing. That would be excruciatingly mean. Especially since I've spent my whole life trying to figure out who he is.

My mom's face remains unchanged.

"Tell me something, EJ. Has today been particularly odd at all? Anything seem different?"

I freeze. How could she possibly know about today's weirdness? Maybe Bruno called her and told her. But then again, how would Bruno know? I didn't tell anyone.

"I can see from your face that I'm right," my mom states matter-of-factly. "Your dad told me that I should be prepared for this day, the day after your thirteenth birthday. He told me—" She pauses for a moment, biting her lip. "He told me that your powers might manifest in different ways, that it might seem scary at first. But he wanted me to let you know that it's normal; all of what you're feeling is perfectly normal."

Normal? Is my mom listening to what she is saying? She is telling me that I'm the daughter of some mythical flying baby, and she wants me to think everything is normal. My mind flashes to earlier, to Bruno's weird personality change and Mr. Fairview's out-of-character date proposal. Both things happened after I touched them. But it could still just all be some weird coincidence, right?

My mom slides the leather binder toward me. Skeptically, I fiddle with the ribbon tying the binder together.

Could all of this be true? Could I really be Cupid's daughter?

No. I shake my head. Impossible. Scientifically impossible, to be precise. Love isn't even something that can be scientifically proven.[46] I mean, how can you prove a feeling? And if love can't be proven with evidence-based research, then fictional love gods definitely do not exist.

"Look," my mom says, pulling my hands into hers. She squeezes lightly. "I know that this is a lot to digest. A whole lot. But it was necessary to tell you, now that your powers are kicking in."

Powers, riiight.

---

46. I think I once read a scientific study that suggested that love is an actual illness, meaning that it's not a good thing. It's the opposite of a good thing. It's an actual disease.

I always knew my mom had an active imagination, but this is bordering on delusional. Mom wants to pretend like my dad has magical powers. That's just fine. I will get as much information as I can while I have the chance. I cross my arms. It's interrogation time.

"What's my dad's real name?"

My mom gives me a funny look.

"Cupid."

Okay, apparently, she's doubling down on that.

"All right, what about his last name?"

A last name that could've been mine.

"He doesn't have one."

I shake my head.

"How is that even possible? What type of person doesn't have a last name?"

"Plenty of people," my mom volleys back.

"Name one," I challenge.

"Prince, Banksy, Beyoncé."[47]

"All those people have last names. Those are just their stage names."

"Well, maybe Cupid is your dad's stage name."

Giving up, I ask one last question.

"What happened to him, my dad?"

My mom turns back toward me with a small smile, her lips thin and pressed together.

---

47. Prince: famous for purple condensation.
Banksy: famous for a blitzkrieg style of art. Also, I'm not even sure if this person actually exists.
Beyoncé: Honestly, Beyoncé is just Beyoncé. No further explanation is needed.

"Gods are not meant to live among humans, EJ. No matter how much they love them."

My mom pushes the envelopes toward me. She clears her throat.

"These are for you. All these things. They are from your dad. He explains a lot. Read them when you are ready."

I touch the yellowed envelopes with my fingertips, tracing the faded ink that spells out my name. My mom is now standing, looking older and more harried than I have ever seen her look before.

"Now I need a promise from you."

My mom is hardly ever serious, but she's staring down at me with a very hard expression.

"Okay," I say cautiously.

"I need you to promise not to use your powers." I start to say something, but my mom holds up a hand. "I know you couldn't help it today, but . . ." She points to the binder. "That should help you. Your dad said it would."

I chew on my lip. This is all ridiculous. First off, my mom decides after thirteen years of making me believe that I'm a test-tube baby to unveil the well-kept secret of my parentage. Then she wants me to believe that my father is a make-believe dude who prefers Huggies to pants. And that I'm pretty much a magical freak of nature.

"Erin, did you hear me?"

I return my eyes to my mother's earnest expression.

"Promise not to use your powers."

Easiest promise ever. Of course I won't use my powers. I can't use something if it doesn't exist.

I square my shoulders and look my mother in the eyes.

"Sure, I promise."

When I get to my room, I take a moment to lean my head against my closed bedroom door. Breathe in. Breathe out. Clear head. Clear mind.[48]

"Okay, get a grip, EJ," I scold myself. I know how my mom is. She lives in a fantasy world. It's what makes her a great writer, and a not-so-great adult. This has to be a prank or some type of Mom-related coping mechanism.

I snap my fingers. That's it. Mom is finding a way to cope with losing Nana. With having to raise me all on her own. I take another deep breath, this one shaky and slightly unsteady as I look over to a picture of me and Nana on my dresser. I pick the picture up, caressing the edges of the frame. Has it already been over two years since Nana's death? Sometimes, it seems like she's just been there, shaking me awake, urging me to get ready to meet the day.

I sit on the bed, staring at the picture.

"What a mess, Nana," I mumble. "This wouldn't be happening if you were still alive."

---

48. I know many people might believe that the art of meditation is some pseudoscience, but it actually really helps when I feel overwhelmed. Don't worry. It's not like I'll be presenting it at conferences or anything.

Nana's presence was a calming force in my life, a balm, really, and with her gone everything feels backward and topsy-turvy. I dump the binder, locket, and envelopes onto my dresser, next to the picture of Nana and me.

"Cupid. Yeah right. Who would actually believe that?"

But what about the tingly feeling you felt with Bruno and Mr. Fairview? a little voice in my head reminds me. *What about how you saw actual colors? Colors that surrounded Bruno and Mr. Fairview and made them act strange?*

"Doesn't matter," I say out loud to myself. "If it exists, then science will have an explanation." I pull out my school laptop and start to research, opening a fresh Word doc to compile my notes in.

Three Possible Explanations for the Strange Things That Have Happened to Me Today
1) I could be developing kaleidoscope vision,[49] a symptom of really serious migraines. Though I didn't exactly have a migraine, so maybe I just had a kaleidoscope vision sans migraine.
2) I felt warm and tingly because I was experiencing heatstroke. Some symptoms of heatstroke include confusion. (Though it is a bit puzzling how I got heatstroke in fifty-five-degree weather.)

---

49. Kaleidoscope vision is a temporary disorder that makes you feel like you're looking through a kaleidoscope.

3) My mother has been under a lot of stress
since my nana died, and an inordinate amount
of stress can make people say and do things that
they don't believe or mean.

Now if you add all these things together, today makes perfect scientific sense.

But it doesn't, a small part of me whispers. This isn't science. It's something else altogether. Something that I might not be able to quantify or measure. Something that defies logic. Something like magic.

No. I shake my head, picking up the binder, the letters, and the locket. My eyes move up to my vanity mirror, and I remember the locket picture. Cupid. My father. Even if all the magic stuff is made up, could that man be my actual father? I set everything back down on the dresser and take a step back. This is all too much.

When I was five, I would ask my mother to tell me something about my father. Anything, really. But my mom would become quiet. There would always be something else that she needed to do. Finally, she got tired of me asking and complained that she would tell me when she was ready. That night, Nana let me sleep in her bed. She let me talk about all my fears and longings when it came to my dad. My nana never met my dad. My mom never introduced them. In the end, before I went to sleep, she plopped a kiss on my forehead and told me that I was fearfully and wonderfully made and that it mattered very little who my father was. And I believed her, because my nana was seldom wrong.

Impulsively, I grab one of the envelopes. It has my name scribbled across the front in faded ink. I rip it open in frustration.

> My dearest Erin,
>
> If you are reading this, you have just celebrated your thirteenth birthday, so, happy belated birthday. If you are anything like your mom, you are a beautiful, creative, free-spirited girl, and that's all I would ever want for you. But this letter isn't about the qualities you may have gotten from your mother. This letter is about the qualities you are going to get from me. Magical qualities, to be specific. Your mother has probably already told you about me and the fact that I'm Cupid, the God of Love. And I know this might be unbelievable at first . . .

"You think?" I scoff, holding the letter away from me a bit. I continue reading.

> But it is important for you to know that you are my daughter, because being my daughter, being half Cupid, means that you have access to some pretty powerful magic. And that magic can be wonderful and amazing, but it can also be dangerous, because love itself can be the most dangerous thing in the

world. I'm not telling you all this to scare you. On the contrary, I'm telling you to prepare you. I wish I could be there in person. I wish I could help you navigate these changes, but for reasons beyond my control, I can't be there. So in place of my absence, I'm leaving you this series of letters and a book I like to refer to as The Cupid Manual.

I peek over at the leather binder, filled to the brim with papers.

You'll find everything you need in the manual. How to use your powers. When to use your powers. How your powers work. It is a pretty inclusive manual. Which is why I'm going to implore you to read the manual in its entirety before attempting to use your powers. It is very, very important that you do so. Your mom says I should keep this first letter brief so I don't overwhelm you. So, I will heed her advice and end it here. Erin, I know you don't know me and that to you I'm simply a god that is giving you unsolicited advice. And while that may be true, I'm also your father and I care about you. So please trust me when I tell you not to use your magic until you have learned thoroughly what it is to be a Cupid.

Yours truly,
Your father, Cupid ♥

Oh god. He signed it with a little heart next to his name. I push away the letter, wrinkling my nose. Who does this Cupid think he is? First off, he's not really my father. I mean, a real father would be here to raise his daughter. He wouldn't write weird letters to her about make-believe magical powers. He would be here giving her actual advice, helping her with homework, and telling her how proud he was of her. Like my nana used to.

"Well, you can't tell me what to do," I spit out. I violently stuff the manual down into my sock drawer.

Suddenly, I know what I need. The same thing I've always needed when I'm upset. My nana.

I'm not supposed to leave without telling my mom, but sneaking out of the house is easy. I've never had to do it before (the reward has never been worth the risk), and today it is particularly easy as my mom is in her room with her door shut. She is blasting what she calls her "calm-down" music.[50] Because of that, it takes me almost no time to get to the garage and get on my bike.

I rarely use my bike anymore. I got it for Christmas when I was nine, and although I'm still a bit on the short side, my knees constantly hit the handlebars when I ride it. Even worse, the bike is a bright pink My Little Pony bike, part of a phase that I'm not proud of. Also, my bike helmet most definitely doesn't fit over my pouffy curls. When I was nine, Nana used to twist my hair, therefore making helmet-wearing more feasible. And no matter how badly I want to get to my destination, I'm not going anywhere

---

50. My mom's calm-down music is just a recording of one of her old high school friends humming loudly while periodically striking a gong.

without a helmet. Luckily (or rather, unluckily), my mom has an antique motorcycle helmet that she found at a yard sale once. It smells like moldy cheese, but it is better than nothing.

I need this. I need to talk to my nana.

I ride my bike toward the cemetery, down the winding roads of my neighborhood. Past the gas station that sells fresh catfish sandwiches on Wednesdays after the owner, Mr. Bendle, goes fishing in the river. I ride past the Mennonite store where Nana used to buy delicious fudge and half-price sandwiches. I ride without stopping, moving up and down on the bike seat when my legs cramp and beg me to stop.

When I finally reach the cemetery, I'm drenched with sweat, but that doesn't matter. What is important is that I talk to my grandmother. I sling my bike against the cemetery gate, locking it with a chain.

"Hey there, EJ," a familiar voice calls from behind the gate. "Should be closing up soon."

"Hey, Ernesto." I flash him a tiny smile.

I've gotten to know Ernesto pretty well over the two years. He's spent most of his adult life working as the groundskeeper for Hallock Cemetery. Sometimes when he knows I'm coming, he'll bake peanut butter cookies for me to eat while I sit near Nana's grave.

"Just ten minutes, Ernesto. I promise."

I give him my puppy-dog eyes, which no adult can resist.

"All right. All right," he sighs. "You can have ten minutes. Just stop making that face."

"Thank you. Thank you so much," I say as Ernesto opens the gate.

I squeeze in, desperate to go to my grandmother's tombstone. Ernesto leaves me as I move toward the back of the cemetery where my nana's plot is laid. I find the familiar tombstone, the one I try to visit every Sunday morning. The only tombstone shaped like a heart. I slide down in the cool, dry grass, moving my fingers over the letters of my nana's name: Elnora Henrietta Brown. Most of her friends simply referred to her as Nora. Nora Brown. Even after getting married to my grandpa Ellis Johnson, she'd kept the name, telling my grandpa that there was only one Nora Brown and she wasn't going to change on account of falling in love.

I cross my legs, turning my full attention to the tombstone.

"I know I'm two days early, Nana. You aren't really used to seeing me on Fridays."

I clear my throat.

"It's just . . ." I pause, unsure of how to continue. "It's just . . ."

I feel the tears sliding down my cheeks before I realize what is happening. And then it's like a dam bursts open, and I'm sobbing.

"Nothing is the same without you. Absolutely nothing. Mom decided to throw me an awful birthday party. It was so embarrassing. Honestly, it's like she doesn't know me at all."

I hiccup, rubbing my eyes with the backs of my sweaty hands.

"And then when I got home after school today, she decided to tell me who my father is. The only problem is that she thinks he's some fictional god. Can you believe it?"

I laugh, a bit hysterical.

"You know how Mom is." My sobs quiet down, and I wipe my face with the corner of my jacket.

"The worst part," I say, my voice almost a whisper, "is that I think there's a part of me that believes her."

"EJ." Ernesto places a cool hand on my shoulder, which causes me to jump.

"Oh," I squeal.

"Just me. It's about time you wrap up. I'll be closing up soon."

I nod. "Thanks, Ernesto. I'm finishing up now."

Ernesto gives me a quick nod and walks back to the front gate. I turn toward my grandmother.

"I have to go. But I guess I just wanted to come talk to you to tell you I miss you and love you."

I wait a beat.

"And I hope you're proud of me."

With that I stand up, brushing off my jeans, and I slowly move toward the gate. When I reach the front, I find Tommy, the night guard,[51] perched against the fence, engaged in an animated discussion with Ernesto. Even though Tommy is a night guard and theoretically should only be at the cemetery after it closes, he frequently shows up during the day to help Ernesto or sometimes to simply hang out.

"Hey, Tommy," I call out.

---

51. Apparently, our town has been experiencing an uptick in grave robbers, i.e., people who dig up coffins to take jewelry off the dead. Hence the need for a night guard. To be fair, most graveyards don't need night guards, but our cemetery is really old, like, it existed during the time of the Civil War old. So there are a lot of aboveground mausoleums.

Tommy's face lights up with a smile.

"Hey, kid."

Even though Ernesto and Tommy are close to my nana's age before she died, they both seem filled with endless energy when they are near each other.

Tommy bounces on the tips of his toes, inadvertently pushing himself closer to Ernesto.

"Never see you this late. Are you visiting your nana?"

"Yep." I nod. I eyeball the blush that creeps over Ernesto's cheeks as Tommy's shoulder accidentally grazes his.

"It was an emergency," I mumble.

"Well, I certainly understand that," Tommy says to me before flashing Ernesto a small smile. They like each other. They totally like each other. Ernesto notices my stare, and he clears his throat, moving forward slightly, away from Tommy.

"Well, come on, EJ. We can head out together." Ernesto puts a friendly hand on my shoulder, steering me toward the unlatched gate.

An idea forms as quick as lightning. I need to know. I have to know for sure if any of this is actually true. I focus on Ernesto's hand on my shoulder. *I wish you would see how Tommy likes you. He really, really likes you.* I feel the warmth rush through me, and a silvery blue mist circles Ernesto like a cloud. He snaps his hand back as if he's been shocked. Ernesto first looks at me in confusion, then peeps behind me at Tommy's retreating form.

"Hey," he says, looking back at me. "Wait here for a second."

He jogs over to Tommy, calling out his name. Tommy stops

walking, turning around to meet Ernesto halfway. I watch anxiously as they talk animatedly, and for a moment I'm suspended in a bubble of hope. Maybe it didn't work. Maybe Ernesto just needed to give him a key or something. But then Tommy and Ernesto hug, and Tommy lets out a full-bellied laugh. My heart sinks. Ernesto gives Tommy one last pat on the shoulder, and he jogs back over to me.

"Sorry. Thanks for waiting," Ernesto says, out of breath.

"No problem," I reply numbly as we move through the opening of the gate.

"Craziest thing. I just couldn't let Tommy go without letting him know how much I like him. I have for ages, but good thing is, he happens to like me too. We're meeting up for a movie tomorrow."

"Great, Ernesto. That's great," I respond, stunned.

My stomach feels heavy, and for a second I worry I'm about to dry heave in front of him. He peers at me in shock.

"Not sure why I just blurted all that out. Sorry, I must be excited."

"It's okay, Ernesto."

As I strap on my borrowed helmet and unlock my bike from the fence, I know without a shadow of a doubt that what my mother told me was real. I'm Cupid's daughter.

CHAPTER EIGHT

Cupid Commandment Number 4: Cupids have a responsibility to use their powers for the good of all parties involved. Using magic for personal gain comes at a price.

I WAKE UP THE next morning in a panic. What a weird, weird dream. I shake my head and stare at the ceiling. I really don't dream about crazy things, especially crazy magical things. Sometimes I dream about things that are far-fetched, like a shark attack or an earthquake that is so powerful that it destroys the planet. But these things are all possibilities in the realm of science. I have never had a dream that was completely out of the realm of probability, that is, until I dream not only that Cupid is real, but also that he is my father.

But it's fine. It's all fine because it was just a dream. Just a crazy dream. Last night must have been a fluke, a coincidence. Part anxiety about my failed birthday and part bad sushi lunch. I slide out of the bed, patting my hair down and pushing the strands behind my ears. Something shiny on the dresser catches my attention.

My stomach sinks. The locket. My locket. Numb, I walk over to it. I pry it open again and look at the pictures, the pictures of a strange redheaded man. The pictures of my father.

"It's real," I mumble. "Everything that happened last night was real. But it can't be. It just can't be."

Then I remember the graveyard and Ernesto and Tommy and my experiment to see if magic was real. And it was. Magic is real. My dad is Cupid. My mom kept it from me. And my nana is dead.

These are indisputable truths. All of them.

My phone vibrates loudly on my nightstand, shaking me from my thoughts. I frown, looking at my digital clock. It is eight in the morning. Who is texting me at eight in the morning on a Saturday? I pick up the phone, scrolling through until I reach my text messages.

Trevor: **5967 Truely Ln. I forgot to send this to you yesterday. This is my address in case you couldn't figure that out.**

Ugh. Pompous, arrogant Trevor Jin.

Me: **Who wouldn't figure out this was an address? What else would it be, Trevor?**

Trevor: Oh, I'm glad you figured out who I was. I was worried you wouldn't.

Me: Eat dirt.

Trevor: Weird pastime. I'm afraid we don't have any dirt in my house to feed to you, but you could always eat the dirt in the backyard if you need it.

Me: Is there something you wanted? Or are you just trying to make me scream at the top of my lungs at eight in the morning????

Trevor: I was giving you my address.

Me: . . . . .

Trevor: It's Saturday.

Me: I KNOW what day it is.

Trevor: We're supposed to work on our project . . . today . . . Saturday.

Crap. I forgot that I'm supposed to go over to Trevor's house and work on our DNA model. Honestly, I've forgotten a lot of things since learning that my dad is a mythical Cupid.

Trevor: I coulllld just do the project by myself. It would be much better that way if we're being honest.

Me: Over. My. Dead. Body. 😠

Trevor: Whatever 🙄 So what time are you coming over? I'm going to start working on the project soon.

Me: Trevor, you legitimately just texted me, and
it is eight in the morning. And I'm thirteen. I don't
drive. I have to wait until my mom wakes up.
Trevor: Your mom isn't already up?

Shame rushes through me. Not all of us have picture-perfect moms who wake up at the crack of dawn, Trevor.

Trevor: Never mind, what time do you think you
will be able to make it over here?
Me: Around 10
Trevor: Fine. I guess that will work. I will see you
then.

I throw my phone down on the bed in frustration.

"I guess that will work," I say, mimicking Trevor's dry, humorless voice. "News flash, Trevor Jin, the world doesn't revolve around you."

I pinch my lips together. Yesterday during science class, I thought that we were actually making progress. Somehow, I thought that Trevor and I could be cordial with each other, not quite friends, but definitely no longer enemies. I was so sure that we had turned a corner, but Trevor was quick to remind me about how wrong I was with his nomination speech.

"Ugh." I lie on my bed, looking up at the ceiling in disgust. "Some people are born with absolutely everything. Great parents with even greater jobs. Access to the best things. Never having to work hard. Being naturally smart. Being completely gorgeous."

Wait, did I just call Trevor Jin gorgeous? It must be the fact that last night I found out that I'm some type of magical unicorn or something. Something must be scrambling my brain.

Suddenly an idea pops into my head, something about what my mom said. Yesterday she made me promise not to use my powers. But what if I did use my powers? What if I used my powers on Trevor? What if I made Trevor Jin fall in love with *me*?

I feel a slight pinch of guilt, but it's quickly replaced with a flare of anger. Why should I listen to anything my mom says? I shouldn't feel guilty about breaking my promise. My mom has literally been lying to me for thirteen years. Thirteen years! All those times I asked about my father, and my mom brushed me off, and she knew the truth. She knew. So what is the harm in using my powers in a way that benefits me?

I pace back and forth in my room, thinking through my plan. If Trevor falls in love with me, he would do anything I wanted him to do, including giving up the presidential nomination, making me the president by default. Then I would be a shoo-in next year for the dual enrollment seat at the high school. I stop for a moment, pulling the locket out of the drawer I'd stuffed it in. I pop it open, looking at the pictures of my dad again, running my finger around the edges of the photos. Maybe I should listen? Maybe my mom has a good reason for wanting me to wait to use my powers. Maybe it is important to read through the entire manual before I use my powers again. Maybe I'll find out that if I use them too often, I'll explode or something.

You know what, whatever. It doesn't matter. This isn't me. I'm not some fairy-tale reject who has to resort to magic to get her way. I'm Erin Marie Johnson. Top of my class. Future scientist and Nobel Prize winner. And future president of the Multicultural Leadership Club. I don't need magical tactics to win against Trevor Jin. I just need me. Me and me alone.

My phone buzzes again, and I go over to check it. It can't be anybody but Trevor.

> Trevor: **Also, please make sure you're prepared to work when you get here and that you have completed the assigned reading. I would hate to have to redo your part of the project when you get here.**

I grunt at the phone in frustration before another text comes through.

"What now—"

I stop when I notice Bruno's name. Bruno and I are used to texting each other nearly every hour when we're outside school, but lately I have gotten either complete radio silence or hurried throwaway texts. I lift the phone so I can read the message.

> Bruno: **Hey, EJ. I know it's early, but I don't know if you have seen this yet, and I know that you'd want me to send this to you as soon as possible.**

I scroll down to the link that Bruno has included in his message. I click it, and the site for the school's newspaper flashes onto my screen. I go down until I get to the information Bruno wants me to see. It's a poll. A poll predicting the outcome of the Multicultural Leadership Club's presidential election. A poll that shows Trevor clearly in the lead, with 60 percent saying they would definitely vote for Trevor, 35 percent showing they would definitely vote for me, and 5 percent undecided. I fling the phone to the other side of the room with a wail.

Trevor doesn't get to win this. I'm not going to let him.

Operation Make Trevor Fall in Love with Me is a go.

Two hours later I stand in front of Trevor Jin's modestly sized yet very pink Victorian house. My mom gets out of the car, joining me on the porch, her hand on her hip.

"Whoa," she mumbles, her eyes sweeping over the decorative porch railings and large bay windows. "So this is where your hero lives."

My brain automatically flashes to when Trevor told me he liked the character Erin, and I push the memory away.

"Stop calling him my hero," I bark. "He is not a hero, and he is definitely not mine."

My mom shrugs, knocking lightly on the heavy door. "He is in my book." She wiggles her eyebrows playfully. My mom is making an effort to talk to me, to try to make me smile. But I'm not ready. Honestly, I feel betrayed. My mom has kept this secret from me for my whole life. And this isn't some little secret. This is about my dad. Half of me. Half of my identity. Contrary to what she may think, my mom and I are not okay. I pout, folding my arms over my chest.

"I see you put on makeup this morning. I've never known you to wear makeup before." My mom looks straight ahead when she says this, a smile spreading across her face. "Is that for the hero? The makeup? The brushed hair? The new sweater?"

I grit my teeth, waiting for someone, anyone, to answer the door and relieve me of this torture. And actually yes, all the dolling up *is* for Trevor, but not for the reason my mom thinks. It isn't because I like Trevor. It is actually the opposite. It is because he is my nemesis, and I'm going to make him fall in love with me. And according to all the nonsense blogs I read in the last hour, looking nice is the first step to making a boy fall in love with you, powers or not.

The door swings open, and I look up into the face of a beautiful woman clad in light blue scrubs. She smiles politely, pushing her short black hair away from her face, and I know instantly that this is Dr. Jin. This is Trevor's mom.

"Greetings, my lady." My mom curtsies. She *curtsies*! She remains frozen in the position as if she is waiting for something.

I lightly elbow her in the side. "Mom," I hiss. "Get up."

Dr. Jin simply smiles, cocking her head. "You must be Erin." She looks directly at me, giving me another friendly smile.

I nod enthusiastically, pulling my mother up into a wobbly standing position.

"And this is my mother."

My mother finally holds out her hand like normal people do when greeting strangers. Dr. Jin grasps her hand.

"Joanna," she offers.

"Sara," Dr. Jin offers back.

"I just love your house. It's very majestic. It reminds me of a house I wrote about once in one of my books."

Don't ask. Please, for the love of god, don't ask.

"Oh," Dr. Jin says, looking interested. "You write books? What genre? I'm an avid reader."

Of course she's an avid reader along with being an amazing doctor.

"Oh well," my mother replies smugly, "it's all very hush-hush. If I gave you my clients' names, then I would have to kill you."

Dr. Jin looks alarmed, her eyebrows rising to the top of her forehead. "Oh my, I'm sorry. Are you in the CIA or something?"

My mom snorts with laughter. "They wish I was in the CIA."

I cannot believe this is my life.

Dr. Jin looks back and forth between us, confused.

"She's a ghostwriter," I supply quickly. "She can't tell you the books she wrote because she signed contracts stating that she wouldn't."

Dr. Jin's smile becomes tense around the corners of her mouth. "Oh, I understand."

"But I could tell you some of the content I write about if you promise not to tell anyone."

My mom cackles. I'm sure everyone in Trevor's neighborhood

is now peeking out of their windows to see what is going on.

Dr. Jin shifts from foot to foot. "Oh, I don't want to get anyone in trouble. If you're not—"

"Oh, it's no trouble," my mom interrupts. "My new story happens to be a love story between—"

"Mom!" I scream, startling poor Dr. Jin. "I have to get this project done."

My mom looks at me guiltily. "Of course, honey. I'm sorry. What time should I come and get you?"

"Two hours should be fine. We should be able to finish everything in two hours," I say.

"Three hours. We will need three hours," a voice says from behind Dr. Jin. I inwardly cringe and lift my eyes to see Trevor standing behind his mom, a cocky grin on his face.

Trevor doesn't look like his normal self. There's something different about him, something that makes him less like a stick-in-the-mud and more like a cute boy who is hanging out casually at home. He's got on a black-and-white checkered T-shirt and khaki shorts. He looks . . . well, he looks amazing. I blink rapidly, trying to push my traitorous thoughts from my head.

"Oh, hello again, Trevor." My mom waves a hand at him.

"Hello, Ms. Johnson," he responds politely.

"Oh, you can call me Joanna. Ms. Johnson was my mother."

In fact, my nana's last name was Brown, but my mother cares very little for facts, it seems.

"So, I'll be back in three hours, EJ. Okay?" My mom pops a kiss down on my head. I flinch back.

"She'll be just fine," Dr. Jin says. She opens the door wider so I can slide inside.

Before I make it, though, my mother engulfs me in a hug.

I stand stiffly in her arms as she whispers, "I know you're mad, but I hope you have a good time, and please remember what I told you."[52] She gives me a meaningful look, and I remain silent.

With one last squeeze, my mother leaves to go hop back into her car, and Dr. Jin is shutting the door.

"Well, kids," Dr. Jin says, clapping her hands together. "I've got quite a bit of work to do in the office today, but I will be available if there's an emergency."

Dr. Jin glances over at Trevor and says something quick and sharp in Korean. Trevor nods and responds. I look at Trevor, gobsmacked.

"It's nice to meet you, Erin," Dr. Jin says, smiling before she leaves Trevor and me alone.

I whip around to face Trevor. "You speak Korean?" I ask.

Trevor shrugs. "Why are you so surprised? I'm Korean."

I roll my eyes, crossing my arms. "That doesn't necessarily mean you have to speak Korean and you know it."

"Well, I do," he says with a smile. "Is that a problem, EJ?"

"No, of course not," I huff. "It's actually really cool."

I can't believe that I just gave Trevor a compliment. Honestly, this means that he has one up on me when it comes to that dual enrollment spot,[53] but I'm not lying. It is really, really cool.

---

52. How did she even know that that was what I was trying to do? Could she be a mind reader? Hey, apparently anything is possible.
53. I only know a very minor amount of Spanish, enough to say "Hi" and "How are you?" and "Please may I use the bathroom?"

Trevor shrugs his shoulders again, turning his back to me. "So you have to take off your shoes while you're in the house." He points to a row of shoes lined up neatly by the door. "It's one of the rules."

"Sure. No problem." I slide out of my sneakers, lining them up next to a pair of black boat shoes. I shift my bookbag from one shoulder to the other, looking at Trevor expectantly. "Where do you want to work?"

Trevor turns around. "We can work in the library. My mom will be in her office, so I think the library should be okay."

"You have a library?" I ask, my mouth involuntarily hanging down near my chest.

Trevor smiles. "It's not really a library. It used to be some type of sitting room, but my mom needed a place to store all her books, so she had shelves put in when she and my dad first moved in."

I don't respond. I simply follow him as he leads me through the hallway to the back of the house. Even though the house is older, and many older houses appear to be cramped, Trevor's house seems to be the opposite. It is bright and airy, and everything has a proper place. It is the exact opposite of my house, where my mom refuses to throw anything away on the assumption that she never knows when she will need it again.

After a couple of minutes, we get to the room Trevor refers to as the library, a spacious room with a teal built-in bookcase along its back wall. In the center of the room there is a small table and two chairs. Along a side wall, a yellow couch is pushed under a picture of a bouquet of flowers.

"It's pretty," I state simply. "I like it."

Trevor gives me a half smile. "It's my favorite room. It's where I usually do my homework."

We're quiet, and Trevor is staring at me oddly, like I have started growing snakes out of the top of my head. Ignoring him, I look up at the shelves, scanning the book titles. Most of the books are nonfiction tomes that have something to do with medicine or science or something else similar, but a couple of the books are fiction, some about witches, one about a man who lived in the woods for thirty days.

"Oh look," I squeal. I pull out a thick book, cradling it with both hands. *Gray's Anatomy*.[54] I flip through the pages, stopping to frown and squint at the diagrams.

"It's not about the TV show, if that's what you were expecting." Trevor is still looking at me strangely.

"Obviously, genius." I close the book and slide it back onto the shelf.

"Don't get mad at me. I was just making sure you knew." He keeps staring at me, his eyes never leaving my face.

"What?" I ask in exasperation. "What are you staring at? Do I have something in my teeth?"

Trevor squishes up his face, giving me another funny look.

"No, it's just . . ." He stops for a moment, examining me again. "It's just—it looks like you have lipstick on."

"I don't,"[55] I answer indignantly. "Look, why are you worried about what's on my lips? Aren't we supposed to be working?" I snap.

---

54. The *Gray's Anatomy* book is a reference book on human anatomy.
55. I am, in fact, wearing lipstick. The color is called Fire Engine Red.

Trevor shrugs again. I'm so surprised. Not.

"I was just going to tell you that it looked nice."

I bite my bottom lip, avoiding Trevor's gaze. He said "nice." Trevor thinks it looks nice. Why is that making me feel all floaty and tingly?

Well then, maybe Mom's beauty magazine is right. Maybe a good lip color is the way to get a boy to fall in love with you. Maybe I won't even need my Cupid powers. Maybe I just need my handy-dandy Fire Engine Red lipstick.

"But whatever you put on your eyes makes you look like an insect. It's actually quite creepy-looking."

Or not.

"Whatever," I reply. "When I want your opinion, Trevor, I'll ask for it."

I plop down at the table, pulling out my biology book, turning to the chapter about DNA. Trevor sits down with a smile, pulling out his binder and flipping through his notes. I bite my lip again, turning my face away so that Trevor can't see my smile. I'm starting to think Trevor likes it when we argue. And if I'm honest with myself, I think I like it too. Trevor keeps me on my toes, and I know I keep him on his.

"So where do you want to start?" I ask casually.

"Let's start with organizing our information, and then we can sketch out how we want our model to look."

I nod and we get to work. After about an hour, we finish a rough outline of our project. We combine our notes and come up with a fairly accurate sketch of how we want our DNA model to look.

"Looks good," Trevor mumbles, holding our sketch up and squinting at it. "Your part looks a bit dodgy, but I can fix that later."

Dodgy? First off, who says "dodgy"? And second, my part is not dodgy. It's perfect.

I swallow my words. It doesn't matter, because I came over here to do one thing and one thing only. Use my Cupid powers to make Trevor fall in love with me. I have to. I absolutely have to. It's the only way I can become the president of the Multicultural Leadership Club. *But this isn't right,* a tiny voice says in the back of my head. And I'm immediately flushed with guilt. I shake my head in frustration. This is Trevor Jin. He's my archenemy, my nemesis. My cute archenemy. Ugh, enough of this. I'm not my cousin Birdie. I do not let my plans get sidetracked by cute boys, even if said boy has ridiculously long eyelashes and a smile that could melt butter.

I fling out my hands and grab Trevor's wrists before I can talk myself out of it.

Trevor's face twists in confusion. "Erin, are you okay? What are you doing?"

I ignore Trevor, closing my eyes and concentrating on the words *I wish Trevor Jin would fall in love with me. Trevor Jin should totally fall in love with me.* A warm, tingly feeling climbs from my arms up through the rest of my body. Unlike the first three times, I'm anticipating the feeling. I brace myself, tightening my hands around Trevor's wrists. After a moment the feeling goes away, and I open my eyes and let go of Trevor. Trevor is staring at me with his mouth open. A silvery mist shimmers around him, flickering in and out.

"Are—are you okay?" he asks nervously.

"Yeah," I say, pushing back some of the frizzy pieces of my hair that have fallen in front of my eyes. "Why? Are you okay?" I ask accusingly.

Trevor sits back, frowning. "I'm fine, EJ. I'm not the one who is grabbing people's wrists and glowing like a light bulb," he snaps. Seeming to realize what he has just said and that it might sound a bit unbelievable, he quickly shuts his mouth.

"I was glowing?" I ask in amazement.

Trevor shakes his head, ruffling his fingers through his hair.

"I don't know. Maybe I've been staring at the same sheet for too long. Let's take a break." Trevor pops up from his seat. "I'm going to the kitchen to get us some snacks. Are you allergic to anything?"

"Just you," I pipe up, but then I immediately become embarrassed, looking down at my feet.

Trevor laughs. "You're so weird," he responds. I glance back up just in time to catch him giving me a probing look. We catch each other's eye and both turn away. He clears his throat. "I'll be right back."

I watch him as he walks away. He doesn't look any different. He isn't talking differently either. He seems like the same Trevor. The Trevor who is not in love with me. Maybe my powers didn't work, but that doesn't seem right either. I felt the heat spread through me, just like it did when I touched Bruno, Mr. Fairview, and Ernesto. And besides, Trevor said I glowed. Glowed! Have I always glowed?

Trevor comes back into the room, interrupting my thoughts.

He carries a silver tray with an array of food spread across it.

"I hope you're hungry," he says, hefting the tray onto the table. The tray is loaded with a variety of things, a colorful assortment of food that I've never tried before. I pick up a small oblong item from the tray. I hold it in my hand. "So what's this?"

Trevor smiles. "A rice cake stick." He points to a small saucer at the end of the tray. "You dip it in the honey."

I dip the rice cake stick in the honey and then bite off a piece.

"It's delicious," I state, almost grudgingly.

"Yeah, they are. They are one of my favorite snacks."

I quickly grab two more, dipping them happily into the honey. "Yeah, they might be my new favorite too."

Trevor's smile is glorious; looking into it is kind of like staring into the sun. His head tilts forward, and I'm drawn to him like a magnet.

"Try this next. They're delicious."

He pushes a white plate forward. In the center of the plate is a tiny bowl of soy sauce, and surrounding the bowl are what look like some type of hash-brown meat patties. They smell amazing.

"What are they?" I ask, dying to grab one from the plate.

"Chamchijeon."

"Chamchijeon," I repeat, and Trevor's breathtaking smile is back. My stomach flip-flops, and I snatch one and stuff it in my mouth before Trevor can notice how I'm staring at him.

Flavor explodes in my mouth, and I groan in approval. This is so good.

Trevor laughs.

This Trevor, this laughing Trevor, is so different from the boy I know, the boy who I consider to be my nemesis. This Trevor is warm and smiley, and this is a Trevor I could see myself being friends with.

"Slow down. The food isn't going anywhere."

His eyes are glittering with amusement, and his smile is stretched across his face. I gulp the rest of my chamchijeon down, my attention frozen on Trevor's face. Has he always been this cute? Trevor holds my gaze, his laughter trickling away. We're staring at each other, and this stare between us is sort of electric. It feels like it's zinging me from the inside out.

"So what's in this?" I ask. I sever our eye contact and focus on the chamchijeon.

"Oh." Trevor's eyes travel over the chamchijeon. "They are pretty much tuna pancakes. There's cabbage, tuna, ginger, eggs." He shrugs. "My mom makes them in batches."

Trevor's eyes are back on me, and I wiggle in my seat. Why am I reacting to him like this?

"And what's this?" I reach out and grab a syrupy-looking cookie. It's sticky, and the sweet smell of it fills my nostrils.

Trevor picks one up and pops it into his mouth. I do the same, enjoying the simultaneous fluffiness and stickiness.

"I change my mind. This is my favorite."

My mouth is still full, but I don't care. The cookie is the best cookie I've ever eaten.

"They are called yakgwa. They're Korean honey cookies."

I sigh, leaning back against my chair.

"Well, these are my new favorite cookies. Maybe my new favorite food, period."

Trevor leans in over the tray, and suddenly he is very, very close to me.

He smiles, and he has a tiny dot of honey cookie on the corner of his mouth, and in normal circumstances I would find that disgusting,[56] but for Trevor it only increases his cuteness.

"So you're telling me"—Trevor's voice comes out slow; it's completely mesmerizing—"that I have just introduced Erin Johnson to her new favorite food?"

I swallow. I know I'm not well versed when it comes to matters of love, but this feels like flirting. Is Trevor flirting?

"I think we should get back to work," I say, so loudly it's basically a shout. Trevor flinches back, eyes wide.

"Okay, okay. Yeah." He hops up to his feet. "Just let me clean up quickly." Trevor takes the tray into the kitchen. When he comes back, I'm already reviewing our sketch, checking the accuracy, but my mind is still racing.

Trevor is just so different. This is a total Dr. Jekyll and Mr. Hyde[57] situation, and school Trevor is definitely Mr. Hyde.

"It's not wrong, you know?" Trevor says, coming back into the room. "I've already double-checked our work."

I snap out of my thoughts.

---

56. It doesn't take much to wipe your mouth with a napkin after you eat. Quite frankly, it is one of the simplest things in the world.

57. *The Strange Case of Dr. Jekyll and Mr. Hyde* is a book about a guy who drinks a potion that splits him into two different personalities: 1) Dr. Jekyll, respected doctor and citizen, and 2) Mr. Hyde, a crazed murderer who no one likes. I realize that this comparison might be a bit dramatic, but I think I make my point.

"There's nothing wrong with triple-checking," I reply, still reviewing the sketch.

"No, I suppose not," Trevor says with a shrug.

Hold on. I pause, examining Trevor carefully. Did he just agree with me? No snappy response? No insult? Maybe the spell is working after all.

I push aside our sketch.

"Trevor, before we get back into our project, I have an important question to ask you."

This is it. This is the moment that makes all this worth it.

"So," I start, looking casually at my fingernails. "I was wondering . . ."

I stop to give him my best flirty look. I bat my eyelashes and give him a huge wink.

"What's wrong with your eyes? Do you have something in them?"

"No, no," I sputter. "I was just—oh, never mind. Look, I was wondering if you happened to change your mind about running for the presidential spot. Maybe there was something"—I flash him a quick smile—"that happened to change your mind."

Trevor's mouth dips down at the corners as if he is concentrating on something really important.

This is it. This is it. He is totally in love with me. He wouldn't dare take the presidential seat from me. Right? Right??

Trevor looks down for a few more moments, his mouth slowly curving up out of the frown. A small noise escapes his mouth, and before I know it, he is doubled over in laughter.

"Good one, Erin." He laughs so hard that he starts hiccuping. "Me, drop out of the race?" His laugh is full, and in normal circumstances it would be contagious, but not now. Definitely not now. "Who knew you were a comedian?"

"Yeah," I respond dryly. "Hardy har har."

Trevor Jin is definitely not in love with me.

We end up finishing the project quickly, and I will not admit this to Trevor, but using the 3D printer was a brilliant idea. Our project looks professionally made, and I'm pretty sure that we will have the best project in the class. Although the spell didn't work, Trevor was pretty nice to me the whole time I was there. I mean, he didn't pull my chair out from under me or anything. He made me *snacks*, which as shocking things go, comes in at the top of my list. I will just have to reorganize when it comes to my campaign. I have to make sure I'm at the top of my game: posters, prepared speeches, little bags of cookies to convince the other club members to vote for me. Honestly, it shouldn't be all that hard.

CHAPTER NINE

*Cupid Commandment Number 11: A Cupid is a
diplomat of love, but that does not mean that they
are immune to love's power. When a Cupid falls in
love, they fall hard and fast.*

BY THE TIME MONDAY rolls around I have a solid plan for my campaign. The first thing I need to do is ask Bruno to design my campaign posters. I tried texting him over the weekend, telling him I had a really important favor to ask him. But he never texted me back, which, to be honest, is completely unlike him. I can only assume that he was too busy with India. Which, don't get me started on that. It's completely rude of him to ignore me when it's all thanks to me that he even has the confidence to talk to her, but whatever. But this morning I should have him all to myself, and then I can tell him my plan, and he can help me create a poster that will blow anything that Trevor creates out of the water.

I'm already outside waiting by the time Isa's car comes up the driveway. I start walking toward the back door of the car where I normally sit before I stop, a shape coming into view. A girl shape. Isa rolls down the window, leaning out slightly toward me.

"Good morning, sunshine. Hop in front today. Ben decided to take the bus this morning, and we have a visitor." She wiggles her eyebrows at me.

"Mom," Bruno retorts in exasperation.

"What?" she responds with complete innocence.

I look through the backseat window and right into the face of India Saunders. She smiles at me, waving a hand. I smile tightly back at her, sliding into the front seat beside Bruno's mom. I glare back at Bruno, who gives me a meek smile. Gee, thanks for the heads-up, Bruno. This is so not the time for this. I have a campaign to plan. Bruno knows this, or he *would* know this if he had bothered to text me back. Now India is sitting in the back in *my* seat with my best friend. We could be planning the poster design right now, but instead Bruno is too busy making moony eyes at India Saunders. Which I realize is completely my fault, but still. I had no idea that India and Bruno becoming a couple would cause me to lose my best friend.

I huff loudly. "So, India," I say sharply, stretching my seat belt so I can turn around to face them. "Why are you riding with us this morning? Did you miss the bus or something?"

India bites her lip. Bruno crosses his arms, glaring at me.

"No, I invited her." Bruno's tone is icy.

"Oh," I mutter. I turn back around as Isa pulls out onto the road.

The quiet is deafening. And hey, look, I know I'm being a brat. I *know*. But this campaign is just too important, and I really don't have time for the Bruno and India love saga.

India leans forward.

"So, did you enjoy your time at Trevor's house?"

I freeze. How does she know about that? I haven't even gotten a chance to tell Bruno about it yet. Not that I'm trying to hide it from him or anything, but I've just been too busy to tell him. Plus, it's not like he's been texting me as often as he used to.

"How did you know I was at Trevor's?" I ask.

"You went to Trevor's?" Bruno's accusation overlaps mine.

We all sit in silence for a moment.

"Wait a minute." Isa's singsong voice rings out from the driver's seat. "Trevor—isn't that the name of the boy from your mom's book, mija?"

"No," I howl. "It's not."

"Oh, no need to get snippy, Erin Marie. I just thought I remembered the name from her book—"

"Back to Trevor's house," Bruno interrupts his mom.

"I'm so sorry," India says. "I just live next door to Trevor, and I saw you over there on Saturday. I didn't know it was a secret."

"It isn't a secret!" I yell over everyone. "I was there because we were forced to partner up on a science project. That's it. End of story. I don't want to talk about Trevor anymore."

The whole car falls silent. India looks awkwardly out the

window. I can feel Bruno glaring at the back of my head.

Isa smiles. "Sometimes it just feels better to let your feelings out. Your aura even looks brighter now."

I sigh, putting my forehead against the window. I know I said this already, but it's worth saying again: I can't believe that this is my life.

When we get to school, I sit in the car for a moment while Bruno and India amble out. Bruno says something to India, and she nods, then heads off toward the front door. Bruno waits for me by the car door with his arms crossed. I sling my bookbag over my shoulder and climb out of the car.

"I see India's gone. That's good. I've got some things I need to talk to you about. Did you get my text messages?"

Bruno holds his hand up to stop me.

"First, EJ, India is not gone. I told her I'd meet her by her locker after I talked to you."

I cross my arms. "You're not coming to our locker? We always go to our locker in the morning. It's tradition."

"Second," Bruno continues, ignoring me, "you were really rude to India this morning, like, extremely rude, EJ. It really wasn't cool."

Okay, he's right. But I'm not going to admit that, because didn't India sort of throw me to the wolves and tell everyone in the car that I was at Trevor's house on Saturday, like it was some kind of date or something? And Bruno has been ignoring my texts and standing me up, all because of India.

"It wasn't cool that India brought up the Trevor thing," I reply frostily.

Bruno throws up his hands. "How was she supposed to know it was a secret? And also, EJ, why was it a secret? Why didn't I know about it? We're supposed to be best friends."

You've got to be kidding me.

"Bruno, I would have told you if you'd ever bothered to text me back."

Bruno grimaces, and he really does look sorry. "Yeah, I just got busy, EJ. I kind of spaced and forgot."

I laugh. "If by 'forgot,' you mean that you were too caught up with India, then you're absolutely correct."

Bruno's skin turns a vivid, angry red color. "Look, I don't know why you are being so mean to India, but cut it out. You're the one who encouraged me to talk to India in the first place."

The accusation stings because it's true. Worse, I used magic to make it happen.

"Yeah, I know," I yell back. "But I didn't know that meant we weren't going to be friends anymore."

Bruno sighs, looking as weary as I feel. I can't even remember the last time Bruno and I disagreed on something, much less had a full-blown argument.

"This is stupid," I say, sagging against the wall.

Bruno gives me a tiny smile, flicking his hair away from his eyes.

"Yeah, it is a pretty stupid argument," he agrees. "But I'm sorry, though, about not responding to your texts."

I return his smile. "Yeah, I'm sorry too, about everything with India," I say.

What I really want to say is *sorry not sorry*, but that wouldn't really be the best-friend thing to do.

"It's okay." Bruno shrugs, giving me another small smile. "We all get grumpy sometimes. Maybe you should eat a Snickers."[58]

I snort, pushing his shoulder. "Or maybe you should eat a Snickers." I glance down at my watch. "You better go catch up with India before you miss her."

Bruno pauses for a moment, looking over at me shyly. "Are you sure? You're okay with breaking tradition?"

I sigh. "Yeah, go ahead, Romeo. We can always talk later."

He smiles. "Thanks, EJ. You're the best."

I continue walking to my locker alone. Which isn't all that bad. It's not like Bruno is abandoning me for India. It's just one day. I can walk alone to my locker for one day. When I get there, I'm surprised to find Trevor leaning against the adjacent locker.

"Hey," I say suspiciously, sliding past him to jiggle my combination lock.

"Hey," he answers. I squint up at him, waiting for him to finish. He doesn't.

"Well, why are you here, Trevor? Homeroom is on the other side of the building."

"Oh." Trevor's cheeks color a bit. "I just came to drop off our project to Mrs. Evans's room so I wouldn't be carrying it around." He jerks his thumb toward the room for extra emphasis. "I didn't want to get it messed up."

---

58. Bruno is referencing our favorite commercial, where eating a Snickers turns you from a grumpy Joe Pesci to a normal teenager.

"Oh," I reply, slamming my locker. It actually makes perfect sense.

Trevor plays with the ends of his bookbag straps, shuffling his feet back and forth. Is he nervous? Yes, yes he *is* nervous. And it is kind of cute. Wait, what? I shake my head, willing the last thought out of my head. Honestly, I need to stop thinking that.

"I was wondering—"

"Did you want to walk to drop it off together?" I blurt out.

Both of us are immediately flushed with embarrassment.

"Yeah, sure," Trevor replies with a small smile.

No, this is part of my plan, I assure myself. Even though my magic doesn't technically work—at least work the way I want it to—it doesn't mean I should give up on my plan to make Trevor fall in love with me. Obviously, I subconsciously know that already. That's why I just asked Trevor to walk together. That's absolutely why. The only reason why.

We walk silently side by side, ignoring the weirdness that we both feel. Because, honestly, this *is* weird. Trevor Jin and I should not be walking together. Ever. When we get to Mrs. Evans's room, Trevor hurries in front of me to grab the door. He opens it, waiting patiently for me to walk through. I stare at him, completely flustered. Trevor just opened the door. I've never known Trevor Jin to ever open the door for anybody.[59] I must have been standing there for a long time, just staring, because he clears his throat.

---

59. To be fair, this is mainly because he's so early to class that he's already sitting at his desk by the time everyone else arrives.

"Are you coming?"

I nod my head, walking into the room. I turn back to look at Trevor.

"Don't think this makes us friends," I whisper, but with a smile.

Trevor gives me a half smile. "Wouldn't dream of it."

The morning speeds by in a somewhat happy blur. Trevor is unusually nice to me throughout homeroom and English. And by unusually nice, I mean there are no snarky replies to any of my comments. And he even lets me answer a question, even though I know that he knows the answer too. By the time we get to science, we're both more than ready to present our project. We already know it will be the best project of the bunch. But there is still something exhilarating about going up in front of the room and presenting our assignment. It makes me feel like a real scientist.

Mrs. Evans runs through the roll fairly quickly. Then she calls for volunteers to go first for the project presentations. Both Trevor and I fling our hands into the air.

"Okay, Mr. Jin, Ms. Johnson. Let's see what you've got."

Trevor quickly goes to the back of the room where we stored our project. He pulls it out slowly, being careful not to knock it against anything. Then he does something really, really strange. He hands it to me.

"Here," he says with a smile. "You hold it."

Smiling back at him, I cradle the DNA model in my hands. We move to the front of the room.

"So," Trevor says, facing the class, his voice becoming crisp and businesslike, "this is our model. As you can see, we opted to do a replication model."

A couple of appreciative gasps sound from the other students in the room.

"And we decided to use my dad's 3D printer to create this. We really just wanted our project to look as professional as possible."

I can hear the pride in his voice. But hey, he has a right to be proud. Our project is amazing, and we worked hard on it.

"I also would like to say that Erin did most of the research for our report, and she double-checked my work. So we were a really great team."

I stare at him in shock. Did he just compliment me? Better yet, did he just share the credit for an assignment?

Mrs. Evans stares at us smugly from behind her desk. "It's almost like I knew best when I put you together as partners." She gives me a knowing look, her eyebrow raised.

Okay, okay, Mrs. Evans. I get it. You were right, and I was wrong. But who would have guessed that I would work together so well with Trevor Jin?

After science class is lunch, and this is the time that Bruno and I usually get to catch up on our day, and it is particularly important that I talk to Bruno today. I have to get my posters up ASAP. Trevor's posters are already peppered around the school. And I have to admit that they are pretty awesome. He used the phrase "A vote for Trevor is a vote for fun-damental rights," and the poster is all clean, sharp lines and monochromatic colors. It looks very much like a Trevor Jin poster.

I go into the lunchroom, moving toward our normal table, but I pause before I can get to it. Bruno is already sitting there, lunch tray in front of him, and India is sitting next to him. India! I move toward the table again, my anger starting to cloud my vision. This is getting ridiculous. First India takes my seat this morning in the car. Then she interrupts my morning talk with Bruno. Now she is going to sit with us at lunch. When will this end?

I drop my backpack loudly onto the stool across from where Bruno and India are sitting. They both jump back in surprise.

"EJ," Bruno says, looking at me with concern. "Are you okay?"

"Yeah," I huff. "Why wouldn't I be okay?"

India turns away from my gaze, clearly uncomfortable.

"Because you're slamming things?" Bruno says. "And that's clearly a sign of someone not being okay."

"Well, *clearly* you aren't as psychic as you think you are," I mumble grumpily.

Bruno ignores me, looking down at his tray. I try to quell my anger at India being at the lunch table. I have more important things to think about, such as Bruno creating the logo for my campaign posters.

"How was your presentation?" India asks politely. She pushes her mashed potatoes around with a fork.

I sigh. This is ridiculous. I don't *hate* India. I just don't know her, and it seems like lately she is hogging a lot of time with my best friend. And maybe that does irritate me a little bit, but I should probably at least try to give her a chance for Bruno's sake.

"It was good," I answer begrudgingly. "I think we're going to get a good grade."

"Oh, EJ is just being modest."

I startle as Trevor plunks his tray down next to my lunch bag. He slides onto the stool next to me. "We blew that project out of the water."

Bruno stares at Trevor as if he has suddenly grown a second head.

"Trevor," I say evenly. "Did your spot get taken or something?"

Trevor's usual spot is a table near the entrance to the cafeteria. He probably sits there so he can make it to class before everyone else. Trevor gives me a crooked smile, which makes my stomach do a weird loop-the-loop thing. I smile back. Wait, stop smiling, Erin.

This is Trevor. Trevor! We do not smile at each other or interact outside of academic environments. Ever.

"Nope," Trevor replies. He bites off a piece of a grilled chicken sandwich. "Just thought I'd sit over here today."

I throw up my hands. "Sure, fine. It seems like this is the hot spot to sit at today for some reason."

"How are you doing, Trevor?" India asks.

God, that girl is just all rainbows, sugar, and sweetness. It almost makes my teeth hurt.

Trevor gives her a smile, and for some reason I feel myself tense. She's already stealing my best friend. She can't have my Trevor—I mean, my nemesis, too!

"Doing well, India. How about you?"

I roll my eyes, sucking my teeth loudly. "Everybody's fine.

Everyone is great. We're all eating lunch together like one big happy family!"

Bruno doesn't speak. In fact, he hasn't spoken since Trevor sat down. His eyes bounce back and forth from Trevor to me, then back to Trevor again. He looks completely and utterly confused.

"Okay, what's going on? Why are you sitting over here, Trevor? Is this a game or something? Are you guys trying to see who irritates who to death first?" Bruno asks.

Trevor shrugs. "I don't know. Maybe I just wanted a change of scenery."

I gaze at Trevor, my mouth hanging open. Is he serious? A change of scenery?

"Sooo," Bruno says, a sly smile playing over his lips, "you're saying you didn't come over here to sit with Erin?"

"Of course I came to sit with EJ," Trevor scoffs haughtily.

He did? My stupid heart does a skipping thing.

"I mean," Bruno continues, "I didn't know you and EJ were friends."

Bruno and I don't have a lot of friends outside of each other. At first our tight circle was out of necessity. Bruno and I weren't exactly turning away hordes of people seeking our friendship. We are oddballs, and we were perfectly content in sharing a close-knit friendship with each other. But then after my nana died, it was almost impossible for me to try to let anyone else in. It was too hard, getting close to someone, loving someone, just to lose them.

Trevor raises an eyebrow. "Well, we can't all know everything all the time."

Bruno doesn't respond. He simply continues eating his food. Soon India turns her full attention to him. She starts asking him questions about his day. I ignore them and look over at Trevor.

"I'm sorry about Bruno. I know he's asking a lot of questions. But to be fair, I haven't gotten a chance to brief him on our, um . . ." I clear my throat. "Change of situation."

Trevor nods, his face all pretend seriousness. "Change of situation. Well, that sounds ominous."

I crinkle my nose. "Well, it wasn't too long ago—I believe a couple of days, in fact—when we were mortal enemies."

Trevor stifles a grin. "Mortal enemies?"

I shrug. "Kind of felt like it."

Trevor chuckles, finishing up his chicken sandwich.

"So how's your campaign going?" he asks.

I frown, pulling out my own bologna-and-mayonnaise sandwich. I bite into it.

"Why do you want to know? Are you planning to sabotage me?"

Trevor laughs, a full, unencumbered laugh.

"Yeah, EJ." For some reason, I now like how he calls me EJ. What's wrong with me? "I have some serious sabotage plans in the works."

I smile a bit as he laughs again. "Really?" I respond, playing along. "Like what? Cross my name off all my campaign posters?"

He smiles. "Nope. Think bigger."

I sit back on the stool, pretending to think.

"Ooh, maybe you're going to erase me from the school system altogether. I can't run for president if I'm not officially enrolled in the school."

"How am I supposed to do that?" he asks.

I shrug my shoulders. "Maybe you're creating some type of goo that makes me invisible when I put it on?"

Trevor laughs again, running his hand through his hair. "You've got quite an imagination."

"Okay," I say, crossing my arms. "What would you do to sabotage my campaign?"

Trevor shrugs. "Hey, maybe I'm just not the sabotaging type."

"Whatever," I reply, happily guzzling down my water. "You're the only person who would be able to sabotage me at all."

"You're probably right," Trevor responds, smiling broadly. "Oh, before I forget."

Trevor shuffles around in his bookbag, finally pulling out a neatly creased paper bag.

"Here, this is for you." He pushes the bag into my hands, his gaze flicking away from my face. I carefully open it. I squeal as I examine the contents.

"You brought me yakgwa? Oh my god! You remembered!"

Overwhelming giddiness slams through me. This is one of the most thoughtful things anyone (outside of Bruno, that is) has ever done for me.

Trevor chuckles. "Of course I remembered. It's not every day someone figures out their mortal enemy's favorite food," he says before he bumps his shoulder against mine.

Trevor just touched me, and what's even worse is that I feel wobbly like a teetering Jenga tower.[60]

Before I can respond, India gives a little cough, and I turn toward her. Beside her, Bruno is eerily quiet. He is staring at us with a mixture of confusion and anger. Trevor looks at me too, then quickly looks away. Just then the bell rings. Trevor hurriedly scrapes back his chair, a stoic, serious look clouding his face.

"Anyway, see you later, EJ. India. Bruno." He nods to each of us.

Bruno gets up as well, leaning over to whisper something in India's ear.

When Bruno stands up, India stands also, gathering her things. She looks at me sympathetically.

"See you later, EJ."

Bruno crosses his arms as I start to gather my trash. "We need to talk."

I fidget nervously under his glare. "Well, we don't have much time. The late bell will ring soon, and you know how I like to be—"

Bruno cuts me off. "It won't take long."

He walks briskly from the cafeteria, and I follow closely on his heels. He stops in front of our shared locker, abruptly turning around to face me, his arms still crossed.

---

60. Jenga is actually pretty fun. It is Bruno's and my go-to Friday night game, but that doesn't mean that it doesn't come without loads of nail-biting tension.

"What is going on with you?" He sounds angry and hurt, and I flinch. "First you're treating India like she's some type of lower life-form. Then there's this secret relationship thing that you have going on with Trevor Jin. Who, by the way, you hated last time I checked."

I cross my arms. "I'm not in a secret relationship with Trevor Jin."

Bruno lowers his voice. "Why are you keeping secrets from me? I thought we were best friends."

My heart sinks.

"It's not like that," I sputter. How can I make him understand?

"Then what's it like?" Bruno says, his voice getting an octave softer. "What's going on, EJ? Talk to me."

Anger hisses through me as I think about the last couple of days and how Bruno has been all but absent.

"Talk to you, talk to you," I whisper-yell. "When, Bruno? Ever since you started hanging around with India, I've kind of just been an afterthought."

Pain lances through my chest, because really, that's my fault too. Bruno flinches back.

"Well, I'm here now," Bruno responds softly. The anger leaks out of me instantly.

"I know you are," I state, rubbing my hand against my forehead wearily. "Things have just been so weird lately. Look, I'm not in a relationship with Trevor. Remember the presidential position I told you about?"

Bruno nods.

"Do you remember how I told you about how Trevor and I are running against each other?"

Bruno nods again.

"Well, I'm kind of trying to make him fall in love with me so he will drop out of the race."

There. I told Bruno the truth. Well, sort of the truth. Mostly the truth.

Bruno stares at me, his mouth gaping open.

"What?" I ask. "Say something."

The bell rings, but for the first time in a long time I don't care.

Bruno stands still, looking at me in what seems like disgust.

Finally, he speaks. "Erin, you can't be serious. Please tell me that you're joking."

I scowl at him. "Of course I'm serious. Why wouldn't I be serious?"

He blinks at me, astonishment coloring every inch of his face.

"Wow," he says, rubbing his hands along his face. "Just wow, EJ."

"What?" I ask defensively. "Why are you suddenly Team Trevor? Trevor started this whole rivalry when he stole my story. He's a horrible person, remember?" I ignore the tiny voice in my head that asks if a terrible person would bring yakgwa to lunch just for me.

Bruno rolls his eyes. "When are you going to let that go?"

Wait a minute, he's acting like I'm some unreasonable brat who's holding on to a grudge just for the fun of it.

"It wasn't just kindergarten," I spit back. "It was the other day, too, during our election introductions. He used my ideas during his speech."

Even as I say that, I know it isn't completely true. They weren't completely my ideas. They were more our shared ideas. But that's just semantics. He should have asked to use them for his speech.

Bruno sighs.

"Come on, EJ. This is drastic, even for you."

"You know how important this election is to me, to my future."

Bruno laughs dryly. "To your future? Really? We're thirteen. You're just thirteen. Sometimes it's okay not to think about the future."

Something inside me snaps.

"Oh *yeah*?"

I could list a thousand different reasons why I'm focused on my future. Like how I want to prove myself as a Black girl and how I can't just be reduced to a stereotype. Or I could bring up my nana and how I want so badly to find the cure to the disease that sucked the life out of her. I could say any of those things, but I say the one thing I know will hurt Bruno the most.

"The future isn't important if you're just going to end up being some unemployed artist."

Bruno's face pales. He looks at me as if he's never seen me before.

"It's better than toying with someone for your own personal gain, EJ. It's way better." He says it quietly, as if the whole conversation has tired him out. Bruno starts to move away from me. "I have to get to class."

"Wait." I grab his hand before he goes any farther. "Wait, Bruno."

I look down at his hand, and I can see the glowing golden light coming from mine. I shut my eyes tightly. *We're best friends. Don't be mad at me. Please don't be mad at me.* I feel warmth cycle through me, this time more quickly. I open my eyes to Bruno. He is giving me a curious look. The orange mist swirls around him like a hurricane.

After a beat, Bruno says, "You okay, EJ?"

"Yeah, I'm fine," I mumble, stunned at what I've (maybe) done. The bell rings. "We're late to class."

"Is it my fault? God, I'm sorry, EJ—"

I stop him. "It's not your fault. Let's just get to class."

It worked. Oh god, it actually worked.

He agrees, taking my arm as we march off to class together.

Later on that night I reflect on the day with a sort of nauseous feeling. For one thing, I feel awful, just plain awful, for what I did to Bruno. After I used my powers on him, he completely forgot that he was angry at me. I mean, he wasn't upset at *all*. I'm a little concerned that the magic rattled his brain or something. And if that's the case, did it rattle everyone else's brains as well? Oh god. What if I have ruined everyone's lives? What if my magic has altered them forever?

I throw myself on my bed and scream into my pillow. This is insane, absolutely insane. What are the odds that I would be the girl who wakes up to find out she has magical powers, powers that can change her friends' lives? I've always been a strong believer in logic and science. For me, unless there is evidence or science to back up someone's argument, I don't even bother listening to it. But now here I am, apparently a half-mythical creature with no logical answer as to why I have what seem to be magical love powers.

Not only that, but there is now the scientific possibility that since magic exists, and there is such a thing as Cupid, other gods or magical creatures exist. Anything could exist. The possibilities are endless.

A knock interrupts my thoughts.

"Erin."

My mom's voice sounds small and tentative from the other side of my door.

I ignore her.

"I was just wondering if you wanted to talk."

She pauses, waiting for me to respond. I remain quiet.

"Okay, I'm here for you whenever you're ready to talk."

Anger flares in me. Okay, great. Now you're here when I'm ready to talk. What happened to telling me about my dad when I asked? Or how about letting me in on the secret that I am a supernatural matchmaker? No, things always have to be on my mom's terms, but not this time. I'm not talking to her until I'm good and ready.

I don't respond, and I finally hear my mom move away from the door.

I push all thoughts of the possibility of other magical creatures from my head. I honestly have enough to deal with, with secretive moms and absent Cupid dads.

My phone beeps, interrupting my thoughts. A smile flashes

across my face as I notice the name. Trevor. I tap my phone, and his message flashes across the screen.

Trevor: **Thanks for letting me crash your lunch today.**

I smile harder, typing out my answer. I can't believe how Trevor is now the person I all of a sudden look forward to talking to.

Me: **It wasn't a problem. You were the best par—**

Nope, erase that.

Me: **Not a problem ☺ Lunch was fun.**

Lunch was fun. Ugh. Who says that?

Trevor starts to write. Stops, then starts again. My stomach tumbles a bit. What if he thinks what I wrote was stupid? Maybe he was expecting me to say more? But what? Great conversation? Loved the company? My English teachers are always telling me to be more specific in my essays. Maybe they were right. The phone beeps, and I look down at Trevor's response.

Trevor: **It was fun! I might have to make it a habit ☺**

A laugh slips out of me as I type my response lightning quick.

Me: You should 😊 😊
Trevor: Then I will 😊
Trevor: We make a pretty good team, EJ.

A picture pops up on my phone. It's a selfie of Trevor with our project. Our model is on a dresser in what looks like his room, and he is smiling. My heart speeds up. He has our project in his room? On display? I smile again.

Me: I love that!
Trevor: We could have shared custody if you want. . . .

I pause, completely bewildered for a second.

Me: Of what?
Trevor: Um, the project

Duh, Erin. I roll my eyes. Of course he meant the project.

Me: Hehe. I knew that.
Trevor: I know you did. . . . You're one of the smartest people that I know . . . maybe the smartest.

Did Trevor Jin just compliment me on how smart I am? Is this the same Trevor who at the beginning of sixth grade said my book report on *Jurassic Park* deserved to be extinct right along with dinosaurs? Is this the same Trevor who is now texting me, complimenting me, putting our partner project on display?

The phone beeps again, startling me out of my thoughts.

> Trevor: **I've got to get ready for bed**
> Me: **Oh, okay. Well, good night, Trevor**
> Trevor: **Good night, EJ**

As I settle into bed, plugging my phone in to charge, I come to a startling realization. The spell worked. It actually worked. I think Trevor Jin is falling in love with me. And really, that should make me feel ecstatic, over the moon even, but instead I feel like a balloon that has been filled with lead. And I absolutely hate this feeling.

I really need to get it together. I'm almost to my goal. I'll be the president of the Multicultural Leadership Club, and I'll get a spot in the dual enrollment program. And I'll do all the things that would have made my nana proud.

So why do I feel like I'm sinking in an insurmountable pit of doom? And what is this feeling?

I stare at my ceiling, mulling everything over. It's only when I'm halfway to sleep that I realize what it is that I'm feeling. It's guilt.

CHAPTER TEN

Cupid Commandment Number 15: Being a Cupid is noble work. As a Cupid, you will be expected to always take the high road. Always.

I WAKE UP THE next morning in a fog. There is something about knowing that maybe Trevor likes me that makes me feel light-headed. But on the other hand, I also feel queasy knowing that I manipulated him into feeling that way. Not just manipulated—*magically* manipulated. So when Mom beeps the horn at Bruno's house to let him know she is outside, I'm extra surprised and frustrated to see Ben stomp out beside him. I'm really not in the mood for Ben.

"No India today?" I ask nonchalantly.

Ben turns around and flashes me a smile. "Nope. *I* talked to her this morning. She had to go in early for dance team practice."

Bruno balls his hands into fists, ignoring his brother while he looks out the window.

"Oh, who's India?" my mom asks. She is always digging around for gossip, even if it is middle school gossip. And now it is painfully obvious that she is trying to bait me into talking to her.

Things are still off with my mom, and I'm not about to be tricked into talking to her.

"Oh, just one of my best friends. We're really, really close," Ben says.

Bruno is now squeezing his fists so tightly that I'm afraid he'll leave nail marks in his palms.

"India is also good friends with Bruno," I interrupt. Even though I don't really want to talk to Mom about this right now, Bruno needs me.

"Oh, how nice is that! You two share a friend."

Ben's eyes gleam. He turns to look at us in the backseat. "Yeah," he says in a mockingly sweet tone. "We share a friend, Bruno."

Bruno is now shaking with anger, his face pressed against the window. Before I know what I'm doing, I reach up to the front of the car, grabbing Ben's left hand.

"Hey," he shouts. "What are you doing?"

He tries to twist free, but I tighten my grip. I close my eyes, ignoring him. I concentrate, letting the expected warmth wash through me. *This is your brother. Your twin. You should be closer to him than anyone else. Stop treating him like this. Stop hurting him.* A sharp red color surrounds Ben in a haze.

"Erin Marie." My mom's dark tone cuts through my thoughts. I release Ben's hand and sit back in my seat, completely winded. My mom looks at me through the rearview mirror, her mouth creasing in a frown.

"I don't know what's gotten into you, Erin, but enough." My mom sounds furious. Her voice shakes the car.

Anger washes over me like a tidal wave. I clench and unclench my hands in fury.

"What's gotten into me? Really, you have no idea what's gotten into me? You're hardly the person to be flabbergasted at a person's actions."

I know I've gone too far, but at this moment I don't care. All of it is too much. My mom's secrets. My powers. My magical dad. All of it.

I look over and catch Bruno staring at me with confusion and a tiny bit of fear. Was I glowing? Did he catch me? Embarrassed, I turn my face toward the window.

When we get to school, my mom gives me one final glare. *We will talk at home,* she mouths to me. Ben doesn't speak at all. He looks utterly confused, and he keeps peeking back at Bruno with a frown. Great. Another failed magical experiment, and now I'm in trouble with my mom for using magic. I groan, walking toward the building, Bruno silently trotting along beside me. When I get to the locker, I turn to face him.

"Look, I'm sorry about what Ben said. I know it sucks that India told him and not you."

Bruno waves his hand in the air, unconcerned. "No, she told

me, and I know she told Ben. They are friends, and that's not what bothers me. It's just Ben being Ben. He's always been that way."

"But you shouldn't have to take it," I complain.

Bruno continues to stare at me quietly for a moment. "Is that why you did what you did to him?"

My body turns ice-cold. "What do you mean? What did I do to him?"

Bruno shrugs, still looking directly at me. "Whatever you did when you glowed. You were glowing, EJ. And I swear, this isn't the first time I've seen you do that."

I grimace, turning away from Bruno. He knows my secret. He knows. I take a steadying breath. Of course he doesn't. He couldn't possibly know my secret.

"What are you talking about, Bruno?" I respond with a shaky laugh. "Glowing? Did you not get enough sleep last night?"

Bruno narrows his eyes on me.

"Don't do this, EJ." He pauses, lowering his voice a little. "You can trust me."

I know that. I know I can trust Bruno. He is the only person that I've ever felt like I could trust, but this secret isn't just mine. It is mine, my dad's, and my mom's. And somehow I don't think I'm ready to share that part of me yet.

For a moment I consider using my magic again. It would make things easier, and it would be so simple. I could just make him believe me.

Bruno continues to wait for me to speak. I can't do that again. I just can't.

"I'm not doing anything," I insist. I grab his arm, steering him away from the locker. "Everything's fine. I promise. Everything is normal."

Bruno doesn't respond. He simply nods and doesn't speak for the rest of our walk to our classes.

When I get to homeroom, I'm late again.[61] Lateness is becoming a habit I do not like. At all. Everything feels so topsy-turvy. I have to get control of myself. Most of the class is already in the room, including Trevor, who gives me a smile when I scoot into my seat. It is a tiny smile, but it still launches a horde of butterflies in my stomach.

"Very un-Trevor-like," I mumble.

"What is?" Trevor asks cordially.

Oh god, I didn't think he heard me.

I shrug. "Well, for one, you smiled at me. I think I can count on one hand how often you have smiled at me over the years."

Trevor looks forward, his mouth twitching at the edges. I smile at his attempt to hide his smile.

"And two," I say, starting to lay my supplies out on my desk, "you didn't comment on my lateness. Very, very un-Trevor-like. Honestly, I'm starting to wonder if you've lost your edge, Jin, or maybe you've just been taken over by aliens or something."

Or maybe this is my magic? a tiny voice in the back of my head reminds me.

Guilt clenches me once again.

---

61. Well, not really late, but late like I wasn't one of the first ones in class.

Trevor laughs, and when I push down the annoying voice of my conscience, I find myself enjoying the sound.

"It's okay to be late sometimes." Trevor shrugs and sits back in his chair. It is then that I notice what he is wearing. Trevor is wearing jeans! Actual jeans!

"You're wearing jeans," I blurt out, then instantly blanch in embarrassment.

Trevor shrugs again, smiling. "Yeah, I'm wearing jeans."

"I didn't even think you owned jeans," I respond to him, completely surprised.

Trevor huffs with annoyance. "Of course I own jeans. I just don't wear them all the time."

"Never," I correct. "You've never worn jeans. Our first day of kindergarten you were wearing a bow tie."

Trevor looks at me, a strange expression cloaking his face. "You remember what I was wearing in kindergarten?"

I slam my mouth shut, turning around to face the front of the room. I cannot believe I just admitted that to him.[62]

Just then Ms. Richmond comes into the room, her long black ringlets swinging behind her.

"Hello, children. How are we all doing today?"

We all murmur incoherently in response.

"Great," she responds. "I have just a couple of announcements, and then I'll let you work on your own for the rest of homeroom."

---

62. To be fair, Trevor was the only one in kindergarten dressed like he was going off to work at the *Daily Planet*.

She nods vigorously while she talks, as if we're all really in tune with what she is saying. None of us really are.

"Okay, just an update on the rest of this week's tutoring sessions. They are being canceled due to back-to-back school board meetings that are being held during that time. If you're a tutor, please make sure to share the information with the student you're tutoring."

I look over at Trevor. He is writing down everything that Ms. Richmond says. Of course he is. The jeans thing is just a fluke. Trevor hasn't *really* changed. I mentally store away that I need to text Carsen, a sweet sixth grader I tutor, who reminds me a bit of myself when I was new to middle school.

Before Ms. Richmond can finish her announcements, the door flings open, and loud music starts to flood the room. Startled, we all turn around to see Mr. Fairview at the head of what looks like the eighth-grade jazz band. He has a wireless microphone in his hand, and he is singing "Can't Take My Eyes Off You" by Frankie Valli[63] (very badly, by the way) while the band plays what kind of sounds like the instrumental to the song.

Shocked, Ms. Richmond clamps her hands over her mouth. "Paul, what's going on?"

We all swivel in our seats to see what Mr. Fairview is going to say.

---

63. It's an old people's love song. Ironically enough, this song was in the nineties rom-com *10 Things I Hate About You*. Also, I'm completely aware that even though I despise rom-coms, my life has pretty much turned into one.

Mr. Fairview ends the song on a fairly screechy (not at all attractive) note.

"Stella." He moves toward Ms. Richmond, signaling for the band to stop playing. "I know that we have had a sort of whirlwind romance. We've only been on a couple of dates, but I've known for a long time that you were the one."

Ms. Richmond is shaking. Oh god, she looks like she is going to cry.

Mr. Fairview gets down on one knee. The class collectively gasps. Wait, what is going on? My heart starts hammering. Oh no, oh no, oh no.

"Will you marry me, Stella, and make me the happiest man in the world?"

I clap my hand over my mouth in horror. Say no. *Please* say no.

Ms. Richmond starts crying. She pulls Mr. Fairview up from his knee.

"Yes, of course. A thousand times yes, Paul."

"Nooo," I screech out. Everyone in the room turns to look at me in confusion.

"I'm sorry," I mumble. "I . . . stubbed my toe."

Ms. Richmond is going to marry Mr. Fairview. Marry! Ms. Richmond doesn't even know that it was magic that made Mr. Fairview propose to her. What if he doesn't really love her? What if my magic wears off and he decides he no longer wants to get married? Ms. Richmond would be miserable, and it would be all my fault. Honestly, this can't possibly get any worse.

After English class, I go to my locker to see if I can catch Bruno, but he isn't there. I pull out my phone and shoot him a quick text. **Hey, where are you?** And then **Can we talk?** I wait a moment for a response, but after a minute, nothing comes through. I make my way to science, my mind still on Ms. Richmond and Bruno.

Trevor is already there, his stuff neatly lined in a row.

"Hey." I set my stuff down next to his, climbing onto the stool.

"We got our grade back from our DNA project." He slides our report over to me. I glance down at the 105 grade and grunt in approval. This type of thing would normally have me fist-pumping with joy, but today, well, today is different. Everything feels wrong.

"Don't get too excited," Trevor replies dryly. "We wouldn't want to start a riot."

I smile at him. "Sorry, normally I'm excited about these things. Obviously, I wanted to get the best grade, and we did, but today has been weird. These past couple of weeks have been weird."

"Yeah." Trevor rubs his hand against his forehead. "I agree. Things have been weird."

Instantly, I feel another pang of guilt. Of course things have been weird for him, too. I used magic on him.

"Hey," Trevor says, perking up. "I have an idea."

"What?" I give him a cautious look.

"Let's go get ice cream after school. The Frozen Cone is just around the corner. We could walk. We could have our parents pick us up afterward."

I stare at him. Is he asking me on a date?

"Not like a date or anything," he amends, his cheeks growing pink. "But whenever I'm having a tough time, ice cream always makes me feel better. So I just thought . . ." He trails off.

I don't say anything for a moment, causing Trevor to shift back around in his chair, his facial features hardening.

"I mean, you don't have to if you don't want—"

"Sure. Sounds fun," I interrupt him. "Right after school?"

Relief floods Trevor's face.

"Yeah, we can meet at your locker if you want to?"

I nod. "As long as I'm back at the school by five so I can catch the activity bus."

Trevor grins. Another Trevor Jin smile. "Scout's honor," he replies. "We will be back by five."

The rest of the day goes by in a blur. At lunch both India and Trevor sit with me and Bruno. Bruno hasn't answered my texts, and he barely looks at me the whole time. When the bell rings, signaling the end of lunch, I try to follow him out of the lunchroom, but he loses me in the crowd of people. By the time the end of the day arrives, I'm frazzled and disheartened. This day is not going the way I planned it to, not at all. I used my magic, again, and worse, I lied to Bruno about it. I have never lied to Bruno before. And Bruno knew, and 1) he's probably disturbed and disgusted because I'm some type of freak, and 2) he hates my guts for lying to him. I'm so lost in my thoughts that I don't hear Trevor as he comes up behind me.

"Hey, ready to go?" He gives me a smile. Honestly, he should just do that more. He really does have a nice smile. It's amazing how seeing his smile makes the rest of the day melt away.

I slam my locker shut, shouldering my backpack.

"Yep, ice cream. With you. Not a date," I blurt out.

Why did I say that? Oh god.

Trevor chuckles. "Yeah, thanks for clarifying, Erin."

"EJ," I correct. "My friends call me EJ."

A curious expression flickers across his face.

We walk toward the front of the building. When we get to the door, Trevor jogs in front of me so that he can hold it open.

"Thanks," I mumble, flushing with embarrassment.

"You're welcome," Trevor replies, looking away quickly from my glance.

As we walk outside, I see Isa's car and Ben and Bruno walking toward it together. I already sent my mom a quick text letting her know that I was going to stay after school, so Isa isn't expecting me. Ben and Bruno look as if they are deep in conversation, and it looks like Bruno is laughing at something Ben has said. Weird. They almost look as if they are enjoying each other's company, which hasn't been a thing that they've done, not since, well, not since their parents' divorce.

"Hey," I shout, waving my hand at both of them.

Ben lights up with a smile (okay, weird) and waves back (weirder). Bruno gives me a brief nod before frowning and looking away. I cringe, pulling my hand down out of the air.

Trevor looks at me curiously.

"Friend trouble?"

I shrug noncommittally. "We're arguing. It's nothing serious. At least, I hope it's not."

We start walking away from the school. The ice cream shop is only a few blocks away, but the weather is abnormally crisp for an October afternoon. I pull my sweater tighter around my body, hopping from one foot to the other to keep warm.

"Here, hold on." Trevor stoops down, placing his bookbag on the ground. He shuffles around for a minute before pulling out a purple NYU sweatshirt. He tosses it to me.

I look at the sweatshirt. "You own a sweatshirt?"

"Yeah." Trevor's cheeks grow pink. "I use it for gym, so it might stink, but that's all I've got."

"Thank you," I reply sincerely. I shrug on the sweatshirt, noting how it in fact doesn't stink, but smells like a combination of laundry detergent and peppermint gum.

We continue walking, and I try not to think about how nice Trevor is being or about the fact that I'm wearing his sweatshirt.

"So, do you want to go to NYU[64] or something?" I pinch the front of the sweatshirt, where the letters are starting to fade. I didn't think Trevor owned anything that wasn't perfectly pressed and new.

Trevor shrugs, his mouth pinching a bit at the corners. "Yeah, I guess. I mean, I don't know. It's where my parents went to school. It's where they met."

I nod enthusiastically. "NYU is a great school. You'd probably be able to get into any medical school that you wanted to."

---

64. NYU, also known as New York University, is an amazing school in New York.

Trevor grimaces. "Right," he mumbles.

What is that? Why did he look so disgusted when I mentioned medical school? Ever since I've known Trevor, he's talked about becoming a doctor like his parents. I mean, when we were in first grade doing a future careers assignment, Trevor presented a whole PowerPoint on how he was going to be a cardiothoracic surgeon.[65]

We reach the ice cream shop, and Trevor holds the door open for me again. We step in, and I immediately sigh with contentment. I love the way ice cream shops smell: a mixture of melted chocolate, vanilla bean, and freshly baked waffle cones. Trevor excitedly goes toward the see-through display that houses the different ice cream flavors. I go over to stand by him.

"If I had to guess," I say, putting my finger on my chin thoughtfully, "your favorite flavor is something like vanilla or maybe chocolate."

Trevor peers at me, a wink of humor in his eyes. "You'd be wrong." He points toward the green ice cream behind the glass. "It's actually pistachio."

I gasp, pretending to be horrified. "Eww, Trevor. Who likes pistachio?"

"Me," he responds, laughing. "I like pistachio. It's delicious. What about you? *Your* favorite flavor is probably like vanilla or strawberry or something."

I stick my tongue out at him. "Nope, wrong. It's cookies and

---

65. My presentation was on becoming a princess. We already went over how I was less refined at the tender age of six.

cream because it combines the two best desserts into one delicious cone."

"Cone?" Trevor wrinkles his nose. "You're going to get a cone?"

I fold my arms, giving him a stern look. "Trevor Jin, do you not like cones? The cone is the best part."

"Agree to disagree, EJ," Trevor quips with a small smile.

We each order our ice creams, pay, and find an unoccupied table near the window.

At first we just dig into our ice cream, saying very little as we enjoy our food.

"How's the green sludge?" I ask teasingly.

Trevor puts another huge bite of ice cream into his mouth, and I giggle.[66]

"It's delicious. How about you? Enjoying your paper-thin, cardboard-tasting waffle cone?"

I giggle again. "It's great." I stop laughing, my voice taking on a more serious tone. "I'm serious. This is great. Thank you for asking me to come."

Trevor blushes, dipping his head toward his ice cream cup. "You're welcome," he mumbles.

We're quiet for a moment before Trevor interrupts the silence.

"So do you want to talk about it? I mean, whatever's bothering you?"

I peer up at Trevor's face, and it seems like he genuinely cares.

---

66. I'm giggling!! I don't think I've ever giggled in my life.

I shrug, biting into my waffle cone. "Bruno and I have been friends since before I can remember. His mom and my mom are best friends. But lately . . ." I pause for a moment. "Lately, things have been different."

Trevor nods, encouraging me to go on.

"Well, so Bruno has had a crush on India Saunders for a while now, but he's never really talked to her because she's good friends with his twin brother, Ben."

"And Ben and Bruno don't like each other, right?"

"Nope, Ben is pretty much a top-notch bully. He seems to love making it his life's mission to make Bruno's life miserable."

Trevor nods again. I continue.

"Well, Bruno finally got up the nerve to talk to India, and I'm really proud of him, but . . ." I stop, looking down at the table, feeling a wave of embarrassment wash over me.

"But he's been hanging out more with her than with you lately, and maybe it's been making you kind of irritated."

I look up at Trevor in surprise. When did he become a therapist, or better yet, a psychic? Or moreover, when did he become someone I could spill my guts to?

Trevor is still working on his ice cream, moving the spoon slowly around the cup.

"It's just hard. I'm trying to figure out a way to deal with this new trio we've got going on."

"To be fair, I'm sure Bruno is also feeling the same kind of way about us—I mean me," Trevor says. He stops eating his ice cream, concentrating on the table with noticeably redder cheeks.

"I mean, according to you, we were just mortal enemies." His voice holds a teasing tone. "That's gotta be hard for Bruno to get used to."

I blink. He is right. This is probably weird for Bruno. I have always been firmly on the Anti-Trevor Team, but now it seems like I've changed my mind, almost overnight.

"You're right." It comes out like an afterthought. I didn't even really realize I said it out loud.

"I'm what?" Trevor's eyebrows shoot up to the top of his forehead.

"You're right," I repeat sullenly.

"Wow." Trevor has a ridiculously wide grin on his face. "I don't think I've ever heard you say that before. Can you say it one more time just so I can record it?"

I ball my napkin up, throw it at him, and laugh. "Whatever. It's a onetime thing. Don't expect it to happen again."

He joins in on the laughter. "Don't worry. I won't."

We transition back into a comfortable silence for a few moments.

"What about you?" I ask. "You said it's been a weird week for you, too. Do *you* want to talk about it?"

Trevor twiddles with his spoon for a few moments, scraping the now-soupy bits of ice cream at the bottom of his cup. He shrugs half-heartedly.

"I don't know. I guess it's the campaign."

My heart sinks. The campaign I haven't even started on yet. The campaign I've essentially put on the back burner. The campaign that pretty much determines my whole future.[67]

He looks up at me to see if it is okay to continue, and I nod.

"Well, my parents, mostly my dad, don't think I'm doing enough to win. I mean, I've already made the posters. I've put together my speech, but it's still not enough."

Trevor hangs his head down low, his normally brushed jet-black hair falling over his eyes like a curtain. A really cute curtain. Ugh. Stop it. Stop thinking those thoughts.

"Well, if it makes you feel any better, I haven't even completed my posters."

"Really?"

"Nope, not a single one. I was going to get Bruno to design them for me. He's a really great artist, but since we've kind of been in this weird space lately, I didn't think it would be wise to ask him. So you can tell your parents you're miles ahead of me. Worlds, even."

Trevor gives me a small, grateful smile.

"Thanks, EJ," he replies with a sigh. "It wouldn't matter, though. My dad would say that the only person that I should be in competition with is myself. That's the only way I'll achieve greatness." Trevor's voice drops into a low timbre. I assume he is mimicking his dad's deep voice. Honestly, it doesn't sound like bad advice. It sounds like something I would tell myself. But I can tell by the droop of Trevor's shoulders and the tightness around his mouth that he doesn't really think it is great

---

67. Okay, I might be being a teensy bit dramatic here, but hey, it is super important.

advice. So I remain silent and continue listening.

"Sometimes I wish they'd just ask me what I thought about things, you know? Like maybe I don't want to be president of the Multicultural Leadership Club. Maybe I want another minor role, like treasurer, or maybe I just want to be in the club and enjoy it without pressure."

Hold on, Trevor doesn't want to be president? I never would have thought, not in a million years, that Trevor wouldn't want anything other than being at the top. I mean, I assumed that because that's what I want. Isn't this the basis behind our whole rivalry?

"Don't get me wrong," Trevor says, looking up at me. "My parents are great. They love me and all that, and they just want what's best for me, but sometimes it's a lot."

Trevor's eyes stay connected with mine.

"My grandparents on my dad's side came to the United States when they were in their early twenties. Neither one of them spoke the language, and they had very little money. They worked hard for everything they had. And they raised my dad and his sister with that same work ethic. Work hard to make your family proud. My mother's parents died when she was five. She was raised by her grandparents. So she also worked hard to make them proud.

"It's just a lot of pressure, you know? Trying to live up to these specific expectations. Sometimes I feel like they don't even really know me."

I know that feeling. I have a mom who thinks that I enjoy

parties with heart piñatas, and I have a dad who I don't really know at all. I also have a mom who keeps secrets. Important secrets about absent dads and magic.

"I get it," I blurt out.

"Yeah?" He peers at me from underneath his ridiculously long eyelashes. I mean, how is it fair that some boys can get eyelashes that are lovely and long, and I'm stuck with eyelashes that you can barely see?

"Yeah, I do," I respond. "I don't think my mom gets me at all. We're sooo different. It feels like maybe I was swapped at birth or something."

Trevor laughs a little. "Nah, you weren't swapped at birth. You look just like your mom."

I smile at the compliment. "Well, you haven't seen my dad."

Uh-oh. I didn't mean to say that. I definitely didn't mean to say that. Everyone in this town knows it's always been me and my mom and, before she died, my nana, and most people know that I have no idea who my dad is. Maybe Trevor won't realize my mistake. Maybe he will gloss right over it.

"Hold on." Trevor sits up a little straighter. "You know who your dad is?"

Or not. Okay, how am I going to salvage this? Of course I can't tell him the truth about my dad, about him being Cupid and everything, but maybe I can at least tell him a version of the truth. Something really close to the truth.

"Okay," I sigh heavily. "If I tell you this, you can't tell anyone else."

"I won't," he pipes up immediately.

"I'm serious," I squeak. "Absolutely nobody."

"Pinkie swear." He holds out his pinkie, his face very serious.

Hesitating, I hold out my pinkie too. He leans across the table, closing the gap between us, entwining his pinkie with mine. I feel a tiny zap when we touch, and I pull back from him quickly. Flustered, I quickly clear my throat.

"My mom told me about my dad last week. She gave me some letters he wrote me before he left, and she gave me a locket with his picture in it."

Trevor frowns in concentration, his fingers tapping against his chin.

"That's a lot," he finally says.

"Yeah," I mumble. "It's weird because I look just like him. Well, almost."

I think about his pale, glowing skin and my own brown skin.

Trevor sits back in his seat, pushing back until the front two legs of the chair are in the air.

"Wow, EJ. Just wow."

"I know," I respond.

"And your mom just dropped this on you—you said last week, right?"

"Yeah."

"So around your birthday?"

He remembered? Honestly, I'm impressed.

"One day after."

He nods.

"It's so weird, you know?" I blurt out. "Because my mom has

always been super secretive about my dad, and now all of a sudden, she wants to spring all these surprises on me."

I let out a breath. Maybe this was what I needed. I needed to be able to vent to someone, someone I trust. And as much as I'm loath to admit it, Trevor is that person.

"I know it sounds ridiculous. My mom finally telling me something that I have been asking about forever. But I guess, maybe, I wish she had done it sooner, you know?"

Trevor nods his head. "No, I understand." He pauses for a moment. "Have you told anyone else?"

"No, and please don't tell anyone. I'm still trying to process everything."

Trevor smiles. If I didn't know better, I would say that he looks pleased to be the only person who knows my secret.

"Don't worry. I'll take your secret to the grave. I take pinkie promises very seriously."

He holds up his pinkie, smiling. I smile back. I know he won't tell anyone.

Trevor examines his watch as it makes a strange beeping noise. He looks up at me solemnly, as if a mask has slipped back into place.

"Well, EJ. Looks like it's time to head back."

I nod, not completely understanding the rush of butterflies that fills my stomach when he holds out his hand to help me up.

"Let's go," I agree. He simply nods as we walk toward the door of the shop. The butterflies continue to tumble as I realize that even though we're outside, and I don't need any help, Trevor still hasn't let go of my hand.

* * *

When I walk into the house, my mom is there waiting for me on the sofa. She doesn't smile. She simply points to an armchair opposite the sofa.

"Sit."

I obey, sliding into what was once my nana's favorite chair. I fold my arms across my chest in defiance. "You wanted to talk?"

My mother's lips are tight, and she, too, has her arms folded across her chest.

"Erin, I know that you are going through a lot. Trust me, I know the news I shared—"

"You mean the news you dropped on me like an atomic bomb?"

My mother's lips become even tighter.

"Erin Marie," she says, a low warning.

I huff, sitting back in the chair.

"Now, Erin," my mom begins again. "Most of the time you're very trustworthy. I mean, I can't ever recall getting bad reports from your teachers, but what you did in the car today, to Ben, was selfish and immature—"

"Immature?!" I burst out of my seat. "I'm the immature one? Really? I have to remind you to clean up your room and not to spill ketchup on your shirt, but I'm the immature one?"

My mother stands up too, anger flooding her features.

"There's more to maturity than ketchup stains. Maturity is knowing when to listen when someone older and wiser gives you advice."

"Yeah, okay. Well, Mom, like, maybe next time you want to give me advice, you should try giving it a bit earlier, like, maybe thirteen years earlier."

My mom sighs, sinking back down into the couch.

"Just go to your room, Erin," she says tiredly, waving her hand.

"I was already going," I reply. I go up the stairs to my room, making sure to slam my door when I get inside.

I lean my head against my bedroom door, breathing heavily. I don't think I've ever slammed a door in my life. When Nana was alive, it was out of respect for the house she and my grandpa had worked their whole lives for. She used to love telling me that Grandpa built this house from the ground up, that the brick and mortar were filled to the brim with their blood, sweat, and tears. But with my mother, it's different. She's not my nana. And some-times I struggle with showing her the same respect.

My phone vibrates in my pocket. I pull it out, and all thoughts of the argument fade as Trevor's name pops up on the screen.

Trevor: **Did you get home okay?**

Now my heart feels like it's playing a game of double Dutch. I quickly type out a response.

Me: **Yes. You?**

Is that a ridiculous question? I mean, obviously he made it home. Why else would he ask me if I made it home okay? How is it this hard to text a boy? I mean, especially since the boy is *Trevor*. Trevor, who held my hand and smiled at me like I was the only person in the room. Ugh. Get it together, Erin.

A few seconds later . . .

> Trevor: **Yeah, I really enjoyed hanging out with you earlier** ☺

I can feel the flush creeping up my cheeks. He had a good time. Trevor Jin and I had a good time together. If someone had told me last year (I mean, even last week) that I would be thinking this, I would have automatically assumed that they had a screw loose.

> Me: **Me too. It was sort of the best part of my day.**
> Trevor: **You must really love ice cream lol**

It's not the ice cream. Shut up, mind. Shut up.

> Me: **Yeah, I guess I do** 😬
> Me: **Did you ever imagine this would be us? I mean that we would be texting each other and stuff after Kinder-geddon?**
> Trevor: **Kinder what??**

Oops, of course he doesn't know what I named our feud.

> Me: Oh yeah, I named our first day of kindergarten
> Kinder-geddon, after what happened with us.
> Trevor: . . .
> Trevor: Okay, I'll bite. What happened with us?

Is he being for real right now? There's no way he doesn't know what I'm talking about. I mean, we've never technically talked about the feud before, but I thought this was just something that was obvious.

> Me: You can't be serious. This is our rivalry origin
> story. The reason we despise each other.
> Trevor: I don't despise you.

A pause. There it is again, my heart pounding like it's competing in a triathlon.

> Trevor: Do you despise me?

Despise you? I can't stop my heart from racing when I think about you.

> Me: Well, obviously not anymore 😒
> Trevor: So let's hear it. Let's hear this villain origin
> story.

And for a moment I'm lurched back in time. I'm five again, swimming in the hurt of the realization that my new friend has stolen something precious from me. He's stolen my story, and not just my story, but my memories, memories with Nana. I shake off the thought and concentrate back on the texts.

> Me: RIVALRY origin story, not villain. That's a completely different thing.
>
> Trevor: LOL. If you say so.
>
> Me: I do.
>
> Trevor: So . . .
>
> Me: You really don't remember??
>
> Trevor: 😳 I just always figured you "despised" me because you were supercompetitive.
>
> Me: No!! We were friends for like five whole minutes. Don't you remember?
>
> Trevor: I guess . . .
>
> Me: We met each other and then we talked about our summer vacations. You went to Disney, and I went to the lake. Ring any bells?
>
> Trevor: Oh yeah. Kind of. I'm going to have to plead the fact that I was five years old.

Okay, in my defense, Trevor wasn't your average five-year-old. I'm pretty sure he came out of the hospital nursery quoting Shakespeare and solving unsolvable calculus equations. What I'm trying to say is that Trevor was pretty much born diabolical (and now has grown up to be diabolically cute).

I take a deep breath, because it seems completely unrealistic that Trevor has forgotten this very vital piece of our story.

> Me: Well, when we first met, I told you about my
> lake vacation with my nana.
> Trevor: Yeah, I think I remember that.

Another small pinch of frustration. I'm so sorry my story about the summer spent with my nana isn't special enough for Trevor to remember, even though he pretty much stole it. Word for word. I continue typing.

> Me: Do you remember what happened after I told
> you about my vacation?
> Trevor: I feel like this is a test. . . .

Furiously, I type my response. He's treating this like a joke. This isn't a joke.

> Me: This isn't funny. You went up to present my
> story. Word for word.

No response, so I continue to type.

> Me: It was like you were mocking me for not going
> on this big, splashy vacation like you did. But you

know what, I don't care, that vacation with my nana
was one of the best vacations of my life.

I'm aware I'm being dramatic. I know I'm pouring out my heart
over text like some overemotional guppy, but I can't help it. The
old hurt is sloshing through me in waves. I hate that the memory
of the summer with Nana is corrupted with bitterness. I watch
my phone for a full minute as dots appear on my screen, then
disappear, then appear again. After two minutes pass and there's
still no text from Trevor, I decide to plug my phone in and call it a
night. Maybe the truth was too much for him. Maybe he thinks I
was silly for reacting like that. Maybe . . .

My thoughts are interrupted by the buzz of my phone. But
it's not the quick, sharp sound of a text. I hurry back over to
my phone, and I almost drop it when I see who it is. Trevor is
calling. I tentatively answer the call, my voice shaking slightly.
"Hello?"

"Hello," he responds.

Trevor has one of those smooth phone voices that you hear on
apps that help you de-stress. It is deep and kind of scratchy, and
completely distracting.

I guess I'm silent for too long, because Trevor speaks again.
"EJ?"

"Yeah." My voice cracks, and I slam my palm over my mouth.

Great. Just great. Trevor sounds like a phone god, and I sound
like a legitimate frog has taken up residence in my throat.

I hear a chuckle.

"You okay over there?" His voice has a teasing quality, and I smile.

"Yeah, I'm okay."

"Good," he responds.

I don't know if you can technically hear smiles, but I imagine I can hear his.

"So." Trevor clears his throat, and the line falls silent for a moment. "I wanted to call you to talk about your last text."

I go still. Trevor is finally going to talk about what happened. Kindergarten. The stolen story.

Before I can respond, Trevor continues.

"First, EJ, I just wanted to say how sorry I am for stealing your story. It's obvious how important it was to you. So I'm sorry. That's it. No excuses. Though I would like to put a tiny reminder in here that I was five."

I chuckle at his last words.

Trevor lets out a deep breath.

"And second, EJ, I also wanted to clear up why I did it."

He clears his throat again nervously.

"I wasn't trying to mock you."

"You weren't?" I whisper. Hope and confusion are swimming through me in tandem. Could I have been wrong about Trevor?

"No." His voice matches mine. "I didn't think your vacation was lame. I thought it was perfect. I stole your story because I wished it were mine."

I search his voice for any hint of sarcasm or spite, but all I can hear is vulnerability.

"Why would you want my vacation? Your parents took you to Disney World."

He huffs loudly into the phone.

"Yeah, we went to Disney, but I didn't spend time with my parents. Not really. My mom was on the phone the whole time we were there, and my dad had to leave to go back to work after the first day. The only person I spent time with was my nanny, Kelly. So, I wasn't mocking your trip. I would have given anything to spend time with my family the way you spent time with your nana."

My chest is tight, and I squeeze my eyes closed. I can see Nana and me, down by the sandy shore of the lake, in the cabin opening windows to let the light in, out at night by the fire-pit roasting marshmallows. And then I think about five-year-old Trevor spending an expensive vacation wondering when his parents would hang out with him.

How did I get this so messed up? I'm normally a good judge of character. I only make judgments based on logic and facts. It's simple. It's science. *But science changes,* a small voice inside my head insists. *It evolves when new information is discovered.*

Trevor clears his throat. "Um, are you still there, EJ?"

He sounds nervous, and I realize I haven't said anything since his confession.

"I'm here," I respond in a rush of breath. "And . . ." How do I tell him all the things I'm feeling? How do I let him know that I understand? That I get it?

He is silent, waiting for me to continue. I shuffle around on the bed.

"Thank you for telling me."

"You're welcome," he says. I can hear his smile again, and it makes me smile in turn.

"And, Trevor?"

"Hmm?"

"You can share my story anytime."

"Thanks, EJ. I mean it." Trevor's voice cracks.

We're silent for a while, but it's not awkward. In fact, it's weirdly comfortable. Trevor is the first to break the silence.

"So I don't mean to change this lighthearted subject."

I snort-laugh. Trevor laughs too.

Trevor continues. "I have a question." He pauses. "But also, don't get too angry."

I gnaw at my lip. What could I possibly be angry at him about? Didn't we just have a breakthrough? I thought this was a pivot of our relationship in the right direction. I wait for him to continue, my foot jiggling in anticipation.

"I know you said you were still working on your posters. . . ."

Okayyyy.

"And I just wanted to know if you wanted any help. Not that you need any help. My help, I mean. I'm just going to stop talking now."

Heat spirals through my chest. Trevor is offering to help me with my campaign. Even though we're running against each other. I pause for only a moment before replying.

"I would love your help."

CHAPTER ELEVEN

Cupid Commandment Number 12: A Cupid's magic is some of the most powerful magic in the world. A person who has been affected by Cupid magic will sometimes do extraordinary things for the object of their affection. This can be both good and bad. Beware.

THE NEXT MORNING, IT is my mom's turn to drive us to school. I have woken up late, bleary-eyed from staying up all night creating posters. They are nowhere near as good as they would've been if Bruno had made them, but they will do. Plus, making the posters gave me an excuse to continue to text Trevor. He dispensed extremely helpful advice on word positioning and slogans.[68] When I told Trevor he was really good

---

68. At first I was so lost that my original slogan was "Be a Pal. Vote for This Gal" (lame, I know). Trevor helped me select the more appropriate slogan: "There is more to me than what you see! A vote for Erin is a vote for unity."

at coming up with slogans and catchy phrases, he told me that sometimes he dreamed about becoming a writer. (How cool is that?) He told me that he'd even thought about signing up for the new creative writing club. But then when I asked him why he didn't do it, he responded that his father would never let him. Creative writing clubs don't help you get into medical school. And then I felt monumentally sad for him, because Trevor is a lot of things, a lot of great things, as it turns out, but his dad seems really homed in on making sure Trevor will turn out to be successful. Work hard. Make your family proud. And putting energy into a future that has no security, no surety or blueprint for success, is the opposite of making your family proud. I thought about how I wished my mother would care about my good grades or all my other achievements instead of being lost in her own little world. I thought about how we both kind of wanted what the other one had, and it made me feel connected to Trevor in a way I had never felt connected to another person (not even Bruno) before.

I even opened up to Trevor a bit about the argument with my mom. Of course, not the part about being a Cupid, but about how my mom kept my dad from me for years.

He was sympathetic, listening and acknowledging me in a way that I had seldom experienced before. In the end, he gave me some good advice on forgiveness and not pushing away the people who love me.

By the time I get into the car, I know that we're going to be late and not just "not-early" late, but tardy-slip late. Mom has already texted Isa, letting her know that she'll have to take the twins in herself. The car ride is quiet, as neither my mom nor I have talked to each other since our argument yesterday.

I hate being late, almost more than anything else, and somehow over the last couple of weeks, I have started making a habit of being late. My mom pulls into the parking lot. She clears her throat.

"Look." She turns to face me. "I know we're both mad, but your nana taught me a very important lesson when I was your age."

I perk up at the mention of Nana. The thought of being late forgotten, I unconsciously scoot closer to my mother. "Nana?"

My mother chews on her lip, a nervous habit of hers.

"Yes, Nana," my mom says. "She would say we could be mad at each other, that was fine. That was normal. But one thing we couldn't do was leave each other without saying 'I love you,' because you never know if you'll get to say it again."

My mom pauses, squeezing her eyes shut briefly. For the first time I realize how hard this must also be for my mom. I lost Nana, but she also lost her mother. She also lost one half of her family. Grief flows through me as I look at my mom.

Her eyes flutter open. She clears her throat again.

"So, I love you, Erin."

Overwhelmed with emotion, I open the door, shifting my bookbag on my back.

I know my mom kept secrets from me, life-changing secrets, but she is my mother, the only one I'll ever have.

"I love you, too," I tell her before I shut the door.

By the time I get to homeroom, it's already five minutes past eight. Five minutes past the start of school. Trevor gives me a tiny wave when I walk in, and I almost sigh in relief. Besides the morning weirdness with my mom, and me being actually late to class, I had a different set of worries weighing on my mind. And those involved seeing Trevor after our conversation last night. But Trevor seems genuinely happy to see me. In fact, I've never seen him smile so widely. My head whips around to Ms. Richmond.

Her hand flutters to her chest. I notice the glint of a shiny new ring, and I grimace. I almost forgot about Ms. Richmond's engagement, the one that happened because I used magic. I've tried to reason with myself, saying that they both liked each other (that much was obvious before I used my stupid Cupid magic) and that eventually they would have gotten engaged. So, really, I just sped up the natural progression of things. But no matter how often I tell myself this, I still feel icky about the whole thing.

"You're late today," Ms. Richmond announces dramatically. She walks up to me, and I hand her the late pass. "I think that might be a first for you, Erin."

I cringe. Everyone is staring at me. I know Ms. Richmond isn't being malicious, but this, this is my idea of torture.

"I, um . . ." I stand still by the door, frozen in place. Before I can say anything, I'm interrupted.

"I'm sorry, Ms. Richmond. It was my fault." Trevor's voice lifts from the front of the room.

"Your fault?" Ms. Richmond and I say at the same time. Ms. Richmond turns to Trevor, confused.

"Yes," he replies, clearing his throat. "I forgot something for our science assignment at home, so Erin had to ask her mom to stop on the way to school to pick it up."

Trevor raises an eyebrow at me as if to say, *Come on, play along.*

I gape at him as the class swivels back and forth in their seats, looking at us as if we've grown extra heads.

Ms. Richmond looks suspicious. "Something for a science project," she confirms.

"Um, yes." I finally start to play along. "Pipe cleaners."

"Pipe cleaners?"

I nod vigorously at the same time that Trevor calls out, "Yes, pipe cleaners."

"Okay." She waves a hand toward my empty desk. I hurriedly go to it and sit down immediately.

"It's just strange, us not having pipe cleaners at the school." She gives Trevor and me a piercing, knowing look. I flinch and Trevor laughs softly.

"You are free to work on your independent assignments." And with that, Ms. Richmond goes back to her desk, sitting down to work at her laptop.

I turn to Trevor with a smile. "Thank you, you didn't have to do that," I whisper.

He shrugs, a gesture I am coming to learn is less about nonchalance and more about hiding his embarrassment. "We were texting pretty late last night," he whispers back. "I knew you were finishing up your campaign posters." He looks at me eagerly.

I nod, pulling out the posters that I completed last night. They aren't exactly how I originally pictured them, but I worked hard on them, and I'm proud of them. I slide them over to Trevor. He makes a small noise of approval, looking up at me.

"They're great," he mumbles.

"Thanks," I respond with a smile. "I'm going to try to hang them up during lunch."

Trevor's forehead wrinkles. "Then when are you going to eat?"

I shrug. "I'll grab a muffin or something."

Trevor shakes his head. He sticks his hand in the air. Ms. Richmond looks up from her computer. "Yes, Trevor?"

Trevor grabs my posters. "Erin has to hang up her posters for the campaign. Is it okay if we go now since we're doing independent work?"

We? My heart stutters. Did he just say "we"?

Ms. Richmond's mouth tightens. "You're going to help Erin with her campaign, Trevor? Aren't you running against her?"

"Yes, Ms. Richmond, but since one of us will become the vice president, we thought it was important that we start working together for the good of the club."

He looks over at me and gives me a wink. Smooth. Very smooth.

Ms. Richmond puts her hands on her hips. "Mm-hmm," she responds. She bends down over her desk, taking out her book of passes. She scribbles something down on the top sheet, ripping it off and waving it in the air.

"Here, just take it. Try not to kill each other."

"We will try very hard not to," I respond dryly. I take the paper from her hand.

"Make sure you do." She gives us both a stern look.

We shuffle out of the room, me holding on to my stack of posters, Trevor holding a roll of tape.

"We could start in this hallway."

Trevor nods. "That makes the most sense." He holds the tape as I slap the papers onto the tiled wall.

"Is this even?" I ask, stretching up. He answers in the affirmative.

After we put up all the posters, Trevor and I walk back to class, taking our time as we stroll around the halls.

"So are you prepared for your speech on Friday?"

The speech. I grimace, turning my face away from Trevor. I know that his question was innocent. He was just making conversation, trying to be helpful, but the truth is that even thinking about my speech makes me anxious. For some reason, I can't seem to find the right words for the speech. I have sat down at my desk for the last two nights, trying desperately to figure out what to say. But every time I try to write, my head becomes filled with other things: Trevor, Cupid magic, my mom, Bruno, my dad. All these things play like a record in my head, looping on repeat.

Trevor notices that I've stopped walking. He turns around, his eyebrows crawling up.

"Hey, EJ, are you okay?"

I nod. It's Wednesday, and I'm woefully underprepared for what could be considered the single biggest day of my life.

"Want to talk about it?"

I sigh. "I made a mistake, putting my speech off for so long. And now, honestly, I don't know what I'm going to write," I admit.

Trevor scrunches up his nose. "Well, to err is human. I think that's how that line goes."

I frown at him a bit. "Who said that, a Kardashian?"

Trevor laughs. "No, I think it was a philosopher or something. I'm not sure."

I bump his shoulder with mine. "I was just kidding. I know it wasn't a Kardashian."[69]

"I mean, if you need help, I kind of already finished mine." He glances over at some lockers, a blush coloring his cheeks. "Not saying that you aren't perfectly capable. I just want you to know you can have my help, if you want it."

I feel my cheeks growing hot too. "I would like that," I reply softly.

We continue walking back to class, our hands accidentally bumping with every step that we take.

Every so often, when our fingers tap, Trevor glances toward me, and I peek over at him. And honestly, I can't describe this feeling of complete and utter bliss. It must be scientifically impossible to feel this way about someone. I pick through my thoughts one by one, dissecting how I feel about Trevor. I shuffle through our conversations, our shared project, the yakgwa that he brought for

---

69. Well, to be completely honest, I have no idea who said it. So to be fair, it could have been a Kardashian for all I know.

me because it's my favorite, the secret glances, the wide smiles. I think about how he took me to get ice cream to cheer me up, how he's been the only one I could really talk to for days now.

By the time I get to class, I realize that I have learned a new, undeniable truth. I, Erin Marie Johnson, like Trevor Jin.

This is bad.

The rest of the day goes by in a blur, with Trevor firming up plans to meet at my house after school so that he can help me with my speech.[70] When we get to lunch, I'm surprised to find out that Bruno isn't sitting at our normal table. I'm even more surprised to find out that he is sitting at Ben's table, right next to Ben, in fact! Which means my magic backfired, like, really backfired, because now instead of Bruno being my best friend, he is best friends with his twin. The bright side of lunch is that Trevor sits with me (I think this may be his new permanent seat), and he walks me to class after lunch ends.[71]

By the time I get home, I'm a frantic mess of nerves. The talk between me and my mother seems to have broken the bubble of tension in the house. Though we aren't all the way healed, we're certainly getting there.

"You didn't clean," I accuse her grumpily, pointing to the dishes in the sink.

---

70. FYI, I hurriedly texted my mom after he confirmed a meeting time. I texted her: Please, pleaseeee don't embarrass me. And also, can you clean up just a little?
71. Forget flowers. The ultimate romantic gesture is walking someone to class, knowing that you might be slightly later than usual to your next class.

My mother grins at me, her smile stretching ludicrously across her face.

"I haven't cleaned the dishes yet, EJ. I didn't think you would be working in the kitchen. Was I wrong?"

I look around our absurdly yellow kitchen and shake my head. "No, of course not."

"I straightened up the living room." She emphasizes the word "straightened," which probably means that she picked up random things and stuffed them in the closet out of sight. "I figured that's where you would want to work."

"Yes, that's okay," I respond, worrying my lip in between my teeth.

"Well, I'm glad it works," my mom says. "It's the only option we've got. Unless you'd like me to rent a house specifically for this occasion." She is having a hard time holding back her laughter. "Only the best for the hero."

"Stop calling him that," I snap. She is enjoying this way too much.

My mom points to my mouth. "Got your war paint on again, I see."

I suck in my lips, hiding the Fire Engine Red lipstick. "Look, should I cancel this *study* session? Is this something you think you can handle?"

My mother stands up straight, smoothing down the ends of her Little Mermaid sweatshirt.

"Of course, EJ. I'm nothing if not professional." She winks at me, and I groan.

"But in all seriousness, I like Trevor. He's a good kid. Did you know that he stayed after the night of the party to help me clean up? He said it was because he liked being helpful, but every time I looked up, he would be staring at the stairs. Why do you think that is?"

Wait. Trevor stayed to help my mom clean up after the party? He volunteered to help? What does that mean?

My mom smiles, examining me with a knowing look.

Before I have time to process my thoughts, the doorbell rings.

And even though I'd never ever admit it to her, I am glad that things are getting back to normal between Mom and me.

I fly out of the kitchen, my mother closely on my heels.

When I open the door, I find Trevor standing there in jeans (again!) and an old gray shirt that has GOONIES written across the top.

"Sorry I'm a little late." His cheeks flush, and my heart does a tap dance in my chest.

Don't get me wrong—professional, well-put-together Trevor is a force to be reckoned with, but this Trevor, this version that seems completely comfortable and vulnerable, this Trevor is the stuff that dreams are made of. It's like Trevor and I have come to some sort of truce. We don't have to pretend around each other. We can just be ourselves.

"I love *The Goonies*," I exclaim. Trevor looks at me in surprise.

"Really? I didn't think it would be your type of movie."

I shake my head. "No, it's one of my favorites."

Trevor smiles at me, still standing outside the door. "Mine too."

"We'll have to watch it sometime," I continue clumsily. "Together."

Like a date, I want to say, but I don't.[72]

Trevor's mouth twitches at the corners. "Yeah, I think so."

"Trevor," my mom says from behind me. Has she been there this whole time? "Why are you standing outside? Come in."

I move back to give Trevor space to enter. My mom smiles so widely that I'm almost sure her face will split in two.

"You two can work in the living room," she pipes up as an awkward silence fills the air. "I'll be upstairs writing if you need anything." She puts her hand on Trevor's shoulder and squeezes.

Trevor smiles at my mom, a genuine, true smile. "Thanks, Ms. Johnson."

She nods, heading upstairs.

I lead Trevor to the living room, where we set our stuff down near the table. I sit on the couch, and Trevor follows suit.

"Who dropped you off?" I ask, pulling out a pencil and a sheet of paper.

"My dad," Trevor mumbles. "He thinks I'm over here working on a science project. He'd disown me if he knew I was helping you with your campaign speech." He laughs humorlessly. "I'm not even kidding."

I give him a small, sympathetic smile.

"Well, if it makes you feel any better, I'm not sure my mom even knows what my speech is about. I don't think she realizes that I'm running for anything."

---

72. So I'm not 100 percent sure what a date would look like. I haven't actually been on one. I do plan on doing a full research mock-up before I go on my first date so that I can be prepared for it when it happens.

"Oh, I'm sorry," Trevor says. "Is it because she's too busy?"

I let out a terse laugh. "I wish. It's because when I talk to her, her head is always in the clouds. It's like having a mother who consistently lives in another world. I don't know. It's like she just doesn't get me, you know?"

I peer over at him. He nods.

"Yeah, I get it." He pauses. "When I write, the world kind of melts away. It feels right. It feels like I have a purpose or something."

I nod, because this is how I feel about science. This is exactly the feeling. I feel necessary, important, like I matter.

"My halmeoni, my grandmother, used to read me stories every night before I went to bed. They were these wonderful stories full of magic and adventure, and they made me feel like I was a traveler and that I could travel through all those stories. They made me feel like I could be anyone I wanted. Anything I wanted.

"Halmeoni used to tell me that I could be anything I wanted, even though my dad already had everything planned out for me since the moment I was born. But Halmeoni would read me those stories, and she would tell me I should follow my dreams, and it just stuck. It stuck with me even after she died."

I sit back on my heels, examining his face, which seems softer somehow.

"My nana made me feel like that too. She made me feel like I could fly if I wanted to. My nana is dead too."

Trevor and I look at each other for a moment, neither of us talking.

Connection. The word buzzes through me like a tidal wave.

We're connected in a way that I could never be with Bruno. Bruno and Ben still have their abuelas (three, in fact), and their grandmothers visit them often.

"So." Trevor clears his throat.

"So," I parrot back, avoiding his gaze in embarrassment.

"Your speech," he offers. I nod. "What do you have so far?"

I cover my face with my hands. "Is 'nothing' an acceptable answer?"

He laughs. "Sure it is. If it is the truth."

I look down and smooth my piece of paper out on the table.

"So how do you think I should start?"

We spend about an hour brainstorming, then write a draft, then finally fine-tune that draft. After we finish, Trevor convinces me to rehearse what I'm going to say. We go through my speech three times until I have it almost perfect. It is around dinnertime when we finally finish.

"I think we've gotten a lot done. You're ready."

I agree. "Do you think you are ready?"

Trevor's face falls a bit, his eyes wandering over to look at a spot right behind my head.

He runs a hand through his hair. "Yeah, yeah. I think I'm ready. I'm just not sure—" He sucks his teeth. "I don't know. It's stupid. I guess I don't really want to do this, and it sucks because you obviously do. You have great ideas." He flings a hand toward my speech. "I mean, really great ideas, and all I want to do right now is write." He heaves a huge sigh. "I wish I could."

"But your parents . . ."

"Yeah, my parents."

He looks resigned and broken, and for a moment I just want to hug him to make his pain go away. But I know that won't help, not for long, anyway.

"Well, sometimes we have to put ourselves first, and we need to do the things we love to do. No matter who tells us we can't," I say.

"My grandmother used to tell me the same thing. She always said that sometimes I just need to put myself first."

I nod. "Your grandmother sounds like a smart woman."

"She was," Trevor whispers back. I push his shoulder with mine.

"Don't worry, loser. You won't win anyway. You are competing against Paxton Middle School's best student."

Trevor smiles. "I think you mean second-best student."

"Yeah, we'll see," I quip, pushing his shoulder again.

A horn beeps outside, and Trevor shrugs on his bookbag.

"I've gotta go. My dad gets irritated if I take too long."

I nod, walking him to the door. Trevor and I both pause.

"Thanks for your help, Trevor," I say sincerely. He looks over at me, fidgeting, moving from one foot to the other.

"So, do you think it would be okay if I sent you some of my writing? It would mean a lot to me if you'd just look at it. I mean, you can be honest—"

"Yes, I would love that," I blurt out. "I mean, that would be great." I take a deep breath and try again. When did I become one of those girls who turns into a blabbering mess when trying to talk to a boy? "I would like that."

Trevor's smile could set the room on fire. It is that bright. "Cool," he responds with forced nonchalance. "Very cool."

"Yes, cool," I repeat.

It's weird. I spent all this time in this rivalry with Trevor, thinking he was the absolute worst, but as it turns out, none of what I originally thought was true. Kinder-geddon, Trevor's hatred of me. None of it. As it turns out, Trevor Jin isn't the absolute worst. In fact, he might be the best.

Later that night I receive a text from Trevor.

> Trevor: **Hey, are you still up?**
> Me: **Yeah, it's only eight o'clock**
> Trevor: 😳 **I always figured you'd be a person who'd go to bed really early.**[73]
> Me: **What a weird thing to think about a person.**
> Trevor: **Maybe that's just how I am** 😌
> Trevor: **So did you still want to read my writing?**
> Me: **Duh, yes!**

I wait and wait. Dots appear and then disappear on the screen while I hold the phone.

After about five minutes, a group of texts come through.

---

73. Rude, but also true. I actually do go to bed around eight or nine most nights.

Trevor: I wrote this last week. It's not edited or anything, but can you look at it?

Trevor: The Definition of Me

I'm not the perfect son, though that is not what most people believe.

They see the outside of me, as visible as the bark of a tree.

But underneath, there is sap so clear and sweet that it would hurt

your teeth. I'm equal parts terrified and excited, smart and ignorant,

hero and villain. I'm all these things. A bundle of endless contradictions.

It's like the story that I thought was finished is still writing itself.

I'm not expecting the wet tears that crawl down my cheeks. I hold on to the phone, cradling it in my hands.

Trevor: EJ, are you there?

Me: That was the best thing I've ever read.

Trevor: Thank you . . .

Me: Good night

Trevor: Good night

I click off my phone, staring up at my ceiling. One thought runs through my head like a freight train. I like Trevor Jin. I like

Trevor Jin. I *like* Trevor Jin. And I think Trevor likes me. This is the revelation to end all revelations. I start to imagine Trevor and me as a couple, all the things we would do: study dates at the ice cream shop, hangouts at the library, sitting in class sharing inside jokes.[74] But as soon as I start thinking about what this could mean, a small voice interrupts my thoughts.

None of this is real. Trevor doesn't really like you. You used magic on him.

And it's true. I used magic on Trevor, and I thought it failed. But it clearly worked. I run through how different Trevor has been acting since the day we worked on the project at his house. He is definitely nicer, that's a given, but there's something else about him. Trevor seems like he genuinely cares about me. And not just like a friend. But I can't trust Trevor's feelings, because they aren't real. They are manufactured by me. By the time I finally close my eyes, I feel miserable. I have my first genuine crush, and I'm not even sure he likes me.

---

74. I've only shared inside jokes with Bruno.

CHAPTER TWELVE

Cupid Commandment Number 7: A Cupid's powers do not always work. Specifically, if you have two individuals who have a strong, underlying attraction to each other, the magic is deemed unnecessary, as the individuals have all the natural magic they will ever need to cultivate their love.

THE NEXT DAY IS weird and tension-filled as 1) Bruno is still not talking to me, and furthermore, he now seems to be a permanent member of Ben's friend group, and 2) I now know without a doubt that I like my former enemy, and to make matters worse, I'm not entirely certain he really likes me (on account of my magic).[75] By the time we get to the end of the day, I barely remember anything that has happened, and I'm grateful to fall into bed.

---

75. I spend most of the day trying to avoid Trevor, because liking someone who only likes you because of magic really sucks.

When Friday comes around, I'm a nervous wreck, a complete, utter nervous wreck. The bell rings, and I trudge out of my last class of the day. We're supposed to meet Ms. Richmond in the auditorium right after school. The speeches start at four o'clock sharp, then the club will be able to cast their votes. I will know within the hour who has gotten the presidential spot. Either Trevor or me. Oddly enough, this isn't what is bothering me. The funny thing is that I wouldn't mind if Trevor won, because I know that he will be a great president, because honestly either of us will make a good president.[76] I guess the thing that is bothering me the most is the fact that this isn't what Trevor really wants, and that sucks because he deserves to do what he wants. And I guess it is also bothering me that I care about the fact that Trevor isn't getting what he really wants. Last week, hadn't he been my archnemesis? Everything is backward now.

"Hey, nervous?" Trevor comes up behind me wearing a pressed robin's-egg-blue shirt and ironed black dress pants. I smooth down the front of my own formal red dress. We both brought formal clothes from home to change into.

"A little," I admit. I clutch my speech tighter in my hands. We only have about five minutes before we go onstage, and I'm up first. Ms. Richmond booked the auditorium so that friends and family could watch the speeches. I know for certain that my mom is coming (even though she is still quite clueless on what I'm running for), and Trevor has mentioned that his parents are also

---

76. To be honest, I'm glad that my original plan to get Trevor to drop out of the race failed. Trevor isn't the guy I thought he was.

coming. We're tucked in the back of the stage, waiting behind the heavy black curtains.

"I'm nervous too," Trevor responds. He straightens his tie. I give him a small smile.

"You'll do great," I say. Trevor straightens his tie again, something I begin to realize is a nervous tic.

"You will too," he says. I put a hand on his shoulder, and he looks down. Then he covers my hand with his. I jump back in surprise.

"Sorry," I mumble.

"No, don't be." Trevor gives me a quirky half smile. I could get used to Trevor's smiles. No, no, no. I'm not supposed to be thinking about Trevor's smiles or anything else about Trevor, for that matter.

Ms. Richmond comes in from the stage, parting the curtains to get through.

"All right, my darlings, it's time. I'm just going to make a short little announcement, and then I'll introduce you, Erin, since you're first."

I nod mutely. It's fine. Everything will be fine.

"It looks like the whole school came to this event. The auditorium is packed."

My stomach sinks. Trevor and I share a panicked look. Why would the auditorium be packed? There are only about thirty kids in the club at most. Why would there be a room full of people?

"I guess my suggestion for giving kids extra credit for attending really stuck. I'm glad. I think this is a great advertisement for our club. Anyway, ducklings, break a leg!" Ms. Richmond snorts with laughter as she moves behind the curtain back onto the stage. I peek out, looking out into the audience. Behind the glare of the bright lights, I can see that every single seat is filled. Every single one.

"Oh my god. I can't do this." I step back into the wings, letting the curtain fall heavily against the wall.

Trevor's hand lands softly on my shoulder. He smiles at me and then gives me an encouraging nod. "You'll be fine. We will both be fine."

His hand feels warm and safe. And I know that I'm supposed to be the one with the magic, but Trevor's hand does wonders to comfort me.

"Thanks." I lean into his hand and breathe.

"Hello, everyone." Ms. Richmond's amplified voice fills the auditorium. Automatically, the crowd becomes silent. "I wanted to thank everyone for taking the time out to be here this afternoon. This is a big event for our club, and we don't normally have this big of a turnout.

"As many of you may well know, we have two excellent candidates vying for the presidential position of our Multicultural Leadership Club. Our club's mission statement includes an earnest effort to bring unity through diversity and education. And I wholeheartedly believe that both of these candidates are fine representations of this motto. So, without further ado, I'm going to introduce our first candidate, Erin Johnson."

A volley of claps fills the auditorium. I gulp, clutching my paper. It is now or never. I can do this. I was born to do this.

I walk out onto the stage on unsteady legs, blinking rapidly at the brightness of the stage lights. I walk up to the podium that Ms. Richmond stands behind. She holds out a microphone to me. *Good luck,* she mouths. I clutch the microphone, placing my speech down on the flat part of the podium. I blink into the silence, then hold the microphone up to my mouth.

"Hello," I try to say, but the microphone squeals in protest. The audience grumbles, many people covering their ears. "Sorry," I blurt out, pulling the microphone away from my mouth. "Sorry about that. Thank you, everyone, for coming. My name is Erin Johnson, and I'm running for president of the Multicultural Leadership Club." I pause to scan the audience, my eyes landing on my mom in the front row in a very normal sweater and leggings. She waves at me, giving me a thumbs-up. Isa is sitting next to her, her phone held up to record me. Beside Isa sits Lou, her hair pulled back out of her face in a tight bun. And beside Lou sits Ben and, and . . . I stare out into the crowd, my heart swelling. Beside Ben sits Bruno, the corners of his lips resisting a smile.

"Bruno," I call out, right into the microphone. "Hi." Oops. I didn't mean to say that out loud. "I'm sorry. I'm sorry. Back to my speech."

I straighten my spine, glancing down quickly at my notes.

"Many people wonder what the point is of having a Multicultural Leadership Club. Why have this type of club at all? Does it really help to point out people's differences instead of concentrating on their similarities? I've been told multiple times over my years here at PMS that we're all the same, that we're all human. But although we're all human, that doesn't mean that each and every one of us isn't different or unique in our own ways. And it doesn't mean that our differences shouldn't be celebrated and respected. For example, did you know that there are thousands of different ways to say 'grandma' around the world?" My eyes gravitate to the spot where I know Trevor is standing in the wings. "But that doesn't mean that we love our grandmothers any differently or any less, for that matter, whether they're called Nana or whether they are called Halmeoni. And the same goes for everyone. We're different in various ways, right down to our very DNA, and that's important and that should be celebrated, not hidden."

I push aside my notes, stepping toward the middle of the stage, the microphone still up near my mouth.

"I love this school. I love this town, but we have to acknowledge that everyone doesn't always feel accepted here, and I want to change that. First"—I hold up my pointer finger—"I promise to rally for a new mascot, one that the students get to design and create together. Second, I want to make sure that we're celebrating all the aspects of diversity at this school. That means decorating doors for Hispanic Heritage Month, handing out ribbons for Down Syndrome Awareness Month, making sure students have time off for holidays such as Yom Kippur[77] and Ramadan[78]

---

77. Yom Kippur is the holiest day of the Jewish year. It is a day when participants make amends and ask for forgiveness of their sins.
78. Ramadan is a holy month for Muslims where they fast and pray.

without it affecting their attendance." A couple of claps sound from the audience. One loud "yeah" interrupts my speech. "Having meaningful assemblies where we aren't watching the same two plays on Martin Luther King Jr. and Rosa Parks every year during Black History Month." More claps, and one girl who looks suspiciously like India even stands up. I take a breath.

"Third," I continue, my voice just a bit softer, "I will advocate for bringing back the Diversity Carnival, an important event that used to be a staple for PMS."

Everyone is on their feet clapping now. A few wolf whistles fly through the air.

"In conclusion, I would love to be the president of the Multicultural Leadership Club. I think together we could bring about real change at PMS. Thank you."

I walk off the stage to resounding claps. Ms. Richmond comes out from behind the curtain, gently taking the microphone out of my hands. "Good job," she says with a smile.

I scoot behind her, coming face-to-face with a smiling Trevor. "You did great," he whispers over the crowd's lingering claps.

My face feels like it is on fire. "Thank you," I reply earnestly.

"What a great speech. Let's give another round of applause to Erin." Ms. Richmond's voice filters backstage. "Up next, we have Trevor Jin."

The audience claps politely, and Trevor stiffens, not moving forward.

I touch his elbow. "Hey, it's your turn."

But Trevor is pale and pensive. He looks down at me, and I

can see that his eyes are filled with alarm and a little bit of fear.

"Hey." I cup his hand in mine, and I can feel the sweat crowding between his fingers. "Everything will be fine. You'll be great. You always are." The last part slipped out. I didn't mean to tell him that. I look away. "Sorry," I mumble.

"For what?" He smiles, squeezing my hand so I will look up at him. "For thinking I'm great?" he teases.

"Trevor?" Ms. Richmond calls from onstage.

"Guess that's my cue," Trevor says with a grimace.

"You'll do great," I offer. He shrugs. It is only when he walks toward the stage and disappears behind the curtain that I notice that Trevor isn't carrying any paper or note cards. Has he memorized his speech? Quite honestly, I wouldn't be surprised if he has.

I pull aside the curtains just a bit so that I can see Trevor standing behind the podium, the microphone in his left hand.

"Hello, everyone. Thank you for coming today. This is an extremely important event for our club, and I can't tell you how much it means that all of you decided to spend your afternoon listening to our speeches."

Somebody from the audience coughs out, "Extra credit." A couple of people laugh in response.

"So that's why I'm going to start my speech with an apology."

The room grows still. What? An apology? What is Trevor talking about? I clutch the curtain with one hand, not worried about if the audience can see me. Ms. Richmond, too, moves forward, coming up behind me to look out at Trevor.

Trevor continues. "I want to apologize for wasting your time.

I no longer want to run for the president of the Multicultural Leadership Club."

My stomach sinks. No, this can't be happening. This can't be.

The audience erupts with noise, some people gasping, others laughing, some outright booing.

Trevor holds up his hands, and the room falls silent again.

"I'm not dropping out of the race because I don't care about the club. I'm dropping out for the exact opposite reason. I'm dropping out because this club is very, very important. In fact, it's so important that it deserves someone who has the passion and drive to take the club to new heights. This club deserves a president who will come up with fresh new ideas, a president who will fight for those ideas to become reality. A person who really cares." He takes a long, unsteady breath. "And that person is Erin. She will be the best president this school has ever seen." Trevor turns around to look at me peeking behind the curtain.

This is my fault. All of this. Trevor would never have dropped out if I hadn't used magic on him. Goose bumps are crawling up my arms, and I feel physically ill.

Trevor turns back toward the audience. "Thank you for coming today to listen to us speak."

He starts to back away from the podium, but Ms. Richmond grabs my elbow and drags me across the stage before he can walk off. She gives Trevor an odd look of pity, and I look down at my shiny black shoes, refusing to look Trevor in the eyes.[79]

---

79. Because I'm a coward. I'm such a coward.

Ms. Richmond gently pries the microphone out of Trevor's hands.

"Well, that certainly was a twist, wasn't it? I'm all for a good plot twist. Let's give a hand to both of our candidates." Light applause follows. "Normally, this would be the time I would tell you to take out your phones and vote for our next president, but since Trevor is formally withdrawing from the race . . ." Ms. Richmond looks over at Trevor to confirm that he still wants to pull out.

Please change your mind. Please change your mind. Trevor nods once. He is also looking down at his shoes.

"All right, then, so we don't have to do an official vote. So help me to congratulate the newest president of the Multicultural Leadership Club, Erin Johnson."

The crowd erupts into applause. I finally look up, catching a glimpse of my mom, who is jumping up and down near her seat. My eyes move down the row, and everyone's face is full of elation—that is, until I get to Bruno. Bruno sits sullenly with his arms crossed, tight-lipped with anger. As I continue scanning the audience, I notice Trevor's mother. She is frowning, whispering something to a man who sits beside her. The man has his arms crossed, and he shares the same angry frown that I found on Bruno's face moments before. I don't need Trevor to tell me that this is his father. Oh god, his parents, his dad. They are going to be livid. I glance over at Trevor, and he still hasn't lifted his eyes from the stage floor.

"All right, everybody, that's it for this afternoon. I want to thank you again for coming, and we will hopefully see you at our next event. If you are taking the activity bus home today, the buses should be leaving in about ten minutes," Ms. Richmond states.

People start to get up from their seats, stretching and talking among themselves. Trevor finally lifts his head, meeting my worried eyes.

"Why did you do that?" I whisper.

Trevor opens his mouth to speak, but he is cut off by a loud finger snap.

"Trevor." Trevor's father stands at the end of the stage, looking up at him. "Come down here now."

"Sorry," Trevor says. "I've got to go. I owe them an explanation."

I nod numbly. Trevor hops down from the stage, he and his family disappearing into the crowd.

My mother and I don't get home until well after eight o'clock. Before I could get down off the stage, Bruno and his mother disappeared. My mother told me that Bruno had a very important project to work on, and he couldn't wait around any longer.[80] But Ben[81] and Lou stayed to offer me their congratulations. After leaving the auditorium, my mom took me to the Chinese restaurant we normally go to for my birthday, and I actually enjoyed eating

---

80. FYI, I know that Bruno is lying. I know he is upset with me.
81. Yes, Ben actually stayed to offer me non-sarcastic congratulations. The world is really topsy-turvy.

there. It felt like some part of my life was returning to normal, and Mom even acted interested in the club. It all felt very nice. But when we pull into the driveway to our house, I feel the guilt and anxiety start to filter back in. Trevor. His parents looked so disappointed in him, and that was my fault. All my fault. And there was Bruno, my best friend in the world. My best friend who I'd been lying to. He knew that something was going on, and I hadn't told him. I'd made it seem like he was seeing things. What kind of friend does stuff like that? Not to mention India and Ben, and Ms. Richmond and Mr. Fairview, and all the other people who are affected by my magic.

My mom opens the door and gently prods me inside. She heaves her purse on the couch, then turns around to cup my face in her hands.

She looks down at me, her soft brown eyes peering into mine.

"I know it doesn't seem like I've been the best mom. And I know that everything that I told you about your dad has been difficult."

That's one word for it.

"But I made him a promise, Erin, to not tell you about him until it was necessary. He said I needed to protect you. And I will always put that first."

Tears sting my eyes.

She sighs. "I know I don't tell you this enough, Erin. I know sometimes it seems like I'm not paying attention or that I'm too caught up in my own stuff, but I want you to know I'm proud of you. I'm so very proud of you."

It feels like an arrow has been aimed straight into my chest.

My mom kisses my forehead lightly. "Just remember that."

She goes up the stairs to her room, and I stand frozen to the spot, tears running down my cheeks.

How did this happen? How did everything get so horribly messed up? My mom is proud of me, I have won the presidency, but I've never felt more awful in my life. I trudge up the stairs, dragging my backpack behind me. The tears are now freely flowing down my face. Fully sobbing, I push into my room, trying desperately to muffle the sound of my sobs into my elbow.

When I first step into my room, it seems impossibly dark. I blink a couple of times, trying to clear my eyes of the excess tears. Then I see it, glowing like a sleepy firefly in the night sky. My locket. It sits on the dresser on top of the letters and manual from my dad. Sniffling, I brush the sleeve of my sweater across my eyes. I move toward the locket.

"This is your fault," I hiss at the locket.

A laugh escapes me as I realize that I have just blamed all my problems on an inanimate object. I sniffle again, moving to turn on the light.

I pop open the locket, staring down at the picture of my dad.

"I've made quite a mess of my life," I tell his picture. "This is going to sound harsh, but I kind of wish I weren't your daughter right now. It would be easier, you know, not being some kind of weirdo magical abomination."

I examine the pictures in the locket again.

"I need your help, Dad."

I pause, waiting for . . . Honestly, I have no idea what I'm waiting for. Maybe I thought the locket was some type of magical cell phone that left my dad a message whenever I was in trouble. Maybe I thought the locket would talk back.

I shake my head. What's wrong with me? Enough with feeling sorry for myself. I need to back up, stop crying, and figure this out. I slide the locket back onto the dresser, moving away toward my bed. But before I can get too far from the dresser, I'm flung back; a ribbon from my dress is stuck on the handle of my sock drawer. I move, trying to disentangle myself from the handle. The sock drawer flies open, causing *The Cupid Manual* to fall to the ground.

"Oh, come on," I mumble, finally pulling free from the dresser.

I stoop down to retrieve the manual. Okay, message received. It's time I stop hiding from who I really am. I pick up the manual.

Chapter One: Cupid, An Introduction

The Cupid figure is one that has been popularized in recent decades as a symbol of romantic love. Although Cupid is largely responsible for true love matches, Cupid's power extends past the confines of romantic love. In fact, the majority of Cupid's power is used for strengthening relationships. Although romantic love can be included in the category of strengthening relationships, it isn't exclusively romantic. Relationships can include friendships and family relationships, along with other forms of platonic relationships.

The earliest depiction of Cupid comes from classical mythology. Where Cupid, or Eros, is the son of the Goddess of Love, Aphrodite, this earlier Cupid is considered to be the original Cupid and the god from which all other Cupids are descended.

I pause in my reading. Cupids? Plural? There's more than one? So my dad isn't the original Cupid? He is one of Cupid's descendants? I continue reading.

Cupids typically come into their powers around the age of thirteen. It is then that a Cupid starts to exhibit the basic powers of a Cupid, i.e., glowing, minor persuasion techniques, and amplification of emotions.

A Cupid's power can amplify certain emotions that will help the affected party achieve the optimal relationship that the Cupid desires. A Cupid's powers are powerful and life-changing. They should be used with caution.

I read through a couple of other chapters, including something called the Cupid Commandments. I continue to flip through the manual in frustration. This isn't what I need. *Help me find out what I need*, I think. Suddenly, my fingers stop. I look down at the chapter I have stopped at. "Spell Reversals and Other Magical Solutions."

I plop down on the floor, flabbergasted. Cupid magic can be *undone*?

Hurriedly, I start to scan the chapter, trying to find information to help me reverse the spells. Finally, I find it. I read silently.

Each spell you cast as a Cupid is a spell that lives inside you. Your spells take up space in your unconscious thoughts, existing there in case you ever need to reverse them. It might seem like a daunting task to undo your magic, but it is really quite simple if you put your mind to it. See below for a step-by-step guide on how to reverse your spells.

Make sure you are somewhere quiet and serene. You will need a space where you can focus on your task.

Once you've found a space free from distractions, make sure you find a spot to sit or lie down.

Once you are either lying down or sitting, close your eyes. Free your mind of any distractions or thoughts. Make your mind as blank as possible.

Once your mind is completely empty, think of the spell you want to undo. You will know when you have thought of it. Some Cupids say that their spells appear to them as locked doors, completed puzzles, or tiny wrapped gifts. Every Cupid's materialized spells are unique. The one similarity with these spells is that they are reversible in some way.

So the next step is to undo your materialized spell. Open the locked door, scatter the puzzle pieces, unwrap the gift. Make the perfect imperfect. Doing this will undo the spell. You will know when the spell is undone.

I put the book back on the dresser, contemplating what I have just read. I can reverse the spells. All of them. Everything can return to normal. But even as I think it, I know it isn't true. How can things go back to normal when I've already meddled in everyone's lives? What would happen to all the people who were affected by the spells, all the people I care about? Would everyone stay together without a supernatural push? I think about India and Bruno, Ms. Richmond and Mr. Fairview, Ben and Bruno, and then I think about Trevor. We were enemies before I used magic on him, but now we're friends. Good friends. Is there a possibility I could lose his friendship?

I throw myself on the bed, groaning in frustration. It doesn't matter, because honestly, I screwed up, and now I have to do whatever I can to make it right. And face the consequences. Even if it means losing Trevor.

I settle into a comfortable position on the bed, squeezing my eyes shut.

Think nothing. . . . Think nothing. Think nothing.

Okay, maybe thinking "think nothing" probably isn't the best way to clear my mind.

I try again, this time simply letting my eyelids flutter closed. I imagine that I have an eraser, and I'm erasing away all my thoughts, all my anxieties, everything. When my mind is completely blank, I think about the spells I have cast. When I open my eyes, I'm standing in a room that is empty, save for one thing—a long wooden table that holds five beakers, four of which are full of colorful liquids.

I pause for a moment, cataloging each of the beakers: one is filled with a swirling green mist, another is filled with what looks like a vibrant orange fluid, the next beaker is filled with a thick midnight-blue liquid, the fourth beaker is filled with a reddish-brown sludge, and the last beaker is bright, shiny, and completely empty.

Okay, okay. I walk around the long table, tapping my chin. Five beakers, four filled with liquid. I'm supposed to do something here, something to break the spells. I examine the beakers again. Each of them has unique contents with colors that feel almost familiar. As if I've seen these colors before. Then it clicks. These are the same colors that surrounded each of the people I used my magic on. Green for Bruno. Orange for Mr. Fairview. Blue for Ernesto. And red for Ben. The only thing that doesn't make sense is the empty beaker. The beaker that should be Trevor's. I remember the silver color that clung to Trevor after I used my magic on him.

I can't think about this now. I have to figure out a way to break the spells. I focus on the beakers, and I think back to the manual.

Step five. Undo the materialized spell. Make the perfect imperfect. Then it clicks. I walk over to the first beaker, the one with the swirling green mist. I tip it over, the mist escaping up into the air and disappearing. I do the same with each of the others; some easily spill out and disappear, while others (the red sludge) I have to push out with my fingers. When I get to the last beaker, Trevor's beaker, I hold it up in confusion. I turn it over, thinking maybe the liquid is too clear for me to see. But nothing comes out. Because it's empty, completely and totally empty. And a realization hits me like a lightning bolt. Trevor's beaker is empty because my magic never worked on him. That means all Trevor's words and actions, all his help, all his smiles were 100 percent him. No magical assistance whatsoever.

I put the beaker back down. I turn my back to the table and close my eyes, and when I open my eyes, I'm back in my room.

"My magic didn't work on Trevor. Why?"

It doesn't make sense. I did the exact same thing with Trevor that I did with the others. So what was different about Trevor? My phone buzzes, interrupting my thoughts. Hopping up, I pick up the phone, not bothering to check who it is.

"Hello?" I say.

"Hello," a voice chirps.

"Uh, it's not a great time. . . ."

A giggle floats over the line. "It's me, EJ. It's Birdie."

I sigh. I love Birdie. I do. She is my favorite cousin, but I have important things I need to figure out. I don't have time for this.

"Hey, Birdie," I start. "Can I—"

"I know you are going to try to hang up. You are probably busy figuring out the cure for the common cold or whatever. I just want to chat for a second. A millisecond. I just need some advice."

I sigh again. The thing is that Birdie is persistent. I could say no, but she would find a way to turn it into a yes. It's as annoying as it is endearing.

"Okay, Birdie. What is it?"

"Right. Right. I'll be quick. I just, well, I'm curious . . . I mean—"

"Before Christmas, Birdie," I cut her off, exasperated.

"Yeah, yeah. I'm sorry. Okay, so here goes. I want to know how you get boys to notice you."

I slap my palm against my head. Of course, why else would she be calling? Birdie was certifiably boy crazy.

"Birdie, don't you have some friends you can ask or something?"

Birdie huffs. "None of us have boyfriends or girlfriends."

I roll my eyes in response. "I don't have one of those either."

"Oh." Birdie is quiet a moment. "But I just thought, the boy from the party, the one who was staring at you . . ."

This timing could *not* be worse. I snort. "Trevor, the one I compared to a polar bear, you mean? Why would you think that?"

"Because . . ." Birdie's voice is low at first, and then her volume ticks up. "Because I've never seen a boy look at a girl like that, not in real life at least. I mean, I've seen it in movies and maybe once when Uncle Ty got to try an authentic Philly sub—"

"Birdie," I interrupt her, my heart so loud I can barely hear her words. "How did Trevor look at me?"

Birdie is quiet for a moment, like she is collecting her thoughts. When she finally speaks up, it's with a reverent tone.

"I know this is cheesy or whatever, but the way he looked at you whenever you were busy or turned away—well, he looked at you like, hmm, how do I explain it?"

I wait, my heart still slamming against my chest. I clutch my phone so tightly in my hand that I'm afraid I might crack it.

"Try," I encourage her.

This feels important. I need to know how Trevor was looking at me.

"Well, he looked at you like nothing else mattered, like if the world were wiped out by zombies and you were the only two left on earth, he'd be okay with it. Because you were there."

I feel dizzy and euphoric, like I could fly if I wanted to. I squeeze my eyes shut. I hold the phone, shaking.

"Hello? EJ, still there?"

I clear my throat, trying to center myself.

"Yeah, yeah. I'm here."

"So, any advice?"

Right, advice. Birdie wants advice on attracting boys. I laugh, shaking my head in disbelief. Me, a boy expert. Who would have known?

"The only advice I can give you is to be yourself. There's no other magic besides that."

Birdie lets out a prolonged, overdramatic sigh. "I do love you, and you are my favorite cousin and everything, but that's some trash advice."

I burst out with a full-bellied laugh. "Well, Birdie, I'm sorry if that's not what you wanted to hear, but that's all I've got. Unfortunately, there's no magic solution to your problem."

After hanging up with Birdie, I ponder the irony of my final words to her. *There's no magic solution to your problem.* But as much as I relied on my Cupid powers, they caused more harm than good. And then there is Trevor, Trevor who stared at me like I was the only person in the world at my birthday party. The birthday party that happened before I discovered my powers, and before I used those powers on Trevor. I think about the Cupid Commandments from the manual, especially commandment number seven. The commandment about how a Cupid's powers sometimes don't work, especially if both parties are already completely smitten with each other.

I sit down on my bed with a thump, ready to accept the truth, something I've been running from for a long time now. My magic didn't work on Trevor because Trevor and I already liked each other.

CHAPTER THIRTEEN

Cupid Commandment Number 6: To err is human.

To fix your error is Cupid.

I WAKE UP EARLY Monday morning feeling for the very first time in my life like skipping school. I know that I did the right thing by reversing the spells, but honestly, I don't want to see what the results of the spell reversals are.

I contemplate pretending to be sick. My mom would believe me, since I have never ever pretended to be sick before.[82] The problem is that I'm pretty sure she will want to take me to the

---

82. One time I even pretended *not* to be sick when I had the flu. The nurse eventually sent me home after I puked in the lunchroom trash can.

emergency room. Plus, I have to face the music sometime, and there is no point in dragging this out.

Trevor was texting me all weekend, and I've been ignoring him. It's hard having to piece together this new knowledge about Trevor, the fact that Trevor liked me all on his own, without any magical influence. And I know that it must hurt Trevor that I'm not answering his texts. He must be confused, or maybe he even thinks that I'm mad at him for dropping out of the race. Neither is true, and I am going to talk to him today. I'm going to set things straight between us. I'm going to tell him everything (well, everything except the magic bits). Trevor and I are going to start with a clean slate.

My mom drives me to school, skipping our ritual of picking up Bruno and Ben. When I ask her why we aren't picking them up, she simply gives me a sad smile through the rearview mirror.

"I think Bruno is going through something, honey. He just prefers for his mom to take him from now on."

My heart sinks. Of course he does. Not even my best friend wants to be around me.

Right then, it feels like a dam bursts open and I find myself desperately wanting to talk to my mom.

"Mom, I finally read the manual. I'm sorry it took so long. I just—I don't know. At first I didn't believe it. It just sounded ridiculous. But then things started happening, and I knew. I knew that all of it was true. I knew my dad was really Cupid."

My mom pulls up to a stop sign, and she puts the car in park. She turns around to give me her full attention.

And to my horror, I feel tears building behind my eyes, and I know that I'm very close to sobbing.

"I don't know why he'd leave me. Didn't he want me?"

Tears are now streaming down my face, and I am hiccuping, and it's all just a mess. My mom leans over the console, pulling me into her arms.

"Oh, EJ, he did want you, and he does love you. He always will."

As predicted, I'm now sobbing. I lean into my mother's purple sweater, and I cry into her. My mom is shushing me, rubbing my back in tiny circles, the same way Nana used to do to put me to sleep when I was little.

When I stop crying, Mom pulls away, wiping my face with her fingers.

"He did want you," she says again. "Gods can't live among humans. Bad things happen. He left to protect you."

I nod. I get it. I do. But maybe I don't want protection. Maybe I just want a dad.

My mom sighs, seemingly guessing what I'm thinking.

"You'll always have a piece of your dad through his letters, your manual, the locket. And I'll get better at telling you about him. I promise."

I nod again.

"And I am here, Erin. As long as I'm on this earth, I will always be here."

I choke on a sob as I pull my mom into another embrace, and we stay that way, locked on to each other, until the sound of a blaring car horn forces us apart.

When we arrive at school, I make a beeline to Bruno's and my locker. I open up the locker and notice that Bruno has already taken out his school supplies. He's beaten me here. He's beaten me here so he won't have to talk to me. Well, I'm not going to let him ignore me any longer. Across the hallway, I see India in her normal morning spot talking to Ben and the rest of their friends. I maneuver my way across the hallway until I'm standing right in front of India.

"Erin." India blinks at me in surprise. "Hey."

"Hey," I respond shyly. I know I haven't been the best person to India, and it sucks, but I'm going to change that, starting now. "How are you?" I ask.

India blinks at me again. "Fine," she responds slowly. "And you?"

I shrug. "I've been better," I answer.

India gives me a supportive look. "Well, I enjoyed your speech on Friday. It was fire, honestly."

"Thank you." I give her a tiny smile. I shift from foot to foot. "So have you seen Bruno? He isn't at our locker, and I really need to talk to him."

India's face immediately falls. She turns her head away from me, snapping her eyes shut.

Ben comes over to stand behind her. He puts a hand on her shoulder.

"She hasn't talked to Bruno all weekend. He's ghosting her. Can't say I didn't warn her."

I glare at him, my cheeks becoming warm. So much for this best-friend, brother-bonding thing that has been happening lately. Ben is officially back to being a jerk. I move away from them, flashing India a sympathetic look.

"I'll talk to him, India. Don't count him out just yet."

India's eyes flutter up. She gives me a grateful smile. "Thanks, Erin."

"It's EJ," I respond. "My friends call me EJ."

I find Bruno alone in the art room, lights off, bent down over his sketchbook, scribbling feverishly.

"Bruno." I step in front of his table. His head snaps up, and for a moment his eyes catch mine and narrow. Then his gaze falls back down to his artwork.

"Bruno," I try again, this time pleading. No response. Not even a glance up this time. "Bruno, are you just going to ignore me? Are you going to pretend I don't exist? Your best friend?"

Anger bites at me, hot and sharp.

Bruno stops drawing, carefully organizing his supplies and shoving them into his bag. He gets up when he is finished, slinging his bag onto his shoulder. He walks around me, not even giving me a second glance.

"Oh yeah?" My anger is an uncontrollable flare at this point. "So you really are just pretending I don't exist? Is that how you solve your problems, Bruno? By pretending they don't matter?"

By this time, we're out in the hallway. Bruno picks his way through the crowd, trying to lose me.

I speed up, making sure to stay right on his heels. "So this is how it's going to be? Me chasing you? You running away from your problems? Really mature."

Bruno continues to stomp through the hallway, his mouth becoming tighter with each word I scream.

"I get it," I yell. People are now turning around to look at us with interest. "I guess this is what you do, Bruno. With me. With Ben. With India. You're scared, so you run away."

At the mention of India's name, Bruno freezes. Not realizing that he's stopped walking, I smash into his back and fall ungracefully to the floor. Bruno looks down at me, fury etched on every feature of his face.

"You"—he points at me accusingly—"don't get to talk about India. You never get to talk about India. Not after what you did to Trevor."

I peer up at him, my mouth open in surprise.

"I don't even know you anymore, Erin." Bruno runs his fingers through his hair in frustration. "I know you are competitive. I know you want to succeed. I get it. I do. But that's not everything. It shouldn't be everything."

I flinch as if Bruno has slapped me.

"Look, what you did to Trevor was wrong. It was wrong on so many levels. Making a guy like you so he'll drop out of a competition is pretty gross, EJ. I know you don't really like Trevor, but, man, nobody deserves that. And the EJ I know . . ." Bruno sighs in tired resignation. "The EJ I *knew* wouldn't do that, no matter how much she wanted to win."

I hang my head down in between my knees. He is right. It was an awful thing to do, and he doesn't even know the half of it. I take a deep, steadying breath and pull my head up. I look up to find Bruno's pale face gazing at something behind me.

"I'm sorry, man. I didn't mean to shout that out for everyone to hear."

I freeze, my heart skittering in my chest. I turn around slowly and find myself looking up into the face of Trevor Jin.

CHAPTER FOURTEEN

Cupid Commandment Number 9: Cupids may be descended from gods, but that doesn't mean they are gods. Cupids make mistakes as easily as any other human.

BRUNO WON'T TALK TO me (check). Trevor won't talk to me (check). My life is ruined as I know it (triple, quadruple check). After Bruno spilled my secret to half the school, and most importantly to Trevor, Trevor wouldn't even look at me. Before I got to class, Trevor had already spoken to Ms. Richmond about our seat assignments. He switched seats with Amy Longhorn so that he could have the seat in the back corner of the room, the farthest seat away from me.

I come into homeroom, furious with myself, Bruno, and

Trevor. Amy Longhorn settles into the seat beside me, clearly miffed with the change.

"There's a reason I like to sit in the back," she huffs. She turns around to give Trevor a look of pure irritation.

I ignore her, pulling out my phone.

> Me: Trevor, can we talk?
> Me: I'm really sorry. I want to explain.

I look back and see Trevor's phone vibrate on his desk. He frowns, picks up the phone, and starts silently reading the messages. After a moment, he clicks off the phone and shoves it into his bookbag. Sullenly, I turn back around in my seat. Fine. I guess Trevor really isn't talking to me.

"Students," Ms. Richmond says, her voice breaking.

My eyes shoot up to Ms. Richmond's face. Oh no. What's wrong? Ms. Richmond's face is swollen, her eyes puffy and a miserable shade of red.

"Homeroom is going to start soon." Ms. Richmond is stuttering, gulping down sobs.

A girl in the front row raises her hand.

"Yes-sss, Alison," Ms. Richmond says, now openly sobbing.

"Um, are you okay?" Alison asks tentatively.

Ms. Richmond starts sobbing harder, and the class looks around at one another in shock.

"It's just . . . It's just that Mr. Fairview and I had a tiny argument this morning, children, nothing to worry about."

I feel dizzy with guilt. This is all my fault.

"He just seemed so different around me. All I did was comment on it, and he said we should take a break."

She starts sobbing again, and my heart sinks.

"Sorry, kids. Too much information." She flushes, trying to clean the snot off her face with the sleeve of her shirt. I dig into my backpack, pull out my unopened individual pack of tissues, and hand it to her.

"Thanks, Erin," she says, blowing her nose loudly.

Don't thank me, I think. Everything is horrible. And quite frankly, it is all my fault.

By the time lunch comes around, I'm resigned to sitting by myself, as Bruno doesn't even show up for lunch and Trevor moves back to his normal spot. So it is somewhat of a pleasant surprise when India plops down at my table.

"Hey." She sets her tray down right across from mine.

"Hey." To be honest, I have been preparing myself for wallowing in my own misery, and I'm not quite ready to engage in friendly conversation.

"Do you mind if I sit here?"

I shake my head.

She sits down on the stool. "I heard what happened earlier in the hallway. With Bruno and Trevor." India's mouth turns down at the corners. "Bruno should never have yelled at you and tried to embarrass you like that. I don't know what's gotten into him."

"No, it's my fault," I insist. "Don't blame Bruno."

India peers over at me skeptically.

"No, really," I assure her. "It's me. I have been awful lately. Honestly, I have. In fact, India, I owe you an apology. I really do. When you and Bruno first started hanging out, I acted really jealous, which isn't right. Bruno's crazy about you. He has been ever since you moved here."

India sighs, moving her spoon around her creamed corn. "EJ, you might be to blame for what happened in the hallway earlier, but I don't think you are to blame for Bruno ignoring me for the past couple of days. I mean, are you?"

She looks up at me, doe-eyed with hope. Hope that I have to squash. I sigh.

"No, no, I'm not the reason Bruno isn't calling you." At least not directly. Without the magic, Bruno has settled into being afraid again. He is letting his doubts take over, and he is pushing India away.

"That's what I thought," India responds, her voice holding a steely resolve. "But enough about that." Her voice switches back to cheery and upbeat. "Have you talked to Trevor since, you know, everything happened?"

I grimace, biting down on my turkey melt. I shake my head quickly. I swallow my food before answering.

"No. I've tried texting him, but he's ignoring my texts."

A pain shoots through me as I look over to where Trevor is

sitting alone. He isn't eating. He is simply pushing a french fry from one side of the tray to the other.

"Give him time," India answers. "Is it true, though? Did you really try to get him to like you so that you could convince him to drop out of the race?"

I squirm uncomfortably in my seat. Part of atoning for your wrongdoings is admitting you were wrong in the first place. That is an important first step.

"Yes, at first that is what I set out to do," I admit. "But . . ." I pause. I don't know how much I want to admit, how vulnerable I want to be with India. "I don't know. It did start like that, but it definitely ended up being something else." I flush with embarrassment. "I think we became friends."

India's eyes twinkle with amusement. "Mm-hmm, yes. I'm aware. Any fool can see how he lights up when you come around."

"What? No, he doesn't."

"Girl, yes, he does." India leans down onto the table, her chin in her hands. "I know I've only known you guys for three years, but I can tell when someone likes someone, EJ. I think the whole school can tell that he likes you."

I play with the edges of my sandwich, pushing it away, suddenly not hungry anymore. I think about Trevor's empty beaker. "It doesn't matter anyway. He's never going to talk to me again. Matter of fact, neither is Bruno."

India's wistful expression drops off her face. The bell rings and she stands, picking up her tray.

"You don't strike me as the type of girl who gives up without a fight. And those two guys"—India backs up toward the trash can—"are worth fighting for, EJ. So maybe you need to regroup and strategize, but you don't stop fighting. Never stop fighting." She gives me a parting smile before leaving.

I sit at the table for a minute longer than usual. I was wrong before. India is actually really, really smart.

I had a hand in messing everything up. So it is up to me to fix it. And I'm going to start with Bruno.

After school I convince my mom to drop me off at Bruno's house, though she keeps insisting that I can't push myself on people when they are upset, and quite honestly, this is the exact opposite of how she treats me when I'm upset with her. So I really don't understand why I'm getting unasked-for advice. When we get to the house, I hop out of the car, leaving my bookbag in the front seat.

"When should I be back?" my mom calls out the window as I go up to the door.

"Can I text you?" I call back.

"Erin Marie." My mom holds a fluttering hand to her chest. "You mean to tell me that you are going to play something by ear?"

I roll my eyes, but I'm smiling. "I guess, Mom."

My mom lets out a low whistle. "I guess things are changing, aren't they?" She speeds off out of the driveway.

Taking in a steadying breath, I lift my hand to knock on the door. Before I can, the door flings open, and Isa stands in front of me in a neon-purple sweat suit. She looks down at me with a smile.

"Erin," she breathes. "I thought that was you, mija. I heard your mom's janky car pull off. She really needs to get that roto fixed."

"I think you mean 'rotor,' Ms. Isa," I correct her gently.

"Yes, that's it. She needs that thing fixed. Oh, why are you standing outside? Come in."

She pulls me in, taking my coat off and throwing it on the couch. I lift my eyes shyly to meet Isa's.

"Is Bruno here?"

Isa smiles down at me, her lips twitching in amusement.

"Yes, he's here. He's in his room right now, sulking."

I nod, as if this was information I already knew.

"May I go up and speak with him?"

"Yes, yes, of course." Isa shoos me away. "You don't have to ask. I just hope he talks to you. He hasn't talked to anyone since he got home."

"I hope so too," I reply. I hurry up the stairs, racing past doors until I get to the last room on the left. I pause, suddenly scared that Bruno will turn me away. And then that would be it. That would be the end of our friendship. And quite frankly, that scares me more than anything.

I knock, holding my breath in anticipation. I hear some shuffling from behind the door, and then it flies open. I register the surprise on Bruno's face. He stares at me first with raised eyebrows, and then his face falls and he just looks tired.

"Come in," he mumbles, moving aside to let me through.

I shuffle into the room that I have been in a thousand times before. I glance around at the anime and K-pop posters covering every inch of his wall. The artist's desk he received for Christmas two years ago is covered with charcoal stains and unused paper. All of it is as familiar as my own room, but for some reason it feels different. I feel almost like a stranger. I take a seat in my favorite spot, an old beanbag[83] chair in the corner of the room. Bruno sits on his desk chair.

"So, EJ, what are you doing here?"

I take a deep breath. Bruno is my best friend. My absolute best friend. I trust him with my life. It is time for me to start trusting him with my secrets.

"Bruno," I begin, at the same time that Bruno says, "EJ."

We both shake our heads, laughing. "You go," I offer.

"Look," Bruno says. "I'm sorry about Trevor. I shouldn't have said those things in the hallway. I let my anger get the best of me. I didn't mean to do that. And for that I'm sorry."

He hangs his head down, his long black hair falling in waves over his eyes.

"No, I'm sorry, Bruno," I reply softly. "That wasn't your fault. It was mine. What you said was true. I was being an awful, selfish brat, and I hurt a lot of people I care about, including you."

Bruno pushes his hair out of his face, looking up at me.

I continue. "Bruno, I haven't been honest with you, and I need to be. But first, I need to know that you aren't going to freak out."

---

83. Bruno absolutely can't stand the beanbag chair. It was a present from Lou when they first moved into the house. Bruno wanted to get rid of it, but I convinced him to keep it, mainly because I was the only one who sat in the chair, so it kind of made it a special seat just for me.

Bruno sits up, his back straight. "What's wrong, EJ? Are you okay?"

I nod, waving away his concern. "Yeah, I'm fine. Just promise you won't freak out and also that you won't say anything to anyone, not even your mom, especially not your mom."

Bruno sits quietly for a second, then nods.

I exhale, and then I tell Bruno everything. I start with the weird feeling I got the day after my birthday, and how when I touched him and Mr. Fairview, they seemed to become brave and conquer their fears about love. So much was different. And how I couldn't stand that I hurt him. By the end of my confession, I'm crying and Bruno is pulling me into a hug.

"I'm just so sorry for all of it," I mumble into Bruno's shoulder. He pats my back consolingly.

"You are human, EJ. Well . . ." He pauses, blushing. "Mostly human, anyway. You are supposed to make mistakes. Look at me. Look at how I'm treating India."

I pull away, sniffling. I slide my hand across my nose. "Yeah, why are you ignoring her? She's pretty hurt by it, by the way."

Bruno shrugs, looking down at the floor again. "I don't know. I just get . . . I get nervous. I have all these thoughts, like, 'Does she like me because of me, or does she want me to be more like Ben?' I don't know."

I huff in annoyance. "Of course she likes you for you. If she liked Ben, Ben would be the one she was staring at in the hallways. She likes you, doofus."

I push his arm playfully. He smiles.

"But how do you know that your magic didn't make her like me, that she really wasn't just, like, enchanted or something?"

"Well, one, the manual my dad left says that two people have to care about each other for the magic to work. Two, I didn't touch India; I touched you. And three, I removed the magic, and India has been pining after you in the cutest way all day."

Bruno's face lights up. "She has?"

I nod. "She has."

For a moment, Bruno looks overjoyed. He hurriedly grabs his phone. "I should text her."

I shrug. "You could, but I have a better idea."

Bruno puts his phone down. "Yeah, what's your idea?"

I hop up clumsily from the beanbag chair. I move over to his bookbag, picking it up and placing it on the bed. Bruno looks at me in confusion.

"I should do her homework?"

"No, dork." I open his bookbag, pulling out his sketchbook. I push it into his hands. Understanding flashes on Bruno's face.

"You should show her what you think of her. Show her your art."

Bruno nods tentatively, as if thinking it through.

"Besides, what girl wouldn't be flattered to star in her own comic series?"

Bruno laughs, ruffling my hair in the way that he always does. It feels familiar. It feels normal.

* * *

The next day, I feel slightly better and slightly more on track. Isa comes to get me in the morning with both Bruno and Ben in the car. Ben doesn't speak to either of us, but Bruno tells me about his plan to apologize to India. By the time we get to school, Bruno is sweaty from nerves.

"Calm down," I whisper to him as we walk to our locker. "Everything will be fine. Just be honest and show her your sketchbook. Easy enough."

"Yes, easy peasy," Bruno scoffs.

"Lemon squeezy," I finish our childhood chant. Bruno smiles at me.

At that very moment, India comes from across the hall, walking with a girl I recognize from my health class. Bruno freezes, his hand clutching his sketchbook. As if India can sense us, she turns around. Her eyes land first on me, then on Bruno. Her smile melts away, and she lifts her hand in a small, awkward wave.

"It's now or never," I hiss, pushing Bruno.

Bruno moves toward her, dragging his feet as he goes.

I stand back, watching as he approaches India. Nervously, he speaks to her. India crosses her arms over her chest, her face sliding into a frown. I'm too far away to hear what they are saying, but I can see that Bruno is gesturing emphatically, pausing every so often to make his point. I see India shake her head, her lips pursed, her left leg jiggling. Bruno pulls his hands through his hair. Finally, he pushes his sketchbook into India's hands. She opens it, and he flips to a page. India stares down at the book, her mouth hanging open in surprise. Bruno says something else, and India holds the book to her chest, then pulls Bruno in for a hug.

I let out a sigh. Bruno looks up from the hug, giving me a thumbs-up. One down, only a couple more to go.

I turn back toward the other end of the hallway and almost run smack-dab into Ben.

"Sorry," he starts to mumble, but then his eyes snap up to mine. "Oh, it's you."

He doesn't say it with disgust so much as a tired resignation.

"Yeah, it's me," I respond. Ben rolls his eyes, preparing to move around me to get to his class. Before I can stop myself, I move directly in his path, blocking him from going around me.

"What are you doing? Move. I've got to get to class."

I hold my hands out palms-up, as if I'm calming a rabid animal.

"Just give me a minute. I want to talk to you about something."

Ben stiffens, his face falling a fraction.

"What's wrong? Where's Bruno? Did something happen? Is he okay?"

Ben's eyebrows are drawn together, his shoulders taut with worry. Even with all their arguments, and their distance, Ben loves Bruno. Honestly and truly loves him.

"Nothing is wrong," I quickly interject. "I just need to talk to you for a second."

Ben looks at me skeptically, but then he shrugs. He steps out of the middle of the hallway and leans back against the lockers.

"Okay. What's up?"

A lot, I want to say. *I see right through you. You don't hate your brother. You love him, but you don't know how to fix this rift*

241

between you. But I don't say that, because I know Ben will close himself off to me and not talk at all.

No, I will have to go about this in a different way.

"Look, I need to talk to you about something, but I need you to promise me that you won't tell Bruno I told you."

Ben perks up. He pushes away from the lockers eagerly.

"Okay," he says.

Bruno will forgive me for this, because even though he doesn't say it, I know he misses the closeness he and Ben used to have. Heck, sometimes I miss it. But Ben is Bruno's brother, and they are family, even if that looks a little different after their parents' divorce.

"Bruno misses you, Ben."

Ben's face flickers with emotion before his mouth settles into a frown.

"What are you talking about, EJ? I'm right here. Why would he miss me?"

"You know what I mean, Ben. He misses you. How you guys used to be."

Ben's eyes fill with hope, his lips quirking up just a bit.

"He told you that?"

I shake my head. "He didn't have to."

I pause briefly. Weighing what to tell him.

"Did you know that Bruno still keeps the picture of the two of you in his wallet, the one where you were Ninja Turtles for Halloween?"

Ben's face softens. "I remember. That was the year where we

got in trouble for smuggling pizza into our room after we went to bed. Mom was so mad. We blamed it on the fact that we were Ninja Turtles and we couldn't live without pizza."

I smile. I remember too. I was so jealous of them. I had dressed up as a witch, so I didn't have an excuse for sneaking pizza into my room. Nana would never have ever allowed it.

"Look," I say. "Bruno needs you. He might not say it, but he does."

Ben is silent for a moment before he sharply nods. It's not a miracle, but it's a start.

It wasn't an easy thing to convince Ms. Richmond and Mr. Fairview to go to the English workroom at the same time. It took quite a bit of trickery, manipulation, and just a slight bit of forgery.[84] But it worked! It totally worked. I got Ms. Richmond and Mr. Fairview into the same room together. Here's what I did. During class transition, I snuck back into Ms. Richmond's room and left a note on her desk stating that she needed to meet the principal in the English workroom at exactly ten a.m.[85] I also delivered a similar letter to Mr. Fairview's office. Bam. It was like magic. They both arrived in the workroom at the exact same time. I didn't technically spy on them, but I did peek through the window in the door to make sure they were talking to each other,

---

84. I had to sign the principal's name on the bottom of each note. I don't want to talk about it.
85. No, I wasn't taking her out of a class or anything. She has a planning period during this block. I checked.

which they totally were. At the end of what looked like a very heated conversation, they both started laughing, and then they collapsed into a hug. It was very successful.

At the end of the day, I feel a sense of accomplishment, and yes, it feels good, but there is still something missing, a big something. And I know it's Trevor. He continued to ignore me throughout the day, sometimes going as far as claiming to be sick so that he could go to the clinic to avoid running into me in the halls.

Honestly, it was miserable.

I'd come to look forward to Trevor's surprisingly sweet smile and his helpful texts. I missed everything about Trevor . . . I mean, everything. Even pre-Cupid-chaos Trevor. At least that Trevor talked to me (even if we mostly argued). This Trevor, the now Trevor, wouldn't even look at me for more than a second. Whenever he did happen to meet my eyes, there would be a second where his mouth would fall and his eyes would flicker with sadness. But then his face would shutter closed, and he would turn away.

There's only one place I want to go after school lets out. One place that can make me feel better. The Frozen Cone.

When I get to the shop and open the door, I'm met with the same sugary-sweet smell from last time. But this time, instead of flutters of hope and anticipation, all I feel are remorse and painful reminders of what was. Sighing, I move up to the display case where the ice cream is kept.

"Welcome to the Frozen Cone. How can I help you?"

I pause for a moment. My eyes sweep the flavors. What am I doing? I always get cookies and cream. Always. It is my absolute favorite flavor. But . . .

My eyes land on the light green ice cream.

"Miss?" the cheerful salesgirl inquires. I can tell that she is thinking I'm going to be one of those difficult customers. One of those people who asks to sample every single flavor before they settle on a small cup of vanilla.

I laugh under my breath. Trevor would have liked that. In fact, he would have teased me and said that that did sound like me. And I would have assured him that that sounded more like him.

"Miss." The salesgirl is now decidedly less cheerful. Her arms are crossed, and she is giving me the stink eye.

Excuse me. I'm just having a crisis over here. I clear my throat. I quickly make a decision.

"I'll take two scoops of pistachio in a waffle cone."

The salesgirl rolls her eyes and then works to fill my order. Once she finishes, she shoves the cone into my hands. I turn around to find an empty table to sit at, and I come in contact with a familiar face.

"Ernesto," I squeal in surprise.

Ernesto's face breaks into a grin, his eyes crinkling at the corners.

"EJ! I didn't know you came here."

"Yep," I say, sliding into the chair opposite him. I don't tell him how I only just discovered the ice cream shop. And only because of Trevor.

"It's still light outside. Shouldn't you be at the cemetery?"

Ernesto shrugs. He takes a bite of his ice cream.

"I hired someone to work part-time, so I can take some days off."

I know how big that is for him. Ernesto's father, Dido, managed the cemetery before him, and he never took a day off. Ernesto still aims to make his dad proud, even though he's been dead for over twenty years. He told me all this the first Sunday I visited Nana's grave. He was trying to distract me from my grief, and it worked.

"That's good. You deserve a break."

I take a small lick of my ice cream cone. And oh my god. Oh my god. It's actually delicious. It's more than delicious. It's absolutely amazing. I start taking bigger licks, smearing ice cream all over my chin.

"Whoa, slow down there," Ernesto says with a chuckle, pushing a napkin toward me. I give him a small smile in thanks, and I wipe off my chin.

"What made you hire someone part-time?"

Ernesto hesitates for a second. He swirls his spoon in his cup.

"It was Tommy," he says with a sigh. "He wanted to spend time with me, and with our alternating work schedules . . . well, it just made sense."

My heart dips. Why is Ernesto sighing? Has something happened? Then I remember. I broke the spell I'd cast on Ernesto.

"Is everything okay?" I ask tentatively. Ernesto's eyebrows pinch together, and he lets out another sigh.

"Yeah, everything is okay, or at least it will be. Tommy and I just had an argument about work. To be honest, I'm not sure I want to keep the part-time worker. My father put a lot into the cemetery. A lot of time and love. I'm not sure I'm comfortable leaving it in someone else's hands."

He pauses. He shakes his head as if to clear it.

"To tell you the truth, I don't know what got into me the last couple of days."

My magic, that's what. I have to fix this.

"Ernesto, if your dad was anything like my nana, and from what you've told me, he was, then he'd want you to be happy."

Ernesto rubs his lips in thought. After a moment, he looks up and smiles.

"Yeah, I think my dad and your nana would have gotten along just fine."

I nod eagerly. "Yes, so you should just tell Tommy—"

Ernesto holds his hand up with a tiny smile.

"Hey, EJ. It's okay, really. Let's talk about something else, if you don't mind."

"Okay." I lean back in my chair, a bit deflated.

I can't help him if he doesn't want to talk.

Ernesto notices my disappointment, and he clears his throat with a half smile.

"EJ." Ernesto leans forward, propping his chin on his wrinkled hands. "I feel like you are like the granddaughter I never had. And that's special to me. So I'm going to tell you something. Something that I learned from living for many, many years."

I listen, waiting for him to finish.

"What is meant to be will be. The universe has a way of making sure everything falls into place."

I laugh, pulling back from the table.

"You sound like a fortune cookie, Ernesto."

His eyes spark with amusement. He stands up, grabbing his trash with one hand and squeezing my shoulder with the other.

"When you get to my age, everything you say starts sounding like a fortune cookie. Got to head out, kid."

He tips his hat at me and walks out the door. I eat the rest of my ice cream, thinking back to what Ernesto said.

The universe has a way of making sure everything falls into place.

I get up from the table, depositing my used napkin into the trash.

Well, maybe sometimes the universe just needs a little help.

CHAPTER FIFTEEN

Cupid Commandment Number 1: The most important rule for a Cupid is largely considered a cliché, but even clichés have to get their beginning from somewhere. A Cupid should always believe in the power of love, because love conquers all.

THE NEXT DAY, I walk into science at my normal time. Mrs. Evans, busy at her desk grading, barely gives me a passing glance. She is disappointed in me and Trevor, that much is clear. Earlier in the week, she assigned a new partner project. Mrs. Evans said we all needed a refresher in body systems. So she assigned projects where we had to relearn different body systems. Trevor and I got assigned the cardiovascular system.[86] Unknown to me, Trevor talked to Mrs. Evans privately, convincing her that it was

---

86. Surprise. Surprise. The cardiovascular system deals with the functions of the heart.

necessary for us to do this assignment separately. She agreed, and Trevor was free from having to talk to me. And we both have to present our individual projects. It will be a competition, just like old times. Except this time, I have a plan. A plan that will show Trevor how sorry I truly am.

The classroom is fairly empty, and Trevor is sitting at our table, quietly organizing his supplies. I clear my throat before I sit down, hoping he will look at me. The only sign that Trevor has heard me at all is the tiny tic near his jaw and the tightening of his mouth. This has been our routine all week.

I sit down, scooting closer to Trevor so that only he can hear me.

"Trevor," I hiss. He continues to ignore me, flipping back and forth through our science notes.

His project is pristine. It's a poster board with an outline of the human body. The cardiovascular system is color coded and labeled perfectly. Trevor's eyes flick over to the empty space in front of me. His eyebrows fly up in surprise. He's wondering where my project is. But I'm not ready to bring it out quite yet. Trevor turns his head, promptly going back to giving me the cold shoulder.

"Trevor." I poke his arm with the eraser side of my pencil.

"*What?*" His face is heated with irritation.

Mrs. Evans looks up from her desk. "This time before class could be used for better things beside chitchat. You do have a presentation coming up in a few minutes."

Trevor sheepishly lowers his head.

"I'm sorry, Mrs. Evans. That was my fault," I offer.

Mrs. Evans grunts in annoyance and goes back to the papers on her desk.

I scoot closer to Trevor and lower my voice. "Trevor, I just wanted to tell you how sorry I am."

Trevor's eyes remain trained on his notebook. "Erin, I know you're sorry. Do you know how I know you are sorry?" He lifts his eyes, meeting mine. "I know because of the dozens of text messages you sent. I know because of the multiple voice messages. I know because of the way you look at me like a puppy from across the room. I get it, okay? You're really sorry."

"But I'm . . . ," I whisper back. "I'm really sorry. How do I prove it to you?"

Trevor's face is hard and unyielding. "Erin, I trusted you. I more than trusted you. I opened up to you about my family, about my writing. I thought we were friends. I really believed we were friends, EJ."

"We're friends, Trevor," I insist, trying to capture his hands with mine. He pulls back, anger rushing through him once again.

"Friends?" His voice teeters. "We're friends, huh? Do friends trick each other into dropping out of a race? Do friends lie to their friends? Make them think that they care? Is that friendship to you?"

Mrs. Evans clears her throat from across the room, and Trevor lowers his voice.

"Erin, all you care about is being on top, coming out number one. Being the perfect student. And fine, you win." Tiredly, he rubs his hands across his face.

I feel my heart tumble and spin. I've hurt Trevor. I've really hurt him. He trusted me, and I betrayed that trust. I put my own needs and wants above his. And that's not what a friend does.

The bell rings, signaling the start of class. Everyone dutifully places their projects on their desks: poster boards, plastic models, and other materials. Every last student completed this ritual, everyone except me. Trevor glances at me, his brow furrowing in concern. He turns around to face me.

"Look, I'm still not talking to you, but you do have your project, right? You've never forgotten your assignments before."[87] Hope surges through me. Trevor's worried about me. People don't worry about people who they don't care about. I pull my bookbag into my lap, hugging it close to my chest.

"Yes, I have my work," I respond.

Trevor doesn't say anything else. He simply nods and turns back around in his chair. I breathe in deeply, trying to steady my nerves. This will all be over soon, one way or another.

"Okay, class." Mrs. Evans moves toward the front of the room. "It's time to start our body systems presentations." She glances down at the silver clipboard in her hands. "Looks like we're starting with the cardiovascular system. So that is Mr. Jin and Ms. Johnson."

---

87. Trevor was right. In the sixth grade, I had to go to the hospital because I got conked unconscious during a game of dodgeball. I still completed my English paper that was due even while hooked up to the hospital IV.

Mrs. Evans stops, pursing her lips. "And this will be our one presentation that will be doubled, as Mr. Jin and Ms. Johnson couldn't figure out how to work together."

Mrs. Evans's glasses slide down her nose in an obvious sign of disapproval.

I flinch and peek over at Trevor, who is staring ahead, stone-faced.

"Which one of you would like to go first?"

"I will." Trevor hops up from his seat, clutching his poster board like it's the last life raft on a sinking vessel.

His presentation is quick and efficient. He talks about all the parts of the cardiovascular system: the arteries, the veins, the capillaries, and of course the heart. Trevor's definitions and explanations are precise and thorough. To put it simply, his project is perfect. But this isn't a competition any longer. Trevor means much more to me than any school competition, and it is time for me to show him. He finishes his presentation, and the class politely claps as he makes his way back to his seat.

My heart hammers in my chest as I clutch my bag even tighter. I'm having second thoughts. No, I'm experiencing more than second thoughts. I'm experiencing sheer, unhinged panic. What if this goes wrong? What if I embarrass Trevor and he ends up hating me? What if I embarrass myself and I end up having to move schools?

Mrs. Evans clears her throat. She has one eyebrow raised and her hands on her hips.

"I'm sorry," I croak. "Did you say something?"

Mrs. Evans clucks her tongue at me as if I'm the silliest girl in the whole school.

"I said, we're ready when you are, Ms. Johnson."

"Right. Right."

I unzip my bookbag, pulling out my crumpled report[88] and a medium-sized heart piñata.

Now Trevor is openly staring at me in shock. Mrs. Evans is also looking at me with a frown as I move up toward the front of the room.

I smooth out my report before handing it to Mrs. Evans, who, for her part, looks as if she's just had a run-in with the Ghost of Christmas Past. She glances down at the paper, then back up at me.

"Are you feeling okay, Erin?"

It's the first time I've ever heard Mrs. Evans sound genuinely concerned.

"Yes, I'm fine, Mrs. Evans." I awkwardly hold up my heart piñata. "I'm just going to start my presentation now."

Mrs. Evans still looks bewildered, but she doesn't say anything else as she moves away from the front of the room.

Everyone is now staring at me. My classmates aren't used to this version of me. The me that has been changed by not only my Cupid powers, but Trevor as well.

I shuffle my feet, willing myself to regain control. I might be changed in some ways, but I'm still the girl who can command a room when I give a speech.

I clear my throat.

---

88. Normally, my reports are bound in color-coded binders—a different binder for each class. But I have been understandably off my game this week.

"Hello, everyone. So I did the cardiovascular system as well. But instead of repeating what was pretty much a perfect presentation, I'm going to concentrate on one organ from the cardio system, the heart."

I pause, and the room waits for me to continue.

"Most people would consider the heart one of the most important organs in the body."

Everyone in the room gives blank stares.

Okay, here goes nothing.

I hold the papier-mâché heart piñata out in front of me. The heart is covered in pink and red tissue paper and sequins.[89]

"Hearts are fickle things. They may not be the strongest muscle in your body, but they are the hardest-working."

Most of my classmates look confused, some look bored, others intrigued. Trevor hasn't stopped looking at the piñata in my hands.

"They're also extremely sensitive. The heart is prone to overwork itself and stop, and sometimes it even breaks."

"That isn't science," Tori Cifer loudly whispers from the front row. "That heart isn't even anatomically correct."

"Did she hit her head or something?" someone else whispers.

I ignore them and continue.

"I used to only think of my heart as an organ, something that was necessary for survival."

Trevor has now lifted his eyes to mine, and I keep my gaze on his while I continue.

---

89. The heart piñata is left over from my birthday party.

"But I recently discovered that my heart is so much more. My heart can race at the sight of someone. It can pound from joy. It can break from heartache."

I'm clutching the piñata like a lifeline.

"None of that's even true." Tori is louder now. "Your emotions come from your brain," she says, all snark.

"Oh, shut up, Tor," someone responds. "She's trying to be romantic."

Trevor is quiet and expressionless. The only indication that he is affected at all by what I'm saying is the slight pink color of his cheeks.

"Look, I'm not perfect. I realize that. I messed up recently, and I hurt someone I really care about, because I was worried about being perfect and being number one." I inhale deeply, continuing. "I was wrong, really wrong. And I need everyone to know that I'm not perfect, and I'm willing to make mistakes and learn from those mistakes."

The room is quiet again, and everyone is volleying looks between Trevor and me. My stomach is flipping because this is the hardest part. This is the part where I open myself up for possible rejection and heartbreak.

I walk toward Trevor's desk, and the silence presses against my ears. I pause in front of Trevor, who is now doing everything in his power to avoid my gaze.

Now or never.

"So I want to give you my perfectly imperfect heart, because there's no one else I'd want to have it."

I hold out the lopsided heart piñata with shaky hands. No one moves as I stand there frozen in place while Trevor studies the literal heart in my hands. I hate cliché sayings like "Time stood still," but honestly, it feels like time has frozen and been erased from the room. It's just me, Trevor, and this ridiculous papier-mâché heart.

After what seems like a decade, Trevor's face melts into a smile. He reaches for the heart, and I'm flooded with happiness. He takes the heart from my fingers.

"So you forgive me?"

Trevor laughs. "I think I have to at this point. I've never had anyone give me an anatomically incorrect heart before."

He winks and I laugh.

"As great as this Hallmark movie moment has been, do you think you and Mr. Jin could wrap it up so other students can present?" Mrs. Evans says.

I spring back from Trevor, and he pulls the heart into his chest.

"Sorry, Mrs. Evans," I splutter. "I'm finished."

Mrs. Evans frowns. "As touching as that whole display was, you do know that the presentation is ten percent of your overall project grade?"

I know. I won't be able to get higher than an A− for the first time ever. But this is important. Everything isn't about being number one all the time. The people I care about are more important than a grade.

"I know," I respond.

When I move into my chair next to Trevor, I notice that he is still cradling the heart in one arm. He looks over at me and gives me a crooked smile. Then he glances at my hands clutched tightly in my lap. Slowly, he moves his free hand under the table toward mine, palm open. For a moment I'm confused, unsure of what he's trying to do, but then I understand. I unlatch my hands and stretch out a hand to meet his. Our hands lock, and our fingers interlace. And we smile at each other, because there's nowhere else we would rather be.

A CONCLUSION (SORT OF)

OF COURSE TREVOR JIN has a gorgeous, sleek mountain bike. Of course he does. I roll my eyes as he huffs his way up the slight incline of my driveway. I tap my wristwatch playfully.

"You're running late, Jin," I tease. "The world must be ending."

He studies the bike, pulling down the kickstand with his foot.

"Yeah, Creative Writing Club[90] ran long today. I read the poem you suggested I share."

---

90. Trevor's dad wasn't particularly excited about Trevor joining the Creative Writing Club, especially after Trevor dropped out of the race for president of the Multicultural Leadership Club. Trevor decided he didn't want a leadership position after all. But his dad eventually came around when Trevor mentioned how the club could strengthen Trevor's writing abilities and that could be an asset when it comes time to write college essays.

He's already flushed from the bike ride, but I still notice the darker pink that inches across his face. He dips his head down in embarrassment.

"The one about new beginnings?"

"Yeah." He gives me a crooked smile.

I give him an answering smile. "Good, that's my favorite."

Trevor shuffles forward shyly and holds out his arms. I melt into them. This is new for us, the hugging. But it's my favorite thing to do when I see him.

I lean onto his shoulder, giggling as I catch sight of the fancy bike again.

I pull back a little, examining his hair. It's poking up in odd places from where he hastily pulled off his helmet. It's adorable.

He's watching me, his crooked smile stretched across his face.

"Whose bike is that anyway?"

I don't think I've ever seen Trevor ride a bike before.[91]

"Actually, it is mine." He laughs as I roll my eyes again. "My dad got it for me last Christmas. He thought it would help me with stamina when I needed to stay up to do late-night study sessions."

I snort. "He didn't say that."

Trevor's smile widens. "Yes, he did. He was confused as to why I wasn't happier about it."

This time my laughter is loud and sharp. Trevor is giggling too.

"Your dad can be a bit ridiculous."

---

91. When we were in elementary school, Trevor used to spend his recess time doing extra schoolwork beneath a tree.

"Trust me. I know."

We're quiet for a moment, and Trevor eventually moves back over toward his bike. "So are you ready?"

I glance over at my bike, and I'm suddenly extra conscious of how it's two sizes too small. I pick up my helmet and lob it back and forth in my hands.

Trevor watches my nervous fidgeting for only a few seconds before coming over to extract my helmet from my hands.

"This is cool," he breathes. "It looks like one of those helmets from a spy movie."

My heart pinches because I know he's saying that to make me feel better. I take the helmet from his hands and unceremoniously strap it onto my head.

"Are you ready to meet my nana?"

Trevor puts his helmet back on.

"Yep, I've been excited for it all day."

And I know he is telling the truth because he knows how important Nana is to me. He knows how significant it is that I'm introducing him to her. It means that I trust him.

It takes us a full ten minutes longer than it normally takes me to get to the cemetery. Even with his new bike, Trevor is far less adept on a bike than I am. We have to stop multiple times for him to catch his breath. By the time we reach the cemetery, he is covered with a fine gloss of sweat, and he is panting slightly.

He swipes the back of his hand against his forehead.

"How do you go so fast?" he pants, taking a water bottle from a holder on his bike.

I shrug. "I don't know," I respond, my eyebrows wiggling. "I guess it's just science."

We both break out into a fit of giggles.

"Hey, kids. Just in time for some blondies. I made them this morning."

Ernesto lets us into the cemetery. He takes a full minute introducing himself to Trevor, shaking his hand, and jovially smacking him on the back.

Once he finishes, he beckons us to follow him to the yard house where Ernesto completes most of the administration work. When we get there, I'm surprised to see Tommy in front of the yard house, his back pressed against the door.

"Hey, kid. Long time no see."

I flash a smile at him and introduce him to Trevor.

Tommy hands me a plate of blondies.

"Good seeing you," he tells me warmly. "And nice finally meeting you," he says to Trevor.

I flinch at the word "finally." Okay, maybe I brought up Trevor once or twice. Trevor gives me a cocky smile.

Finally? he mouths at me.

I shrug my shoulders and giggle. Fine, maybe I did talk about him quite a bit.

Ernesto's gaze bounces back and forth between us, a smile lighting up his face.

"Well, EJ, you know where to go. Do you need anything else?"

I shake my head, but I change my mind right before he turns to leave.

"Ernesto." He turns expectantly. "So, it worked out, everything with you and Tommy?" I whisper so that only Ernesto can hear me.

Ernesto gives me a small smile. "I ended up keeping the assistant. You were right. My dad would've wanted me to be happy."

He winks at me.

I laugh gleefully, delighted for him and Tommy.

"Anyway, enjoy your time with your nana, kid, and again, nice to meet you, Trevor."

Trevor and I make our way to Nana's graveside, and I suddenly find myself almost shaking with nerves. I know Trevor isn't technically meeting my nana. I get that she has passed away and that it's just her grave that I'm visiting, but I can't explain it. Every time I visit and talk to her, it makes me feel whole again. I feel like she can hear me, that she's listening to me while I talk to her by her graveside. So it's important to me that Trevor takes this as seriously as I do, because Nana was and will always be an important part of who I am.

Trevor picks up the pace until he's standing next to me. He cautiously glances at me, and then without saying anything, he slips his hand into mine. I squeeze his hand in response. Trevor knows I'm nervous, and he is doing his best to assure me that everything will be okay.

By the time we get to the gravestone, I'm practically vibrating with nervousness. Trevor gives my hand one last squeeze before letting go.

I clear my throat, shuffling my sneakers in the dry grass. I squeeze my eyes shut, then open them.

"Nana, I want to introduce you to Trevor. Trevor, this is where I come to talk to my nana."

There's a brief pause, and I hold my breath, unsure of what Trevor is going to say or do. Is he going to think this whole thing is ridiculous? Is he going to want to stop hanging out with me because he thinks it's weird that I still visit Nana's grave after all this time?

Trevor steps forward, his hands in his pockets, jiggling his left foot. I realize for the first time how dressed up he is. He's wearing a sweater-vest with a bow tie and black dress pants. Even though he tends to dress formally,[92] he never dresses this formally, not unless it's a special event. Then it hits me. Trevor dressed up to meet my nana. I clutch my chest. This must be how the Grinch felt when his heart grew three sizes.

Trevor clears his throat and then begins speaking. "Hello, Mrs. Brown. I'm glad to finally be able to meet you. EJ talks about you all the time."

Trevor glances back at me and gives me a tiny smile.

I'm dizzy from the inside out. My stomach is doing flip-flops. Trevor has turned back to Nana's gravestone, his head cocked to the side, his hands still in his pockets.

"I guess it's just really important that we meet, because, well, because I think your granddaughter is amazing, and, well—"

Trevor fiddles in his pocket and pulls out a wrinkled sheet of paper.

---

92. Since we have been hanging out, Trevor has been loosening up more and more when it comes to his wardrobe.

"I kind of wrote something." He looks back at me, his eyes asking permission.

I nod at him.

"All right, this poem is called 'In Honor of.'"

I stand quietly, the plate of blondies heavy in my hands.

When he starts reciting the poem, I have to strain to hear over him, over the wind. His voice has grown soft and lilting.

"This is in honor of a girl I've known,
since days when crayons melted
between fingertips and hugs were
given without expectation. This is in honor of
a girl I admired enough to challenge,
whose smile could ignite a fire
across a deserted field.
This is in honor of a girl
who will change the world
all in honor of a woman who
shaped hers."

I don't realize I am crying until I feel the heavy drops sliding down my face.

Trevor turns around, his eyes widening slightly at my tears.

He reaches me in two strides.

"EJ?" he asks tentatively. "Did I do something wrong?"

I set the plate of blondies down on the grass. "No," I mumble. I grab him and pull him into a hug, and at first he's so surprised, he's stiff and unmoving, but then he breathes out a sigh and wraps his arms around me, laying his cheek on the side of my head.

"I was afraid you wouldn't like it." His head dips down near my ear.

I pull back from him slightly.

"You're right." Trevor's face immediately crumples. I quickly add, "I didn't like it. I loved it." His face lights up with pleasure, and he pulls me in for another tight hug.

"I was worried that you would think it's too much."

"Nuh-uh." I move out of his hug and pick up the slightly jostled blondies.

"It was perfect. You're perfect," I say.

"Far from perfect," Trevor replies with a smile.

"Well, I'm not perfect either. That's why we fit together. Like peanut butter and jelly."

He plops down on a grassy spot near Nana's gravestone. I sit down beside him with the plate.

"More like yakgwa and pistachio ice cream."

He laughs warmly, picking up a blondie and stuffing it into his mouth.

"That one doesn't make sense. Those are two of my favorite foods."

"Yep." I grab a blondie and bite off half of it in one bite. "But now they're mine. So it makes perfect sense."

"Whatever you say," Trevor says playfully, pushing his shoulder against mine.

"Ooh, I have one," I exclaim, my mouth full of blondie. "We go together like—"

"Like Erin Johnson and Trevor Jin."

I giggle. "That's it exactly." I slip my blondie-free hand into his.

We spend the rest of the afternoon eating blondies and talking to Nana.

It's only when we're halfway back to my house that I realize there has been a fundamental change to the way I look at the world. I've come to realize that there are a lot of great things about the world, but I have four that I think are the most important. One and two, friendship and love. We couldn't survive without them. Three, good foods like yakgwa and pistachio ice cream. And four, Trevor Jin.

THE CUPID COMMANDMENTS

THE CUPID COMMANDMENTS ARE a set of rules and truths that a Cupid must follow. Following these commandments will help you become your best Cupid self.

> **Cupid Commandment Number 1:** The most important rule for a Cupid is largely considered a cliché, but even clichés have to get their beginning from somewhere. A Cupid should always believe in the power of love, because love conquers all.
>
> **Cupid Commandment Number 2:** A good Cupid knows that their *Cupid Manual* is worth its weight in gold. Cupids must know their manuals inside out.
>
> **Cupid Commandment Number 3:** Cupids know that there is a very, very thin line between love and hate.
>
> **Cupid Commandment Number 4:** Cupids have a responsibility to use their powers for

the good of all parties involved. Using magic for personal gain comes at a price.

Cupid Commandment Number 5: A Cupid's powers normally manifest around the age of thirteen. A new Cupid should be careful that they are not unconsciously using their powers.

Cupid Commandment Number 6: To err is human. To fix your error is Cupid.

Cupid Commandment Number 7: A Cupid's powers do not always work. Specifically, if you have two individuals who have a strong, underlying attraction to each other, the magic is deemed unnecessary, as the individuals have all the natural magic they will ever need to cultivate their love.

Cupid Commandment Number 8: Cupids are ambassadors of love. They must be champions of all things related to love. Every day is Valentine's Day for a Cupid.

Cupid Commandment Number 9: Cupids may be descended from gods, but that doesn't mean they are gods. Cupids make mistakes as easily as any other human.

Cupid Commandment Number 10: A Cupid, much like a person in love, must always be prepared for the unexpected.

Cupid Commandment Number 11: A Cupid is a diplomat of love, but that does not mean that they are immune to love's power. When a Cupid falls in love, they fall hard and fast.

Cupid Commandment Number 12: A Cupid's magic is some of the most powerful magic in the world. A person who has been affected by Cupid magic will sometimes do extraordinary things for the object of their affection. This can be both good and bad. Beware.

Cupid Commandment Number 13: For a Cupid, there is nothing more noble than the pursuit of a quality education (except for maybe the pursuit of love).

Cupid Commandment Number 14: Love is patient. Love is kind. So a Cupid must be those things too.

Cupid Commandment Number 15: Being a Cupid is noble work. As a Cupid, you will be expected to always take the high road. Always.

ACKNOWLEDGMENTS

I've known I wanted to be a writer since I was ten years old. My fifth-grade teacher, Jean James, created a reading space for our class. She built forts with blankets and tents. She put up lamps and fairy lights. It was a magical place where I could get lost in the worlds of Judy Blume, Carolyn Keene, and Gertrude Chandler Warner. Reading these texts helped me forget the anxiety of adolescence. It was then that I knew that I wanted to write for kids too.

It wasn't until I was an adult and I started writing in earnest that I realized how much of a collaborative activity writing truly is. And because of that, I have a whole host of people to thank for helping this book come to fruition.

First, I would like to thank my superstar agent, Chloe Seager. She was this book's first cheerleader and advocate, and there isn't anyone better I could have in my corner.

Next, I would like to thank Jessi Smith, my magical editor. Jessi helped flesh out Erin and Trevor's story in a way that I never would've thought of. She's an absolute genius! Also, my thanks go out to the entire Aladdin team. They made me feel like I was a part of the family from the very beginning.

Thank you to Stephanie Singleton for her breathtaking cover illustration, which nailed the book characters perfectly, and thank you to Heather Palisi for designing the book jacket of my dreams.

ACKNOWLEDGMENTS

There are so many people in my personal life to thank that I can't possibly name them all without missing someone. So, thank you to my family and friends, the ones who supported my dreams even when it seemed like they wouldn't come true. Thank you to my work family for being an unending well of support and helping me unwind on the beach.

And finally, thank you to TJ, Nia, and Chase, the three people who make up the majority of my universe.

Overall, I'm just so overwhelmingly grateful for everyone who believed in this book.

ABOUT THE AUTHOR

Nashae Jones is a freelance writer and an educator. Her pieces have appeared in publications like *HuffPost*, *McSweeney's*, and *Yahoo! Voices*, among others. She currently lives in Virginia with her husband, two kids, two cats, and one dog. She is passionate about diversity initiatives, especially in children's literature. Visit Nashae at NashaeJones.com.